WILD

a Deep 8 novel

_____

KENZIE MACALLAN

WILD

ONE

Sean
_____

A METALLIC CLANG echoes as I duck into the alley, my heart pounding with the storm brewing overhead. Rain lashes against my skin, cold and sharp as shards of glass. The wet city air wraps around me, suffocating yet alive with the pulse of New York. My grip tightens on the brown-papered package under my arm.

The sharp click of footsteps follows me. Calculated. Too steady to be random. I quicken my pace, weaving through the maze of alleys, adrenaline ignites my every step. Shadows shift behind me, but I don't look back. I learned long ago that hesitation is a death sentence.

A hiss of brakes and a burst of neon light fill the street as I emerge onto the Westside Highway. Yellow cabs zip by, indifferent to my plight. I slip into the crowd of pedestrians, blending into the chaos of the city. When I reach the revolving doors of my building, I glance over my shoulder.

No one is there.

The numbing comfort of solitude greets me as the elevator doors slide shut, my penthouse looming above like a sanctuary I don't deserve. I step inside, my soaked clothes cling to me like a second skin, and the package feels heavier.

The deadbolt clicks behind me, the sound a brittle reminder of how isolated I've become. I set the package on the floor and punch the code into the keypad. The silence of my bachelor den swallows me whole, broken only by the hum of the refrigerator and the distant rumble of thunder.

The brown paper tears away under my impatient hands, revealing her face—Jess. Her violet eyes seem to follow me, daring me to confront the demons I'd buried alongside her memory.

But fate's cruel irony had other plans.

Her haunting portrait has caught up with me. In a past riddled with chaos and ambivalence, there's only one desire I want from this purchase: peace of mind.

Her portrait glows under the dim spotlight on the mantle, an oasis of color in a room painted in darkness. My hand hovered over the canvas, aching to touch the paint as if it could bring her back.

She smiles, looking over her shoulder with a carefree laugh frozen in time. But I know better. That smile hides her pain. The pain of rejection, of fighting a world that judged her for her skin, her spirit, her everything.

I sink onto the couch, the weight of my past settling over me like a lead blanket. Though I vowed never to let past events drag me down, it has dictated every one of my decisions.

I yearn for the woman in the portrait to shed some light on my one-dimensional life because the last time I saw her, she was a girl. It's a window to a past I had to run from to save her, but I can't remove her from my soul. A ribbon of questions weaves through my mind. Where is she? Who is she with, and what is she doing with her life? Losing her spark of light was one of my biggest regrets.

A vivacious woman replaces the girl in my memories, her hair flowing around her like a cape, teasing the viewer to come and play. The innocence she radiates vanished from my life years ago. The casualties of war molded me into a hardened soul until there was no room for light and goodness.

My phone's sharp vibration jolts me back to the present, and I swipe right to send it to voicemail, assuming it's another one of my hookups. At this rate, I'll die as a bachelor. Nothing wrong with that, I suppose. If my father was any indication of our gene pool, it would be best if I didn't reproduce. The phone flies through the air and bounces on the blue suede couch. Who the hell buys a blue suede couch? A lonely ex-Navy SEAL.

After leaving the Navy, I spent years building my security company, MBK Global Security, with Beck McKenzie and Peter Bryan. I work hard and have loyal friends, living in the greatest city on Earth, The Big Apple. It doesn't change the fact that I'm sitting here with no one to share my life with.

What started as an itch has turned into a full case of hives I can't ignore. The void gnaws at me. The more I ignore it, the bigger it gets. Restlessness is my constant companion.

My phone's insistent vibration interrupts with a special ringtone, signaling my secure line. A chill races down my spine. Few people use that line.

With a resigned sigh, I pick it up, my tone crisp. "Knight here."

"Sean, it's Neil McFadden." Neil, a heavy hitter at Scotland Yard, heads up the MI6 division, but don't call him M.

"I told you I'd call you tomorrow morning," I reply.

3

"You need to take that trip to Afghanistan," he says, his voice unyielding as steel.

"I told you—"

"I don't care what you told me. Accept the assignment and leave tomorrow."

"I declined the offer for a reason. Not setting foot in Afghanistan is a lifelong goal." I run a hand through my hair, pacing to the window. Everything on the street below is small and far away. Eight million people in this city, yet loneliness wraps around me like a vice. My lifestyle is a comfortable existence, but I've never been happy with the status quo. I always push myself to the limit.

"You're the only man for the job." Silence hangs in the air.

"You could pick anyone else from the team," I offer.

Neil sighs, his patience fraying. "Don't play games with me, Sean. There's someone from your past involved in this."

My pulse quickens. "Who?" The only people I keep in contact with are from my SEAL team, and they know how to take care of themselves.

The rustle of papers distorts the line. "That's on a need-to-know basis. This is an off-book operation. Here's the brief: an agent has gone dark, and they're not alone. There's a hacker and one other who need to be rescued."

"Not gonna happen," I say, the edges of the phone biting into my curled fingers.

The word "rescue" sends a jolt through me. I'd spent years pulling people out of impossible situations, but Afghanistan wasn't just a battlefield—it was a graveyard of broken promises.

He's done his research. The warrior in me screams louder than rational thought. I cave. Neil dangles the bait that hooks me. Rescuing is in my DNA, thanks to growing up in a crappy home life. My code name, Wild, is a testament to my crazy rescue plans, but I was always under control. However, my temper remains unpredictable.

My first rescue happened at age five. I have zero tolerance for bullies, especially when it involves girls. I had seen too much of that at home. Before I knew what was happening, my fist reared back and connected with his nose. He was never a bully around me again.

The power to save became my drug of choice, a healing salve for a tormented childhood. Each rescue took me farther away from an abusive family life where I had no control and made me feel empowered. The silk thread of fate spun around me tighter and tighter.

"Funny how you called just as I got that assignment. Coincidence? I don't think so." I understand how the spy game works. Spies have their fingers in everybody's business.

Neil's voice sharpens. "Didn't you get the memo? There are no coincidences in life. After years of training, you know that. His private jet is waiting for you. Safe travels." He hangs up.

The line goes dead, leaving me alone with the weight of his words.

Joining the Navy and becoming a SEAL seemed like a fitting path, but it became a double-edged sword. Afghanistan is a crucible of war, where young soldiers learn hard lessons and are reshaped into hardened warriors.

Weak men become strong, and the strong survive by burying fear deep. Things I witnessed defy description. Hell on Earth doesn't describe what happens in the tale. The only things to hold on to are sleepless nights and the shakes. No one came to save me. No one ever does.

In the end, it doesn't matter your skin color or beliefs.

We fight for survival and to live a decent life. A decent life has evaded the Afghan people for years.

I stare at the portrait of Jess, her eyes filled with a light I no longer deserve. Afghanistan. The word swirls in my mind, stirring memories I keep hidden away. Memories of sandstorms and gunfire, of lives saved and lost.

Fate dictates it's time to face my demons. The angel peers down at me from the painted canvas as I leave her behind again, her smile both a comfort and a torment. Maybe someday I'll have the courage to find her.

"I'll come back for you someday," I whisper, grabbing my go-bag from the closet.

But this time, I'm not running away from my demons. I'm running toward them.

TWO

Sean
————

THE RAIN HAS STOPPED as I step onto the tarmac; the jet waits like a ghost of my past. Jess's smile stays with me as I climb the stairs, each step pulling me closer to the demons I'd sworn to leave behind.

The hell I'm about to step into is familiar territory. When I left Afghanistan ten years ago, I swore there was no going back. This time, it serves a different purpose. As hard as I try to leave the past behind, it latches onto me. Each time I cut a tentacle, it regrows a new one, grabbing me from behind.

From the looks of Kabul, nothing much has changed. I'm about to reenter my worst nightmare, scars and all. The city comes into view from the high-end Falcon 5X, a far cry from the military cargo plane from years ago.

Drawing a deep breath, memories flood my mind from my last tour. The first bomb attack, when blood and human remains sprayed me from head to toe, left a dark stain on my soul.

Generations of children born into this way of life don't

know there is anything else. Used to the whistle of bombs and gunshots, they never flinch. The Taliban continues to rule the city as the Afghan military presents a weak front, patrolling nameless dirt streets. Thank God this is a stopover.

Nothing has changed in ten years, but have I changed? I'm coming at it from a different angle this time as a private contractor without the protection of my team. My client has sent the jet for me, which has its benefits.

I'm loaded to the hilt with every portable weapon I can transport in a hidden compartment in my suitcase. Based on my history here, I'm fully prepared for any event, but things are never as they seem.

This is supposed to be a simple extraction of a hacker named Red Enigma. I don't know anyone with that name, but something about this feels off. There are no coincidences.

As soon as the plane touches down, the doors open, and three men make a mad dash to load everything onto a beat-up Jeep and get on the road. I grab my luggage. Given what's inside, I'll be the only one handling it. There are other things in unlabeled boxes that aren't mine.

The sun beats down on our topless vehicle, and dust fills my mouth on our way out of the airport.

Afghan summers are unforgiving. Arid land produces heat that's like an alien life force gripping your skin as it sucks the air from your lungs. The urgency to leave the city vibrates through everyone on the ride.

My client tucks himself away in the Nuristan Province, a national reserve that sits northeast of Kabul in a remote location. The remote location makes it risky. I'm familiar with the terrain of the forest and the dangers of the people who live there, but I'm going in blind, having not been here in over a decade. I'm prepared for the worst-case scenario, but flying solo can be dangerous.

The driver crouches low in the seat next to me, and the two men in the back hold on. We almost make our escape when shots ring out. Our instinct to duck for cover kicks in.

The Jeep hits gaping potholes and jerks wildly back and forth as the driver yells at the people in the street. He slams his foot to the floor, and the Jeep launches at full speed. Our survival depends on our ability to take action.

Looking for the shooter is of no use. Those shots could have come from any of the many glassless windows of bombed-out buildings.

My military training comes back to me in an instant as if I had never left. I rip the gun from my holster and fire a couple of shots to each side. My message is obvious. We are armed and ready.

The gunfire stops, and I turn to the men in the back. Blood trickles from the side of the man's head, sitting behind me. He's slumped over. Another close call I can add to my list. I catch the eye of the man sitting next to him as he shoves the dead man out of the Jeep with his foot. No room for casualties. His body hits the dirt and rolls to a stop. The cruelty of war churns in my gut, but this isn't a time to reflect.

We slow down at the next checkpoint out of town as the guards wave us through without a second glance. My client must have connections because that never happens in Kabul. The driver doesn't even blink.

We're an hour out and nearing the hills when my shoulders fall from my ears, and the men speak in their native tongue of Kati. They laugh as if they haven't just been in a shootout.

Everyone has their own normal, but I'm still on high alert. Some things never change. I remember some words and phrases in Kati, enough to get by but not enough to understand them completely. My SEAL team had a translator when we were out on a mission to scout a village.

We drive into a lush valley, the exact opposite of the war-torn earth we escaped from. Lavender-colored mountains rise on either side, and simple terra-cotta-colored houses dot the landscape. The road runs alongside a fast-moving river with transparent water. An unknown world I didn't know existed opens up in front of me. The landscape reminds me of Vermont, only this area has fewer people, but the view is almost as spectacular.

The driver turns to me and speaks broken English. "You be here?" He nods his head.

I shake my head. "No. But it's beautiful. I never would have guessed this was part of Afghanistan." I force a smile to signify I understand him.

We leave the valley and hit rocky terrain that's more of a goat path than a road. We climb up the side of the mountain. The only thing better than a Jeep in this terrain is a Range Rover, which would make us more of a target. My client knows this area better than anyone, and considering we're friends, he wouldn't put me in harm's way.

At a semi-level spot, the driver stops and hands me a black bag. He motions with his hands to put it over my head. I hesitate, weighing my options. He and the man in the back seat exchange anxious looks. I don't have a choice, and I don't have time to argue. I need to get to my destination to complete the mission.

My head follows suit with my body. I'm back to thinking like a soldier. When you are a SEAL, risk is the edge you ride to save others. I put the bag over my head, praying it isn't much farther up the road. The temperature has gone down the higher we climb, but to say it was cool would be an overstatement. Sweat pours from my face as I hold on to avoid falling out.

The need for this much secrecy raises a red flag. If my friend is wealthy enough to afford the services of my company, then he needs to stay under the radar in this poor, war-torn country. I don"t know what awaits me at the end of this road trip.

THREE

Sean

THE RIDE SMOOTHES out before the driver comes to a stop and cuts the engine. I snatch the bag off my head and wipe my forehead with my arm.

The Jeep faces a house that rises above me like nothing I've ever seen. Outfitted with steel and glass, it juts out of the side of the mountain as if born from it. Gray girders come out at an angle, supporting the structure, making it look as though it floats above the tree line. I stare at it from below.

My client must have a ton of money to get these materials up here to build his mansion in the sky. It serves as a reminder not to underestimate the situation.

The men unpack the Jeep, making their way to the lower part of the glasshouse. I grab my suitcase and take in the view behind me as the valley spreads out below. So much beauty wrapped up in so much pain.

"Wait till you see the view from the top," a familiar voice says from behind me.

My head snaps around as Isaad stands, grinning from

ear to ear. "It's been a long time, Sean. Good to see you. The years have been kind to you." His English is still impeccable as his hand stretches out to me.

I shake his hand and bring him in for a bro hug. "Apparently, the years have been even kinder to you. You have definitely done well for yourself."

"Come inside. I'd like you to see the place." He pats me on the back.

I follow behind, ready to get down to business. There's a guard who scans me with a wand, and it goes off. He says something to Isaad about my gun, but Isaad waves him off.

His security seems a little over the top for a place in the woods. "Is your team available so we can go over the logistics of the security details? I need you to fill me in on exactly what we're doing."

"My friend, always a man of action. We have plenty of time for that. Let's get to know each other the way we are now. Have a drink and a cigar." He turns to me. "I haven't forgotten your favorites. Cuban cigars with Tanqueray and tonic with a twist of lime." He motions to his wet bar loaded with every top-shelf liquor on the planet. He must have some serious pull. Alcohol over two liters comes with jail time, among other punishments.

"Thanks for not offering the green raisin drink that could peel paint off a car. I never could get used to it." My stomach turns thinking about the burn, equivalent to White Lightning moonshine. "I'll pass on a drink until later."

"Suit yourself." He continues walking through his home. "I called this 'House Made from Hills'. I had a vision I needed to create. It took three years to build, but it was worth it. Let me show you the observation deck."

This is a far cry from when I first met Isaad. He was a

successful businessman who worked hard to earn a living. Through a series of events, he had become our interpreter and asset, helping us navigate the culture.

I was part of SEAL Team 6, an elite group of soldiers specializing in hostage rescue and counterterrorism. He had limited political connections, which were necessary to get things moving through the right channels. But from the looks of things, he's a multi-millionaire, maybe even a billionaire. I need to get to the reason he lives in the mountains of the Nuristan Forest.

We walk to the elevator, and he puts his hand on a panel. It lights up as the doors open. He smiles and sweeps his hand, directing me into the elevator. "I can't let just anyone take off with my helicopter." He chuckles.

There's a running tally in my mind, and I save it for later. "Absolutely."

The need to dig deeper gnaws at me, but slow and steady is my only option. I'm usually brawn over brain, but when you train as a SEAL, you learn to balance the two. Head over muscle is what's needed for this op. My training to observe and take action runs deep and kicks in like riding a bike.

The elevator takes us to the roof of the house. The observation deck has a spectacular view of lavender-hued, snow-covered mountains to the northeast, with lush rolling valleys and silver-green hilltops to the southwest. We stand on the landing pad for the chopper.

"You're right. The view is incredible. To think, I was just in Kabul a few hours ago. I didn't even know this was here. You've come a long way, Isaad."

The past doesn't hold only terrible memories. My friendship with him carried me through some tough times. We had known each other well back then, trying to navigate the worlds, supporting one another. We were like brothers, but this is Isaad 2.0.

He hums. "Come, let's eat. You must be starving. I can't imagine you got out of Kabul without being shot at."

"Unfortunately, we lost one of your men. I'm sorry." This loss feels different from when I was a soldier.

You're trained to get set quickly and move on without a thought to anything beyond your next target or mission. The man whose body tumbled away on the dirt road had family and friends. One tick in my direction, and that would have been me. I have no family and only a few close, loyal friends. My heart takes notice of what is at stake in this part of the world. I'm here as a different person, not a young man but an older, more mature man who has more to lose. Maturity and civilian life seem to be my new uniform.

He shrugs his shoulders. "It happens." His well-manicured fingers search the pocket in his shirt and slide a cigarette from the box. He lights it without thinking. Thick ribbons of smoke curl in the air, and his smile disappears behind a haze. The tingle comes back again as I wonder what he's hiding from me.

He continues his tour of the rest of the high-end sprawling mansion, filled with many rooms for many occasions and hallways that appear to end in the mountain. He gets a phone call on his cell and declines it.

"You get cell service up here?" My phone registers one bar for reception. Not enough to receive a call or send one out, throwing another monkey wrench in this mission.

"This is a special cell phone linked to my cell tower. Most people don't get cell service. We'll get you squared away. That's why I called you. You're always one step ahead." His lips curl on one side.

We make our way to a huge dining room with one long

table down the middle. Windows are parallel to the long side and end of the table, giving guests a breathtaking view of the valley. He sits at the head of the table, and I sit with my back to the wall.

As a soldier, you always have your eye on the door. Isaad and I reminisce about the old days with the good, the bad, and mostly the ugly. A few of his men stand at the entrance to the dining room. Their presence doesn't faze me in the least. Never let them see you sweat.

Throughout the evening, women dressed in traditional burqas or chadaree in various colors serve us. The women cover themselves from head to toe except for their eyes. Now and then, the faint scent of wild roses floats in the air, reminding me of Jess, the one who slipped through my fingers. My mind plays tricks on me, probably triggered by the portrait I purchased of her. The feeling of loneliness chokes me even as I'm surrounded by beautiful women.

The red-orange dusk bleeds into a night so black the stars burn brighter than I've ever seen them. We finish dinner with a Cuban cigar and a cocktail. I stick to my one-cocktail rule. When your father is a drunk, alcohol is the enemy that can sneak up on you when you're not paying attention. The air between us is without words. This is the routine leading up to the moment we get down to business.

"Tell me. Did you tell the feds you were coming here?" He watches the ash fall from the end of his cigarette.

"Why would I? I don't work for the government and don't have connections there anymore." We spar to see who lands the bigger punch.

He crushes out his cigarette. "You didn't answer my—"

"No. I've had no contact with any federal agencies before coming here. Why so uptight?" It isn't a lie, but it isn't the whole truth either. That's how the game is played.

He snaps his fingers in the air and motions to one man standing at the other end of the table. "When you're in my position, you can never be too careful. I hired you because you're the best soldier I've ever seen, and I've seen quite a few. I also trust you with my life. We're connected, you and I. Brothers. No?"

I smile and nod. One of his men comes over and places a document and a pen in front of him, which he slides across the table to me. "What's this?"

"It's a non-disclosure agreement. Sean, I'm going to warn you. You may not like what's going on, but I need to know it won't go anywhere." He clasps his hands across his waist and leans back in his chair.

I pick up the pen and start signing before he finishes his sentence. He needs to see that I trust him as well. What he doesn't know is, I don't care about the NDA. I came here for an extraction and nothing more. Our security contract is only for a few weeks, enough for me to complete the extraction.

"Looks good to me." I throw the pen down and slide the document to him.

His lips curl, and he nods. "How about I get someone to keep you warm tonight? It can get chilly up here." He looks over to his men and lifts his chin.

A group of women come into the dining room and line up along the windows with only their eyes showing. I can vaguely make out the curves of their bodies under the draped garments. Having someone keep me warm tonight is the last thing on my mind, but I don't want to be rude. There's one that stands away from the group.

He waves his hand at the women. "Take your pick."

I assess them, looking at each woman individually. They aren't all Afghan women. Some are Anglo with lighter features. But they have one thing in common: the look of fear. My hackles rise, but I can't let it show.

This might be a pleasant way to end the day. Being unattached has its advantages. Maybe I can spare one of them a night with someone else and do some recon at the same time. Then I come across a set of violet eyes that belong to only one person. It can't be. Not here and not now.

FOUR

Jess

MY MOUTH GOES DRY, and my heartbeat picks up. I'm shocked to see him here, but I won't let it show. The hijab covers my face from my eyes down, concealing most of my emotions, but he's always been able to read me like a book.

"What about this one?" He points in my direction with his cigar. He disregards me by calling me "one" as if I'm not a person, but cattle going to slaughter. Maybe that's the point.

This callous man in front of me is not how I remember him. But after many years, I would know him anywhere. The last time I saw him, he was a boy. The person before me is one hundred percent man. His dark, wavy hair and amber eyes aren't the only two features that make him handsome. His smile is something else entirely. That smile is my weakness, and it always has been. The pressure in my chest loosens like a valve on a tire. Seeing him gives me relief, but my guard is up. He was my protector growing up. The question is, why is he here?

"I see your taste in women has not faltered." Isaad motions his hand in my direction. "Come sit with us."

I do as I'm told, taking the seat across from Sean. I'm too guarded to say anything, trying to get a feel for what's going on between them.

"Let me introduce you to Daphne Wilder. She's writing an article about me as the wealthiest man in Afghanistan." Isaad raises his chin as cigarette smoke streams out of his nostrils.

The man smokes like a chimney. If he keeps it up, he might not live long enough to spend all his wealth. "This a Sean Knight, a friend from my past."

"It's nice to meet you."

Sean tries to hide the look of shock and bewilderment from everyone else but me. We lost touch over the years for many reasons, but you never forget the tell of someone you've known from the age of ten. There is comfort when I'm around him. We may go head-to-head, but he was always there for me. What interests me more is the fact that he is an old friend of Isaad.

Isaad continues to talk, unaware of the awkwardness between us as we have a stare-off. I note a flicker of anger in Sean's eyes, demanding to know why I'm here. My face is impassive, but my eyes are asking the same of him. What he seems to forget is I'm not a little girl anymore. I'm a grown woman and can take care of myself.

"Why don't you tell him about who you are and the articles you've written?" His finger skims my cheek through the gauze-like material.

By anyone's standards, Isaad is a very good-looking man, just not my type. I force myself not to pull away. Doing so would only offend him, and I need to stay on his good side. His troubled waters run deep, and I don't want to show fear.

"I'm an investigative journalist and have written many articles for magazines and newspapers, such as Newsweek and the New York Times. Some of them have focused on men in the Middle East who are wealthy and established. We are so used to hearing about the big CEOs and billion-aires of the United States that we forget there is a whole other world out there full of individuals who are wealthy and making a difference. Isaad Narazi is one of those men. Afghanistan needs to be portrayed in a better light. I hope my articles will accurately describe what's going on here."

"I've known Isaad for many years. He's a great guy. Tell me what you've learned so far." Sean's eyes bore into me, begging me to read his mind. He wants me to give him the information he doesn't have on Isaad.

He owns the largest construction company in the coun-try. He's created jobs for the people in many parts of Afghanistan and provides shelter for those who have lost their homes in the unrest." My sweaty hands rest in my lap.

He cuts me off. "Is that what they call it these days, 'unrest'? We used to call it straight-up bombing." He blows smoke rings over my head.

There's no smile in his eyes. His stern look gives him an edge I've never seen before. He seems to have hardened over the years.

I continue. "His company does everything from hauling away the debris of buildings, creating temporary housing, and rebuilding entire communities, including schools. He's highly revered. Some even see him as a hero." Small beads of sweat form on my forehead. That is only part of it, the front he wants everyone to see.

Isaad waves his finger at me. "You are too kind. Do you know she got her degree in journalism from Brown? How do you say it in America? She's one smart cookie."

Sean smiles. "She seems to be. Isaad, I wasn't aware of your successes." Sean's underlying message is, "Thanks for the information." We could always read each other well. At least one thing hasn't changed.

Isaad releases my hijab, and his fingertips stroke my face. My eyes stay glued to Sean in a plea for help.

"Look at her beautiful mocha skin and those eyes. Have you ever seen violet eyes?" He turns to Sean.

"No, I can't say that I have." Sean looks at his cigar, twirling it in his fingers. Either he doesn't care, or he is an excellent actor.

Isaad's eyes return to staring at my face. "Smart and beautiful is a dangerous combination. Wouldn't you agree?"

Sean takes a sip of his drink. "Most definitely. She appears to be both smart and uniquely beautiful." Hearing him say I'm beautiful catches me off guard. I wasn't the girl he picked to be with in the end.

Isaad's fingers fall away from my face. "I'm sorry to say she's not available tonight. She is a guest here and not one of the regulars. So far, she's been reluctant to share my bed with me. I'm hoping she'll come around before she's done with her article. But you may choose from the other women." He folds his hands on the table, waiting for Sean's answer.

It's as if I'm not even in the room. I'm a plaything for him, like all the women here. My blood boils, but I smile to cover it up. I wonder how many are here of their own free will and how many are prisoners without an escape.

"You know, I think I'm going to turn in for the evening. It's been a long day, and the only thing I can really focus on is sleep. I need to stay fresh and alert. Besides, I do like to give my woman proper attention." He winks at me as his fingers run across the table in front of him, and then he looks over at Isaad. He's good at this. Whatever this is.

"Now is your chance. The doors get locked after ten

when the women go to their rooms. I allow them out only during the day." Sean tilts his head and frowns. Isaad waves his cigarette in the air. "Sometimes my men are hungry for more than what's at home. I won't allow that under my roof."

Isaad stands up. "Daphne, thank you for your company. You and the others may go to your rooms." He turns to Sean. "I have some pressing matters to attend to. I'm sure you can find your way to your room. See you tomorrow for our first briefing. It's good to see you again." Sean nods, and Isaad leaves the room before we can stand up.

Sean's eyes remain focused on his drink as if he's deep in thought. I get up, and his eyes meet mine briefly. He must have a lot of questions that I'm not sure I have the answers to. The women walk out of the room in silence, and I follow behind.

Sean's eyes burn down my back. I could always feel him before I could see him. Some things never change, but we're older now and have been estranged for years. I'm not sure where I stand with him.

There are cameras and microphones everywhere. Each of us has our own rooms under the divide-and-conquer method of living under this roof. I may be his guest, but I'm more of a prisoner. Isaad said it was for my protection. Maybe he's right because rape isn't on my bucket list.

Isaad wears heavy armor. His ghosts follow him as if he can't shake them, constantly looking over his shoulder. He suspects everyone. Sean being here throws everything into a whole new spin. Unless he is here to get us out. I can't leave until I'm done.

My plush room with a king-size bed has a view to die for overlooking the valley. I checked the room when I arrived, knowing he would spy on me. A woman from the

West in this part of the world always holds suspicion. There's a walk-in closet and an enormous bathroom. They seem to be the only two places in the suite that don't have cameras and microphones.

Isaad spared no expense on the house. He's made an awful lot of money for someone in construction. Suspicion makes me dig deeper into his business and background. Things seem to be on the up and up, but my gut tells me things are not as they appear. I have another reason for being here. I need to find my foster sister, Pippa.

I peel out of my clothes, letting my curly brown hair fall out of its bun, and head for the shower. The knock at my door stops me in my tracks. In the time I've been here, no one has ever knocked on my door this late at night. With shaky hands, I grab a robe and head for the door.

My nerves are raw after the evening's surprise. "Yes? Who's there?"

"It's Sean. I wanted to say it was nice meeting you tonight. I'm slipping a paper under the door with my information on it in case you need anything." His muffled voice comes through between the door and the frame.

Given his background as a SEAL, he knows he's being watched and listened to by the security equipment in the hallway.

"It was nice to make your acquaintance. Thank you for your concern." I try to sound cheery, but I'm crumbling on the inside. The need to rip open the door and hug him is overwhelming. I'm stuck with nowhere to go, and maybe I'm in over my head.

I pick up the folded paper and open it.

Jess,
I didn't expect you to be here. How you're

in this part of the world is beyond me?! Please be safe. I'll get you out, I promise. Sorry about earlier, but I have an image to maintain. We can't let him know I know you.

P.S. I don't have a good feeling about this. Something isn't right.

Sean

He doesn't understand how much is wrong. I get on my hands and knees and stick my fingers under the door. I hear him gasp, which puzzles me, and then I feel his fingers touch mine. The zing is still there when I touch him.

When I was younger, I ignored the spark. As we got older, the spark turned into a raging flame neither of us could handle.

"Be strong," were his last words before he left.

Footsteps pound down the hall, coming toward my room. I know what's going to happen. They are coming for the paper.

I run to the closet. Tearing the paper into small pieces, I shove it in my mouth and swallow. I've never eaten paper before and don't wish to do it again. The combination of dry paper and no water makes it hard to swallow. I prevent myself from gagging.

They knock twice before unlocking the door. Isaad's head of security, Rakesh, enters first, followed by three men. Do they think I have a black belt in Karate?

Rakesh wears a scowl. "Where's the note?"

I play dumb. "What note?"

"The note that Mr. Knight gave you under the door." His eyes narrow. He's not buying my dumb act.

"Are you spying on me?" I fold my arms in front of me.

He takes a step toward me, getting into my personal space. "Yes. We keep tabs on all our guests."

"That's enough, Rakesh. I can take it from here." Isaad steps from behind the men.

Rakesh looks at me for a beat too long. Suspicion lingers in his eyes. "Yes, sir."

"I'm sorry about that. He takes his job too seriously sometimes. Is everything okay?" He holds my chin tight between his fingers and thumb. I'm not sure if the look in his eye is jealousy or anger.

"The gentleman I met at dinner stopped by to make sure I was all right. He was being kind. That's all." My eyes never waver from his face.

His thumb rubs my chin. "Do you need some company tonight? You look unnerved." He's going to keep trying until I say yes. Hell will freeze over before that happens.

"I'm good, thank you, but I need my beauty sleep."

Charm is not one of my strong suits. I do the best I can with what I have. My introverted tendencies pushed me to become a writer; it's fewer people to deal with on the job.

His eyes scan mine. "Have a good night. Sleep well." He walks out the door, and it locks behind him.

My chest tightens, and my breath shortens. If I don't get a handle on this and distract myself, I'm going to have a panic attack. I hurry to the bathroom, shut the door, and lock it from the inside. I untie my robe, letting it float to the floor.

What I need is a good soak. Warm water fills the tub as I add lavender bath oil to calm my nerves. Easing myself into the tub, bubbles surround me, giving me a false sense of security.

My mind catalogs the things I have seen over the last week and a half. Chinese and Russian men dressed in tailored suits with a full entourage have visited the house on more than one occasion.

Even though I'm fluent in Chinese. I could pick up only bits and pieces of the conversation from a distance. Their words included mines, money, and another word I couldn't decipher.

Then there is my foster sister. I know she's here; I just can't find her, and I'm reluctant to ask questions. My over-analytical mind makes up several scenarios. None of them ends well. I need to get to Sean before it's too late for either of us.

FIVE

Sean
_____

I STOP myself from punching a hole in the wall of my room. What the hell is Jess Wilander doing in the middle of the Nuristan Forest writing an article on Isaad? Over the years, I've been trying to find her work under her actual name. The fact that she has a pen name explains why I couldn't find any of her articles. I'll have to play catch-up and do some research.

The minute I saw her, the stakes of this mission went through the roof. Not only do I need to rescue Red Enigma, but I need to get to Jess, which will be no simple task since they locked her down.

There will be no sleep for me tonight, but at least she's secured away from Isaad's hounds. I've seen firsthand how brutal the local men can be toward women. The first time I encountered it, I had to look away. My stomach rolled as flashbacks of a fucked-up home life came to the forefront. I shake my head to get rid of them.

I strip out of my clothes and head for the shower to wash away the grime of the day. My thoughts drift to Jess.

Years ago, she had come into my world like a ray of

sunshine. What others saw was a biracial girl who sat in the corner of the classroom with her brown, kinky hair framing her face. Thick black glasses hid her soft violet eyes as her clothes hung on her like rags. She wore a white, stained T-shirt with a pair of long black shorts that were at least a size too big. The Chucks on her feet were hand-me-downs with holes at the big toe.

What I saw was a beautiful girl with flawless mocha skin, full lips, and a pair of eyes I couldn't look away from. There was magic in those eyes. We recognized each other as two lost souls, loners out of necessity. I wanted to touch her to make sure she was real. I walked over to her, ready to ask her name.

Brody made it to her before I did. "Well, look what we have here. A little half-breed. Where did you find your clothes, in a garbage bin?" His hand reached for her hair.

I grabbed his wrist and held it. "Hey, Knight, let go!" At the tender age of ten, I had already gotten the reputation for punching first and asking questions later.

"Apologize." My voice was loud enough for everyone to hear me.

"Are you for real? You don't even know her. She's beneath us." Brody was so cocky and entitled.

"Now, or I'll break your wrist, and I think we both know I'll do it." I released his wrist.

"You're crazy!" Then he mumbled, "Sorry," over his shoulder as he walked away.

She looked up at me with wide eyes laced with anger. "Thank you, but I can take care of myself."

I shrugged and sat down next to her. I knew better. "Sure."

We were inseparable after that, and she became my best friend. We shared everything. As we got older, things changed, like they always do, and that's when it got complicated.

Too tired to think straight anymore, I flop on the bed, praying the nightmares won't come back full force since my return to Hades. Tomorrow is going to be a day of carefully navigating a search and rescue.

THE DAY STARTS with a knock on my door at six a.m. I wake up in a cold sweat with the sheets tangled around me. Jet lag won't catch up with me as I tossed and turned most of the night. Off and on over the years, I've had bouts of nightmares from my time in Afghanistan. Being back here has set them off. I stagger to the suitcase and pull out some clothes.

"I'll be there in a minute," I mumble.

My eyes are bloodshot as I pull my fingers through my hair and splash cold water on my face. This is as good as it's going to get today.

When you're trained as a soldier, you learn to live on what you have in the tank, and then you give a hundred percent more. Focus on the mission gets top priority. It isn't anything a strong cup of coffee won't fix. If I remember correctly, the Afghans made the switch from tea to coffee and liked to percolate it.

I open the door to be met by one of Isaad's men. He nods without saying a word, and I follow him to the breakfast nook off the kitchen to meet Isaad.

He sits with his back to the windows, reading the newspaper. Jess is next to him with her head down, staring at her plate of food. She's dressed in red from head to toe in a loose-fitting top and traditional pants or turbaan. I can't understand why she continues to wear the hijab to cover her nose and mouth. Westerners rarely wear traditional clothing in Afghanistan.

"Good morning. Did you have a good sleep?" Isaad's focus remains on his reading material, but dark purple circles surround his eyes.

I sit down without acknowledging Jess. "I've had better. Jet lag can be a real bitch."

"So can nightmares after you reenter the country that gave them to you." He puts down his newspaper and picks up his fork.

Jess's eyes catch mine as they go wide with questions tinged with sorrow.

"I thought I would ask Daphne to join us. You seemed to be interested in her last night. What was on the note, Sean?"

The demand of the question is unusual for Isaad. This isn't the man I knew ten years ago. He grew up and lives in a world where distrust comes before trust. He has become a man who can't trust anyone.

"If there's one thing we've always had, it's trust. It seems like you don't trust anyone anymore. If you want to know, I slipped a note under Daphne's door telling her that if she needed anything to please let me know. I seem to be the only other American here. Would you like to give me a polygraph test to confirm it? But to be honest, they've trained me to beat those too." My words have a bite. His suspicions are without merit.

He puts his fork down and leans back in his chair, taking a deep breath. "I apologize. Things have been crazy lately. I brought you here because I do trust you. When we meet at our briefing, I'll fill you in." His hand points to the chef. "Please order whatever you like. The kitchen is open twenty-four seven."

This guy is wound tighter than a fly in a web. I look over at the chef.

"I'll have a three-egg omelet, two pieces of wheat toast, orange juice, and some fruit. Thanks. Oh, and the largest cup of coffee you can give me."

Jess's head is down as she eats as I acknowledge her. "How was your evening, Ms. Wilder?"

"Fine, thank you." She glances over at Isaad before she continues. "I was wondering if I could interview you for my article. It would complete the picture since you've known Isaad for so many years."

Isaad continues to read the paper, ignoring our conversation. "I'm happy to help you with your article. It seems Isaad has changed since I knew him." This gets his attention as he looks at me with curious eyes, but doesn't comment.

Jess senses the tension and excuses herself, saying she has a lot of work to do. I have a lot of questions for her, but I will wait until the interview.

The breakfast sitting in front of me is piping hot, and I'm as hungry as a bear coming out of hibernation. But I have logistical questions. "How many men are on your team?"

Isaad rests his head on his hands. "I have twenty here and another ten at my disposal."

"So why do you need me?" I continue to shove food in my mouth.

His lips make a hard line. "Things have changed recently, and I need another set of eyes, someone I can trust from the outside. Sean, I'm the same man I was when we met. Living under these conditions can make it look like I have changed. Please trust me as well."

I nod. "I always trusted you, Isaad. You always had my back." He seems satisfied with my answer as he stands next to me and puts his hand on my shoulder. "When you're done, meet me in the conference room. The chef can direct you there."

My mind reels back to a time when Isaad was happier. Darkness and secrecy shroud him now. Money doesn't always buy happiness. This is something more than a security gig. From the looks of it, our escape won't be easy.

The chef directs me to the conference room. A hush comes over the group of men standing around an oblong table in a darkened room. There is a Promethean board on the wall with a photo of a cave with various stats sheets around it. But it isn't an average cave. I know the look of this assault on the earth.

"Everyone, I would like to introduce you to Sean Knight. He's a partner at MBK Global Security and is here to give us a hand. I've known Sean for a long time, and we can trust him." Suspicious eyes give me a once-over. I'm an American, and many Afghans' hatred of us still runs deep. Their trust is going to be earned the hard way.

I nod my head but keep my mouth shut. "Let me bring you up to speed. That's a photo of—"

"The entrance to a mining site and it's sloppy." I move closer to the photo.

Isaad addresses the group of men. "Sean has a Master's degree in Mining Engineering and graduated first in his class. He went to one of the top schools in the US."

Isaad joins me by the screen. "This is the entrance the Afghan government wants you to see. We have a back entrance that we use at night. Ten years ago, miners discovered minerals were abundant in the Afghan ground. Everything from gold, copper, and lithium, but the government can't get it together to extract the one trillion dollars in precious minerals and other metals. Poor security, weak legislation and organizational capacity, and corruption have prevented the development of the sector. We're going to do it for them. That's why I need your help."

"It sounds illegal," I press him.

He shrugs. "No one has laid claim to it, so it's up for grabs."

We spend the rest of the morning discussing the logistics of everything from equipment to the types of rocks and minerals found in the area.

The operation is impressive, leading me to question Isaad's source of income for the operation. The group breaks for lunch, and I take my opportunity to get some answers.

"It would seem to me you need investors in this massive operation. Who are you in bed with, my friend?" I keep it light and the suspicion out of my voice.

The projector shining on the screen lights the darkened room. Little flecks of dust float between us. Translucent smoke obscures my vision as it billows from his mouth, casting us in a haze.

"You don't need to worry about that." He sighs as he crushes out his eighth cigarette of the day. Not that I'm counting, but I'm pretty sure I have the beginnings of lung cancer from secondhand smoke. "I told you, you would not like what you see."

The smoke lifts enough for me to see his set jaw. I need to figure out what his plan entails. "Why don't you get lunch and then find Ms. Wilder? I'm sure she is looking forward to connecting with you, American to American." There's a slight smirk on his face.

The hair stands up on the back of my neck. His words feel as though they hold a different meaning. I step through the haze so he can see my eyes. "Don't be so sure that I won't like what I see. I'm a civilian now. My areas are grayer than they used to be."

His eyes widen slightly, not expecting me to come at him from this direction. He needs to understand that I'm on his side. I step back.

Let me check if your chef can make up a picnic and see if Daphne wants to talk over lunch. I'm looking forward to speaking with her. She seems interesting."

My eyes never leave his face, waiting for an undercurrent of acknowledgment that Jess and I know each other, but he stares blankly.

"Good. We'll see you tonight for our first visit to the mine. Enjoy."

He turns and leaves me to stand alone with the gaping mouth of the mine staring at me.

When mining, you examine the rock and ground carefully and look for patterns or signs of what type of minerals might be present. At no point did he put up a slide of what was inside the mining area.

We discuss everything but what needs to be unearthed. I'm being left in the dark for a reason, but after tonight, I'll have more pieces to this puzzle. I can't let it distract me from my mission of finding Red Enigma.

A shadow at the door catches my attention as I whip around. My hand instinctively goes to my hip, where I carry my weapon.

SIX

Jess

I JUMP BACK and stare at him as he reaches for his gun. "I wanted to see if you're ready for my interview."

My heart cracks knowing he lives in a world where he always has to be on guard.

His hand falls to his side. "Sorry about that. I—" I shake my head ever so slightly for him to stop his next sentence. We're being watched constantly. "Let's meet now. I ordered a picnic lunch just in case you were available."

A forced smile forms on my lips. "Yeah, I passed Isaad in the hall, and he said you were free." He lifts his chin. "Lunch sounds good."

He leads the way to the kitchen while I get an eyeful of his backside. The man is built like a tank, with broad shoulders, solid legs, a butt I could bounce a quarter off, and pecs that stretch his shirt in every area. I'm not a petite woman, and he towers over me. He filled out in high school, landing the position of quarterback. Mr. All-American. That's when things changed between us.

My feelings for him had developed, but he kept

pushing me away, yet he still protected me. The man before me now has changed, and he's a lot to take in.

As an investigative journalist, I've covered a lot of stories in the Middle East and the military. I know that any time dedicated to the military can damage you irreversibly. He's put his hard edges in place to protect himself. From what, I don't know.

I stand behind him, lost in thought as he turns to me. "Is that all right with you?"

I put my hands up to avoid crashing into him. "What? Yeah, that's fine."

"You okay?" He frowns.

"Just lost in thought." He smiles and opens his mouth to say something, but then closes it, remembering where we are.

I've been lost in thought since I was a child. I dreamed of becoming a writer, constantly thinking of stories to write. Some people called me flaky. Writers live in their heads. My spaciness had become a running joke with us.

The chef hands Sean a basket, and we're on our way. I need to figure out how to let Sean know we will be monitored in the woods, too. If we can get beyond the perimeter, we can talk freely.

We walk without talking along what appears to be a path into the forest away from the mansion. The silence between us is uncomfortable and unfamiliar, a direct contrast to how we were with each other a lifetime ago.

Our quiet moments were never silent. We filled them with thoughts, wonderings, and questions that had no answers, but they were never awkward. We fill this moment with all the whys, like why did you leave without saying goodbye?

"At what point can I acknowledge I know you?" His lips curl.

"Just so you know, there are cameras everywhere, even out here. We need to get farther from the house." I stop, shifting my eyes up to show the hidden camera in the tree. "And you might notice a drone now and then. I don't know about microphones."

He nods without looking at the camera. "Got it. So, this will be a fun guessing game as we speak in code. How do you know so much about this place?"

"I've been here for a week. I went for a walk out here a couple of days ago and noticed the cameras, and then a drone followed me, so I kept walking until Isaad sent one of his men for me. Keep your eyes open for a secluded spot."

We come across a spot by a small brook and sit down to unpack the basket. Sean casually looks around for cameras and finds none, but we don't know about hidden microphones.

He stuffs some of the sandwich into his mouth and talks. "What the hell are you doing here? Afghanistan is still dangerous and one of the worst places on the planet for women."

I shake my head. "You still talk with your mouth full."

I unwrap my sandwich to discover it's a tomato and mozzarella sandwich with basil vinaigrette, my favorite. Something flutters in my chest. He remembered my favorite vegetarian sandwich.

"If you talk with your mouth full of food, it's harder for them to read your lips. You know, in case a drone flies by." He gives me a cocky grin with a gleam in his eye.

I pick up a napkin to wipe my hands from the oozing vinaigrette, stalling for time on how to explain my situation in the middle of nowhere.

"Take your time. I have all day." He grabs the bottle of rosé wine, another one of my favorites.

I'm seeing him for the first time in fifteen years, and my emotions are everywhere. I want to grab him and kiss him, then I want to slap him for abandoning me all those years ago.

The cool wine slips down my throat and seeps into my veins, calming my nerves. It might give me the courage to go head-to-head with Sean like we always do. I need to stand my ground and stick to my plan. He'll want to take over as commander-in-chief of our escape as soon as possible. I'll hold my cards close and not tell him I'm here to get Pippa out of her prison.

I take out my notebook and click my rollerball pen, ready to write his answers to my questions about Isaad. When I look up, his eyes are focused on my pen.

His body stiffens. "You kept it." His voice is low, and his eyes soften.

We had gone to a craft fair and came across a wood-turner's booth. He had a collection of handcrafted wood pens. One with a ladybug inlay caught my eye, and Sean bought it for me.

Writing longhand helps me put my thoughts together. There's a flow to it. As my hand moves, so do my thoughts. I never go anywhere without his pen. It's become a part of me like I thought he had become a part of me, but I guess I was wrong.

I shrug it off. He doesn't need to know what it means to me.

"Why don't we start from the beginning, Mr. Knight? When did you first meet Isaad?" I rest my hand on the page, waiting for his response.

We spend the next hour talking about his relationship with Isaad and how he was like a brother to Sean. He appreciated his friendship since he was an only child. They formed a close bond through their experiences together, but when his tour ended and he didn't re-enlist, he went back home. Sean lost track of Isaad through the years, only making contact now and then.

I put my notebook down and hug my knees to my chest. Out of nowhere, a statement pops out of my mouth. "You've changed and not for the better." I wish I could take it back.

He looks away, picks sticks up off the ground, and throws them in the stream. "War will do that to you, but underneath I'm the same person." He turns slowly in my direction. "You've changed too, for the better." I'm graced with his megawatt smile.

I bury my face in my arms, feeling my cheeks warm. Compliments are strange to me. I haven't had many of them in my life, and I'm never sure what to do with them. Being an extreme introvert and having an asshole for a foster father will do that for you.

"Let's try this again. Why are you really here? I don't think it's just to get a story." He pivots his body toward me.

"I came to get Pippa. You remember her?"

Pippa and I formed a bond with each other immediately when I became part of her foster family. We were meal tickets for Edith and Buck, our foster parents, and nothing more. Our only way to survive was to stay together.

He laughs. "How could I forget the wild redhead?"

"Well, in typical Pippa fashion, she's here and needs rescuing, only I can't find her. I contacted Isaad to write an article about him. It was the perfect cover to get into his house and find her." My fingers twist in my lap.

Sean rests his elbows on his bent knees and looks out over the brook. "What makes you think she's here? That would imply Isaad is keeping her against her will. I seriously doubt that."

"It's not a simple answer." The battle of wills begins.

He glares at me. "It never is with you. Tell me what's going on." I'm a little taken aback that he's not arguing with me.

A crack of a stick stops us from continuing our conversation. Sean jumps up to have a look around and draws his gun. He puts his finger to his lips.

After he surveys the area, he comes back. "It's nothing. Probably just an animal." He puts his gun back in its holster and holds out his hand to me.

I grab his hand as he pulls me up, feeling that spark again.

"We can't talk here, but I need to get you information so we can communicate through a shared email. Use a dark web address to get to it."

He stops mid-stride and puts his hands on his hips. "Dark web? What do you know about the dark web?"

I look around, wondering how much of our conversation is being heard.

"Pippa deals with the dark web, among other things. I think she came here to work for Isaad, but something must have gone wrong, or he is keeping her here against her will. His house has more security than Fort Knox, and I can't find her. I'm getting desperate." A sense of foreboding claws at me, tightening in my chest.

His eyes narrow, and he exhales. "Leave it to Pippa to get mixed up in something she knows nothing about. None of this makes any sense. He wants me to look at a mining site tomorrow." He pauses and stares at me. "Let's get you out first, and I'll come back and get her."

My heartbeat kicks up. "No! We need to think this through and find out what's going on here. There are a lot of things that don't add up since I arrived a week ago."

He holds my elbow. "Isaad is a successful business

owner who may have some side businesses that may not be legit. I don't know what he would even want with Pippa. She's not exactly easy to deal with." He shrugs.

I tug out of his grip. "I know he's your friend, and you just got here, but don't turn a blind eye to him. I don't have any concrete evidence, but I can feel it." He nods.

I grab his hands. They curl around mine and hold them in place. This is a different Sean, but the old elements are still there.

"Do you remember in middle school when you saw that boy, Tommy, push Jody? You were livid and tried to go after him."

He frowns. "Yeah, I remember." His amber eyes are like liquid gold, my kryptonite every time I look at him.

"Do you remember why I stopped you?"

"You said you knew she had been bullying him and things were tough for him at home." His brows knit. "What does that have to do with this?"

"Things are not always what they seem, and I need you to trust me. We need to examine things a little deeper. My gut tells me there's more going on here than he wants us to see."

I look down to where our hands are joined. His hands are so familiar to me. I know every vein, every scar. Of all the people in the world to be here, I'm so thankful it's him. But it comes with equal parts of fear. Treading carefully is necessary. Old feelings are bubbling to the surface for me, feelings he knows nothing about.

He lowers his head so our foreheads are touching. "Okay. I'll keep a keen eye and see if I can locate her." He squeezes my hand. "That brook looks awfully inviting. What do you say we roll up our pants and wade in to cool off?" He wiggles his brows in a flirty way I'm not used to from him.

"By the way, why are you wearing traditional clothing? You know the Afghan women have come a long way, and you can dress in regular clothes at the house." He already knows the answer, but he wants to test me.

I walk toward the brook. "I feel like I blend in more if I wear what everyone else is wearing. I get more information that way." He follows behind me.

"Hmmm… you always try to blend in or cover up." He's not letting me off the hook.

I whip around and stop in front of him. "Look." I poke my finger into his hard chest. He's much bigger than he was in high school. A small motor turns over in my chest, and it's hard to breathe. "I won't tell you how to do your job, and you won't tell me how to do mine. I know how to get information from people. It's part of what I do as an investigative reporter. You know how to rescue people. Let's stick to what we know."

He pushes his chest into my finger. "This brings me to my next point. Why did he accept your proposal of doing an article about him if you're an investigative reporter? This wouldn't seem to be your type of article."

The thought had occurred to me, too, but I had pushed it to the back of my mind. "I've written some other pieces about men in the Middle East, maybe that's why he accepted my offer. We need to stay focused, which is finding Pippa."

He puts his hands up, and something shimmers in his eyes. "Sure. It seems some things never change."

"Whatever, Knight."

"That's Mr. Knight in Shining Armor to you, as I recall, Bug." He laughs.

The one sound that speaks to my soul from years ago, and I could never let go of. It's a deep, hearty laugh that can't hide the child within.

I kick off my shoes and roll up my pants. My heart wakes up from its lockdown and takes notice, but I push it away. This is not the time for frivolous matters of the heart. I have a job to do.

"I haven't heard that nickname in years. It brings back memories."

He takes off his boots and socks and rolls up his jeans. "I remember when I gave you that name. You were catching frogs and putting them in buckets. You were experimenting to see which food they preferred to eat." He steps into the brook up to mid-calf. "Come on in. But I'm warning you, the water is not warm." He smiles.

He's infectious and inviting. How many women have fallen for him based on his smile alone?

I go to the edge, step on a rock, and lose my balance, falling into him. He catches me under my arms, and we freeze. "You okay?" he whispers.

"Yeah, I just slipped." I push him away with my hands on his chest.

I'm in the danger zone with this man. He left me once already. I won't let him do it again. Besides, isn't he married?

SEVEN

Sean

AS SHE FALLS into my arms, a memory from our past stabs me. She would call me after her foster father, Buck, had said horrendous things to her, like calling her a half-breed, telling her she was ugly, and that she would never amount to anything except on her back. I wanted to beat the shit out of Buck, but he was a hell of a lot bigger than me.

She thought I had the perfect home, but fear was one of the many things we shared. Fear is a bitch that never lets go, a five-alarm clinger. You can rule her, or she will own you. We thought if we stayed together, we could beat her, but she's stealthy.

I wasted no time scaling the side of the house and crawling in through her window. Her tears and soft cries gutted me every time. I would spoon in behind her and rock her to sleep.

When we got older, she called me less, and I saw her turn in, hiding away from the world. You never forget the first woman who lies in your arms for comfort. I want

45

those days back. I want her back, but I'm going to have to tread lightly. We don't know each other like we used to.

We pack away the picnic in silence, edged with nervous energy that hangs in the air for different reasons. She keeps looking at me as if she wants to ask me something. I'm clueless about the question or the answer.

I take her hand in mine, in need of the connection to my past that keeps me grounded and reminds me of where I came from. She tries to pull her hand away, but I keep it locked in mine.

"Let's make sure you don't fall again. I can't rescue a woman in a cast," I say to lighten the mood.

She doesn't smile or laugh. Instead, she narrows her eyes and tilts her head. She's suspicious of me, but I'm not sure why. She concedes, "Okay."

I stop walking. "I know you well enough to know when something is on your mind, so out with it." She's stubborn and won't give up anything until she's ready.

She strides past me and looks back over her shoulder. "Let's keep walking and see where the day takes us." Her lips curl, but the smile doesn't reach her eyes.

I stare at her full, dark rose-colored lips, remembering the fantasies I've had about them. The one taste I had wasn't enough and scared the hell out of me. What I felt in that moment was sacred to me, something I wanted to hold on to and never let go.

The sky clouds up, and a warm, soft rain drizzles on us. The drops become heavier, drenching our clothes as they cling to us. We run up into the forest, but we're no longer on a path as I help her up the steep incline. Up ahead are cabins built on the side of the hill. We head toward them, hoping to find shelter.

She doesn't seem in a hurry, facing up to the sky,

sticking her tongue out, and smiling. I always admired the tomboy side of her, the side that doesn't mind getting wet. It's the one thing that made it easy to be with her. God, I miss her; I miss us.

We stare at the cabins and both say, "Who do you think lives here? Jinx, you owe me a Coke."

Our laughter fills the air. Her laugh takes up the space in my heart I had forgotten about. I was young and foolish, thinking I was a man, but missing the mark, not brave enough to see things through with her.

"You might have to settle for a beer. Coke used to be scarce." I'm still holding her hand, rubbing it with my thumb.

She pulls her hand free. "I'm sure Isaad has some. He can get a hold of anything." Her voice is icy.

My hand is wet, cold, and empty, maybe not so far away from my heart. "So, I noticed. Let's go up and see if anyone's home." Trying to keep up with her change in emotions is giving me a headache.

"Are you sure that's a good idea?" She wraps her arms around her waist. Her hard nipples push up against her wet shirt. I'm getting hard below my belt.

"Have I ever let you down?" Her eyes shoot daggers at me, and she waits to answer.

She stares at the ground so I can't see her eyes. "No. You've always been there to protect me." She sounds sad and disappointed.

The water streams down her face, and it doesn't make her any less beautiful. "Hey, what's going on with you?"

"Nothing. Let's go." She turns and walks away.

I hold her by her elbow and lead us up to the first house. We look in through the windows. The one-room wooden cabin doesn't appear to have anyone living in it.

There are metal cuffs bolted to the floor with chains attached to them. I jiggle the door handle, and it opens.

I look up the side of the mountain at a line of cabins. They are identical. "What do you think happened? Why is there no one here?" The rain shower is passing, and we're left with a mist.

"That's not your concern." A deep voice with a broken accent grabs my attention. "You need to come with me. You've gone too far." Rakesh is Isaad's right-hand man, who I met at this morning's briefing.

His face twists in a scowl. He's not happy with our being here. He's brought two of his men with him, who don't look as confident. They're dressed in soaking wet fatigues, which I know only get heavier as they get wetter.

Jess jumps back, holding on to my arm, and then straightens up.

My anger comes to the forefront as I push her behind me. "It's a forest. I'm pretty sure we can hike as far as we want to." My fists clench at my sides.

His mouth forms a tight line, and he steps toward me. "We'll see what Isaad has to say."

Jess rubs my arm and smiles at him. "It's fine. I've had enough hiking for today, anyway. Let's head back." Ringlets hang around her face, making her look like some kind of goddess.

She was always good at not letting my anger get the best of me. There were many times in school when she stepped up to get between me and my target. The warmth of her hand on my arm catches my attention. I want her to keep rubbing and tell Rakesh to go to hell.

With all the grace of a bull Brahma, he snarls, "Follow me."

Jess mumbles, "How long were they following us?"

"I knew they were there since we climbed the hill. Stealth is not how I would describe them." I wink at her.

She slips a folded piece of paper into my hand. I turn and frown at her. She shakes her head.

We fall in line behind him as his two goons bring up the rear. We're surrounded by the sound of squishing boots as heavy drops fall off leaves above us.

I glance at Jess, and she gives me a tentative smile with an underlying look of fear in her eyes. I squeeze her hand and she nods. The connection between us is still strong even after being away from each other for years, but fear of true intimacy is a powerful thing.

The forest remains silent on the trek back to the house. As I look up, Isaad glares down at us from a large window. Then he disappears as the glass turns opaque. A glasshouse should be transparent, but this place is anything but.

Rakesh leads us into a tunnel that snakes under the house. I get my bearings quickly. Being underground is my thing. The tunnel goes on for a while, longer than the house, and into the mountain. What other tunnels are under or behind this house?

We stop at a door. Rakesh waves his hand. "Inside."

"Not much for manners, are you?" My nose is within an inch of his face. He grunts but doesn't stand down.

Metal covers the walls from the floor to the ceiling. I knock on the wall to figure out the type of metal. From its feel and sound, it's an aluminum composite. There's only one reason to have a room outfitted like this, so no electronic devices can emit or come in.

Rakesh moves toward me, and I turn to face him. "Sit down. We wait for Isaad." There's something about this guy that rubs me the wrong way.

"Mr. Knight..." I hear Jess's voice, and it brings my attention to her.

Her head's more in the game than mine. She's a thinker. I'm the doer. I sit across from her to curtail any suspicion.

Isaad doesn't take long to enter the room. "What seems to be the problem?" His eyes dart between us.

Rakesh stands up straight. "Sir, I found them out beyond the perimeter where they shouldn't have been, by the cabins. She is out there with a strange man. It is forbidden."

For a second, I see something pass in Isaad's eyes. I'm not sure whether it's anger or distrust. "It's fine." He waves his hand.

"It's not fine. They shouldn't have been out there looking around. Their American rules have no room here. She needs punishment," Rakesh argues.

Jess stiffens. My hackles go up. "What's with you? There's nothing to see unless you're hiding something. And not for nothing, but we're out here in the middle of nowhere. What rules are we talking about? It's not Kabul." I stand up as the chair falls back and clanks on the metal floor. "You touch her, you die," I say through gritted teeth as I point my finger in his face.

Rakesh rounds the table and gets close enough to breathe my air. "You're a piece of American scum. You come into our country and force us to bend to your way of life. This is my country." He pounds his fist on his chest. "You have no rights here," he spits in my face.

My instincts take over as my fist connects with his jaw, but not before he clips my cheek with his ring, splitting it open. I do a roundhouse kick, sending him to the floor on his back. Before he knows what hit him, he's facedown on the ground with my knee in his spine, arms locked behind his back.

My mouth is near his ear, so only he can hear me. "If it

weren't for us, the Taliban would own your ass, rape your women, and have you do their dirty work for them. You're welcome."

"Enough." Isaad's voice is soft but carries power as he makes his demand, but he lets the fight go on a little too long. Why is he watching us?

I move off of Rakesh as Isaad says something to him in Kati. Blood drips down my chin, and I wipe it with my arm. Jess twists her hair around her finger.

Isaad turns to us. "I'm sorry about that. He's an excellent soldier and overprotective. It's dangerous out in the woods. The Taliban are everywhere these days and don't take kindly to Americans. Your safety is my number one priority. It looks like you still have your military moves. Come, let's get you cleaned up."

It was a test to see if I could still handle myself. His faint smile leaves me guessing what's going on. "Just so we're clear, I'll be carrying everywhere from now on."

Isaad nods his head in defeat, maybe somehow knowing it would eventually come down to this.

Jess stands up. "I can take him back to his room and tend to his cheek."

"Very well. Follow me."

I say nothing about the metal room, but my questions linger. More pieces reveal themselves, making me question when I should call for backup.

We make it upstairs, and Isaad leaves us with a dinner invitation. Jess follows me to my room. She shuts the door behind her and crosses her arms.

I'm still running hot from the throw-down with Rakesh. "If you've got something to say, then say it. Otherwise, I have a lip to clean up."

Without a word, she points around the room and then

to the bathroom. Once we're in, she shuts the door and turns to me.

"Bugs. I don't think he's bugged the bathrooms." She stops and glares at me. "After all this time, I would have thought you would have gotten more control over your anger. You have got to get your head in the game because, in case you haven't noticed, our lives are at stake."

EIGHT

Jess

HE MOVES toward me and wraps me in his arms. I take one emotionally stupid move after another, from holding hands to his hug. I stand on tiptoe, pulling him closer to me, not wanting to let go. His enormous body swallows my frame. He cocoons me in his arms with a touch that crackles with electricity.

Once I turned the corner from friends to a lover's attraction, I couldn't go back. The mixed messages are confusing me. I'm in dangerous territory and need to remind myself that he's a married man.

Tears well up in my eyes, but I refuse to let them fall. It may be from the frustration of being near him again or the danger that surrounds us. I've been in many dangerous situations around the world, but this moment is mixed with deep wounds from our past. There are things from that time I want to forget, and there are things that have seared themselves into my memory. He's the one thing I can't rid from my heart, mind, or soul.

I feel him press his lips to the top of my head, and a

shiver runs through me. "It's going to be okay. I'm going to get us out of here. I promise." He holds my face in his warm hands.

"Why are you here?" His hands distract me, but I don't give in to the lust swimming through my veins.

"I'm here to help Isaad with a mining project." I watch as his lie flits across his eyes. He's here for more than mining.

I press to find out more. "I'm glad to hear you pursued something in science. You were always brilliant in our geology classes. But that's not the only reason. You're not that good a liar."

He puts his head down. "I could never lie to you. You don't need to know everything right now. Just know I'm not leaving here without you."

Before I tell him he's already broken his promise never to leave me, he stands back and removes my headdress and hijab. "There you are. I missed you."

He's missed me. Really? I haven't seen him for years, and there's been no contact. His thumb rubs my bottom lip. I bat his hand away.

"Stop that. I miss my old friend Sean. I don't know who you are, but I liked my childhood best friend a lot better." He steps back and frowns. The blood drips off his jaw.

"Let's get you cleaned up. Do you have a first-aid kit?" I distract myself by searching for bandages.

"It's in my suitcase." His voice is monotone.

He holds my arm to prevent me from leaving. "I'm sorry."

His eyes are complex layers of the life he lives, a life I know nothing about. I don't know if I know him anymore. They are a kaleidoscope of sadness, loneliness, and even regret.

I soften my tough exterior and cover his hand with mine. "We have a lot of catching up to do, but we may not have that kind of time. There needs to be some kind of plan."

I bring the first aid kit into the bathroom as he sits on the edge of the bathtub holding a washcloth to his cheek.

"Let me look."

I move his hand, and sparks travel up my arm. My heart rate picks up, and I drop his hand like it's on fire. I've got to shut this down. He's a married man and not available. I'm not sure he was ever available to me. He ran away fast enough to join the Navy. "It looks like it needs stitches."

He points to his ditty bag on the sink counter. "That's what superglue is for. It's in the first aid kit."

"Superglue?" This is new to me.

"It makes an excellent Band-Aid. Just hold it together as you put the glue on it. The things you learn in the military." He winks.

I clean out the place where it's split and hold it together as I apply the glue. As I wait for it to dry, our eyes meet, and I'm close enough to recognize his familiar scent, clean and citrus. I'm used to seeing the anger, but what I see now is the hurt and loneliness. I'm having a hard time reading him. He's messing with my head, and my head is where I live.

After the glue cures, I stand up as his eyes linger on my chest.

"What's wrong with you? You're acting way out of character for a married man. I know you've changed, but I didn't think your morals had taken a holiday." I stand with my hands on my hips, anger boiling.

He laughs. "Is that what you think I am? A married man trying to hit on you? Try a divorced man. My father thought it was funny that I had failed at marriage. He always loved to see me fail." His face hardens as his jaw muscles twitch. The flirtiness leaves his eyes.

My burner switch flips on as the knowledge he's not married sinks in, but I put it away for later.

"How much of a failure could you be? You were a Navy SEAL on one of the most elite teams in the world and have a science degree." I snap back.

His father wasn't there for him growing up. He was too busy working and finding the bottom of a bottle to see his fantastic son.

"Do I even want to know how you know about my SEAL team? That's top-level information." He looks at me with suspicion. He doesn't know what it takes to be a top-notch journalist.

I cross my arms in front of me and examine my fingernails. "When we emailed back and forth, I put two and two together. Also, have you forgotten what I do for a living? I know high-ranking officials who can give me that kind of information."

He wiggles his brows, not letting up for a minute. "You've been keeping track of me."

I shake my head. "Not after you married Madison. I wanted to respect your space and marriage."

He stands up with his hands on his hips. I step back as the wave of attraction hits me full-on. "I call bullshit. We were always going to be there for each other. Madison had nothing to do with it."

Thank God, I'm quick on my feet. He doesn't need to know the truth. "If I'm going to be honest, I didn't like Madison. She wasn't right for you."

What I want to say is, I'm right for you. But he doesn't see that. He doesn't see it now, and he didn't see it then when he took someone else to the junior prom and senior ball. Oddly, those girls weren't better looking than me.

He stares at me for a couple of beats. "You're right. Madison and I were wrong for each other. Is that why you didn't come to the wedding?"

I nod and look down. "Yeah. That and I conveniently took an assignment overseas. What happened?"

I don't acknowledge the pain it would have created to see him marry someone else. Not after our kiss. I wasn't the most experienced young woman in high school, but I know what I felt at that moment as the air rushed from my lungs, my toes curled, and my heart stopped. I haven't had a kiss like that since him, and I don't think I ever will.

He rakes his hands through his hair and sits down. I sit down next to him on the edge of the tub as he talks to the floor.

"She was supposed to be perfect for me. We met at college. She was beautiful, well put together, with the right pedigree. I was going to graduate at the top of my class, marry the perfect woman, and show my dad I wasn't a failure. Then I got shipped off to here. We rarely saw each other, and I kept re-upping, doing back-to-back tours. During my deployment, she drained my bank account and slept with another man. Six years later, we were done. We never really got started."

"I'm sorry." I reach for his hand and squeeze it.

As if he doesn't hear me, he continues. "There was always something missing. It all looked good on paper. Friends called us Ken and Barbie. We were going through the motions because it was what we were expected to do. We never really connected. I was never sure what she wanted from me, so I worked all the time. It kept me from coming home and dealing with my dad."

He looks into my eyes. "I miss that place where you can read the other person's thoughts without trying, where things flowed and felt comfortable. God knows I tried, but I never found that with her." His eyes sear into mine, and we connect at the place where you're sure you've known this person forever.

"You promised you would always be there for me, and then you signed up for the Navy and left." My voice is so small, I barely recognize it.

When he left, a piece of me went with him. A chunk of my heart got cut away, leaving a hole. Whether he knows it or not, he still carries it with him.

His other hand cups my cheek. "I had to leave for so many reasons. Some you know nothing about." His words stun me.

We shared everything growing up and kept nothing from each other. The gruesome details of our family lives were out in the open, or so I thought. His confession throws me off balance from a place where I felt secure and trusted him. There's gut-wrenching pain in his eyes that warns me of an ugly truth I may not be ready for.

The bang on the door startles me. "Stay here. I'll find out what they want."

My fingers twirl in my hair as I wait in the bathroom. Shellshocked by what I don't know about him creates fear about what it might be. I'm not sure I want to know. I've had enough ugliness to last me a lifetime. On the other hand, I can't let him carry this alone.

He comes back into the bathroom. "Our presence is being requested for dinner." He holds out his hand and hugs me again. "You have no idea how good it is to see you." He pushes the hair away from my face. "Let's meet up after dinner. You can put a piece of thick cardboard or wood in the doorjamb to keep it from locking. Then you can come to my room and we can talk more." He lets out an audible sigh.

I leave to freshen up in my room, not looking forward to dinner with Isaad. The strategy of using something to stop me from being locked in will help me find Pippa.

I need to find her location before we can even think of a rescue. My head and heart are spinning after what Sean has shared about his marriage. What does it mean for me, for us? I worry about what changed him during his time in the military, which he didn't even mention.

Dinner is boring and tense. Isaad asks questions about what we saw or didn't see. The two of them drone on about a mine and going tonight instead of daylight. I pretend to listen. Half my brain works on how to find Pippa in this maze of rooms and tunnels; the other half is trying to figure out how Sean and I fit together.

"Did you hear me?" Sean glares at me.

"What?" I'm lost in our bathroom conversation as I try to process the man in front of me.

"Do you want some dessert? I need to turn in and get some sleep before we go out tonight."

His look is intense, and his message gets through. He won't be available tonight, which works for me. I won't be available either.

I place the napkin on my plate. "No dessert for me. Thank you."

He shakes his head to tell me not to leave my room, but I've made my decision. "I think I'll excuse myself and call it an early night. See you both tomorrow. Good night, gentlemen."

Back in my room, I search for a piece of wood or cardboard. I take the cardboard from the back of a pad of notepaper and move to the closet, folding it until it's the size to fit into the doorjamb. To avoid the cameras, I turn the lights off and slip the cardboard piece into the door-jamb. Pulling on my nightshirt, I get into bed.

After a day full of emotions, I must have dozed off because I wake up at four a.m. I put my clothes back on in the dark and check the door. It opens easily as I slip into the hallway. I've noted where the cameras are and try to duck away from them. Making my way down the hall, I check the doors to see if any are unlocked. No luck.

There's a wall at the end of the hall. There should be a solid mountain on the other side. My experience with the tunnels underneath the house makes me curious about any tunnels that may lead into the mountain.

In front of a white wall is a table with flowers in a vase. The flowers are fake, which is unusual because Isaad has fresh flowers everywhere else in the house. I look around for cameras and see none. My skin prickles as adrenaline spikes through my body.

I grab the vase to pick it up, but it's stuck to the table. As I wrestle with it, the panel behind it opens enough to squeeze in between the movable panel and the wall.

I peek behind it and see two well-lit tunnels going in different directions and a set of stairs to the right. There are several doors that men are going in and out of. This is something out of a James Bond movie.

An icy chill skates across my skin. I need to wait for Sean before I move forward. I'm out of my element. Investigative reporting is one thing, but playing spy games is a whole other level.

I close the panel and twist the vase back in place. As I head back to my room, I get halfway down the hall and run right into Rakesh. His eyes widen.

"What are you doing out of your room?" He grabs my arm. His fingers bite into my skin.

I struggle out of his grip. "Let go of me!"

He drags me down the hall, takes out his keycard, and opens a room. He pushes me as I fly across the room and onto the floor.

"You American women do not know your place." His body occupies most of the space in the concrete room with a single bed. He bends over me. "I've seen your pictures online. You like to show your skin."

I don't know what he's talking about because I'm the last person to show my skin. I turn my head and hear the rip of my right sleeve and then the left. My shoulders burn as his nails rake across my skin.

"You don't know anything." I back farther into the corner to escape him.

He backhands me, and my head hits the wall. I see stars for a minute, but I fight to stay conscious. God only knows what he'll do if I blackout. I hold the side of my head.

His face is inches away from mine. "Now that I have you alone, I can do anything I want to you." He stands up and unbuckles his belt.

My vision blurs as I try to focus. Sweat beads on my forehead. I'm trying to think my way out of this mess. "Not if you want to keep your job." He stops pulling his belt and narrows his eyes. "Isaad is very interested in having my story show him in a good light. You're a smart guy. I'm sure you can connect the dots."

He grits his teeth, puts his belt back in place, and grabs my upper arm. "But you forget he won't be happy to hear about you roaming around. There will be punishment." This guy is into punishing women.

He throws open the door and yanks me back down the hall, but not before he says something into his earpiece. We arrive at my room to see Isaad waiting for us. Rakesh says something to him in Kati and pushes me in Isaad's direction.

Isaad motions me into the room and closes the door. He stands with his hands behind his back. His eyes are black as coal and meant to intimidate, only they do much more than that. The way he's looking at me makes me want to run as far and fast away from here as I can. Coldness slithers through the air and grips my throat. This is far more dangerous than I ever imagined.

He takes a step toward me. "Tell me what you were looking for."

"I wanted to talk more with Mr. Knight." I keep eye contact with him.

"You mean Sean." He gives me a knowing smile.

I stand my ground by not looking away from his accusatory eyes. "Yes. But he wasn't there."

He continues to move in my direction, backing me into a corner. "Tell me what else you found on your hunt. Hmm?"

"Nothing but a lot of locked doors. You can't keep me a prisoner here or anyone else." The sweat drips down my sides.

Red silence cloaks the room, screaming the things that aren't being said.

He hums and bends down at eye level. "The things I have in place are to keep you safe while you write your article. Remember your place here. Many people get lost in the forest and never come back again." He's making a promise. I'd better watch myself. My question is, what is he hiding?

He turns to walk out of the room and digs the cardboard out of the doorjamb. Holding up the piece, he says, "I'll see you at dinner, but not before. Good day, Ms. Wilder."

My heart beats so hard in my chest, I feel it in my throat. He'll keep me in here with no breakfast or lunch as if he's punishing a child.

Fear crawls over my body like a heavy blanket ready to suffocate me. I need Sean. I'm in over my head, and I'm not sure how to get out.

NINE

Sean
———————

I MEET up with Isaad and his crew of men around eleven
p.m. This is the best time of night to avoid my PTSD
nightmares, which have only increased since I've been
here.

Excitement replaces the dread of my nightmares.
Scouting a new mine brings me back to when I was in
school and we had to learn various ways of mining. I
learned to listen.

The earth always spoke to me, telling me things as I
look for clues about where to find minerals. Most things in
life come with clues; you just need to know where to look
for them and listen.

Isaad demands that his men wear clothing with no
pockets, so they can't take any gold with them. Given the
poverty in the countryside, they could strip the mine clean
and still not be able to feed everyone.

We'll travel in a caravan of vehicles, driving about an
hour to a gold mine. The mine is to the north of Nuristan
in the Badakhshan Province, an area not familiar to me. I
need to stay sharp and be ready.

We make our way down to an underground garage loaded with Jeeps and Range Rovers. A Jeep with huge KC lights leads the way, followed by our Range Rover and other vehicles. Isaad and I sit in the back and discuss the mine we're about to inspect. His estimated projection of its earnings is impressive. The country could use the much-needed income and jobs.

"The mines are poorly maintained, and they've had many collapses in recent years. No one wants to put money into them because they don't see the return." He turns to me, smiling. "But I do. I have some investors to get the best equipment available to excavate the maximum amount of minerals. Mining illegally is an art form." This is my first clue into the illegal side Isaad alluded to earlier.

We continue to talk about the logistics of mining and profit margins as we bump along the road through trees and over rocks. Isaad tells me he expects to get at least one hundred ounces a day from the mine, which is remarkable. Some of the most profitable mines in the world aren't bringing in that much gold. He stands to make over forty-two million dollars in gold for the year, but there are many things to consider that could hamper his return on investment.

I haven't been able to shake the feeling that something else is going on behind the scenes. The lack of moonlight makes the forest oppressive. The dark, tall trees create impenetrable walls, making it feel like a tunnel. Darkness bears down on me. We would have wrecked by now had it not been for the powerful lights on top of the vehicles.

We slow down as we drive toward a vast hole in the earth, like a gaping mouth that could swallow us in an instant. The SUVs bounce shining light onto the mine, giving it a strobe light effect, highlighting the spiral that leads to the center where the gold is extracted from the earth.

During the day, mines are second nature to me, but there is an eerie effect the mine has at night, almost as if it's sleeping and doesn't want to be disturbed. The road around the outside of the spiral is a bypass to go to the other side and down the mountain.

The vehicles stop, and we get out, sporting our miners' hats with headlamps. In the distance, a generator comes to life, and high-intensity floodlights come on. Shots and yelling ring out. Isaad stands still without a reaction. I draw my gun.

"What the hell is going on?" I try to get a bead on where the shots are coming from, but the echo of the mine makes it impossible.

"Fucking poachers." He yells something in Kati, and the shooting ends. "We just kill them. They have no business here." His lack of compassion for these poor people makes me take notice of who he is now compared to the man he used to be. "It's a kill-or-be-killed world we live in."

I cringe inwardly. "It doesn't mean you need to live by those rules."

He shrugs and puffs on his cigarette.

This is the part I will not like. I'm used to weeding out the enemy, but those days are long gone. The killing of innocent poor people doesn't sit well with me. I head into the mine with more trepidation than I started on this journey. My senses heighten as I notice every nuance in this new environment.

Isaad and I make our way to the backside of the mine. He has cut a hole in the lower side of the spiral. The large machinery is moving, jackhammers are breaking rock, and the trommel screen is running. Music to my ears.

We discuss the various ways to be the most efficient at extracting the gold and the equipment needed to do the job.

We go farther into the mine, and I notice highly unusual triangular-shaped silver pieces. I've never seen anything like it. Crystal gems like diamonds can form in a triangular shape, but not metal. It looks like points on a star. I notice some men picking up the pieces and putting them in a basket. I pick a piece up and rub my thumb over it.

I show the mineral to Isaad. "What is this? I've never seen it before."

He looks away and waves his hand. "It's junk. We call it Stellarium because it looks like a piece of a star. We collect it and throw it out. You can throw it back on the ground. It's worthless."

His eyes have a hard look. He doesn't want me to test him on it. I throw it on the ground and walk away. To find an unknown mineral is highly unusual. The Geological Society would know about it, yet I haven't come across it in their research.

There's shouting farther in the tunnel. Isaad grabs my arm and pulls me with him. "Part of the tunnel has collapsed. We need to see what's going on."

We run toward the mayhem. There's a wall of rock in front of us as the men are trying to remove the rocks by hand.

"Get the bulldozer," I yell to the men. Isaad informs me that they think there are several men trapped behind the collapse.

I motion for the driver to get off the bulldozer and make quick work of removing the rocks.

Once I create a hole, several men walk out from behind the rocks, and others shake their heads. We've lost two of the men. I jump down from the bulldozer. Silence falls among us with only the hum of the generator in the background. They haul out the bodies of the men and load them into one of the Jeeps.

In the commotion, I lean down to make it look like I'm tying the laces on my boot and slip a piece of Stellarium into my sock. I know minerals, and this is not like anything I've ever seen on planet Earth. This is a rare find at this point in Earth's history, and I have to investigate it.

I walk over to where Isaad is talking with the miners. "It doesn't look like your mine is safe from collapse."

Isaad sighs. "The poachers get in here and hack away at it, making it unstable. I'm going to have to get more security out here. We're wasting valuable time."

The miners get back to work like loyal ants, as if the men had not just lost their lives. The way of life I used to live is so distant from me.

Being a soldier put my mind in a different place, hiding behind the gear, guns, helmets, and camouflage. There were orders, a purpose, and a reason to kill or be killed. I'm not in a place where I have to lock down my emotions and pretend life goes on because, for many in Afghanistan, it doesn't go on. Life ends too often, making it the norm when it shouldn't be.

We spend the next couple of hours examining the equipment and talking about the best way to run the operation. A man runs up to Isaad and says something, pointing to the trommel screen.

"It looks like our night will end early. The trommel broke, and we can't get it fixed until tomorrow." He swears in Kati and runs his fingers through his hair.

The ride back to the house is quiet. Isaad seems to contemplate something.

I want to see where his head is at in this. "Out with it. There's steam coming out of your ears."

"You know me too well." Do I? I don't feel like I know him at all. "I wanted to offer you a permanent job here running the mine. It would be better money than you're making heading your security firm."

I turn my head slowly in his direction. "And how would you know how much I make?" He must not know about my stock portfolio.

"I have my ways. Sit with it and we'll talk numbers later." He grabs a cigarette.

"Please, not now. I like my lungs the way they are, cancer-free."

My comment is meant to loosen the tension. He laughs and nods, stowing the cigarette back in the box.

I have no intention of accepting his offer, but I'll wait. I don't need his money. There may be a way for me to use this information. The one call I need to make will wait until tomorrow morning. Neil is going to get an early morning wake-up call.

There's more here than meets the eye, and I have a feeling he knows exactly what it is.

TEN

Sean
_____

SLEEP ESCAPES me like it always does. Not getting in until almost three a.m. helps my brain skip the nightmares. I lay there looking at the ceiling, begging for sleep to take me peacefully. I must have snoozed because when I open my eyes, it's eight a.m.

I roll to a sitting position to get my bearings. In one of the many hidden compartments in my luggage is a Stealth phone, a highly encrypted satellite phone with an intrusion warning. The number I need is on speed dial.

"Sean, how's it going?" Neil's response is curt and tense.

"Cut the shit, Neil. What the hell is going on out here? Don't keep me in the dark." I'm done putting up with his covert bullshit.

There's a pause. "Are you on a secure line?"

"Of course." I don't hide my irritation.

"We're not exactly sure. There are hot spots around the world with some unusual activity. Isaad's compound is one of them. He has a lot of money he's sinking into a gold mining operation, but we can't pinpoint his source of income. There's a digital trail to nowhere."

He hasn't told me anything I don't already know. "Well, he's not just mining gold. There seems to be—" A tone breaks the line, letting me know someone is trying to intercept my call. "Gotta go." I click off, shut down the phone, and stuff it in my luggage.

The knock at the door comes two seconds after my SAT phone gets stowed away. I rush to the door and open it as fast as possible to ease any suspicion. My good buddy, Rakesh, stands with arms crossed.

I lean on the doorframe. "What's up?"

He pushes past me to get into the room and looks around. "Where's your cell phone?"

I grab it off the nightstand and hand it to him, smiling smugly. He swipes at the screen and pushes the buttons. The screen lights up, showing the power-up mode. He shoves it in my direction.

"What seems to be the problem?" I smile with a wide grin.

The scowl on his face tells me he didn't catch me in the act. Oh, well. Better luck next time, asswipe.

"Isaad wants you to join him later for dinner." He takes a step into my personal space. "I will catch you. You're here to spy on Isaad."

I shrug. "There's nothing to catch." He shoves my shoulder as he goes out the door. I call after him, "Have a great day."

"Maybe. I almost had a lot of fun last night." He smiles with a maniacal look in his eye. What the hell does he mean? Goosebumps dimple my arms.

After my encounter with Rakesh, I decide to go for a walk to check out the cabins again. Holstering my weapon,

I put a .22 at my ankle. I recon the area in case I need backup, which seems more and more likely.

I don't get very far before I'm stopped by a guard who points an AK-47 in my direction. Reaching for my firearm is pointless. He'll drop me before I can pull it. He says something to me in Kati. When he realizes I don't speak his language, he repeats it in English.

The menacing look on his face speaks to his hatred of Americans. "Stop. You need to go back."

"I'm not one of your prisoners." I push his AK-47 out of the way. "You have prisoners, don't you?"

He talks into his walkie-talkie as I hear Isaad's name. The burn of someone's eyes hits my back as I see Isaad staring at me from the second floor of the glass house. I wave to him and smile, and then turn to make my way farther into the woods.

I'm interested in the cabins and look into three of them. They share the same design. Bolted chains to the floor with a cuff at the end are long enough to reach the farthest corners of the cabin. There's only one reason to have a setup like this: slavery. The question is who, and better yet, why.

As I enter the glass house, I'm told Isaad requires my presence in the dining room. He sits at the far end with a woman on his right. I sit across from her, opposite the view of the valley.

The vibration of the house is a direct contrast to the serene picture on the other side of the windows. Everyone walks on pins and needles. The woman has her head down and eats her food piece by piece with one hand while holding her face with the other hand. She looks up, and her violet eyes pierce me. *Jess.* Her face shows sheer terror, but she shakes her head minutely.

"Ms. Wilder, how are you today?" I play along to find out what the hell is going on.

Isaad speaks up. "Rakesh caught her leaving her room early this morning by stopping the bolt from locking. Claims she was looking for you." He cuts his meat into equal parts and places it in his mouth without looking at me.

My hackles are up at the mention of Rakesh's name. I need to tread lightly here. "I doubt she's a security risk. Did you do a background check on her?"

"Passed with flying colors. She needs to understand that locking her in is for her own good." He glances at me as if it's obvious.

Jess drops her hand from her face. "And you need to understand that I am not your prisoner."

Isaad puts down his utensils. "As I've said before, it's for your safety." He resumes eating.

My blood turns to ice seeing the welt on her cheek. "What happened to your face?" Under the table, my fingers curl into fists.

Isaad speaks. "Rakesh—"

My eyes are on her. "I didn't ask you. I asked her. What about Rakesh?" I'm seeing red.

The vein pulses in her neck. "He found me in the hallway, and I tripped and fell." Her nose twitches, a dead giveaway that she's lying to me. Her eyes go wide when she sees me smirk.

"Really? Did you fall? Rakesh never put his hands on you?" My words stir the pot.

She glances at Isaad. "He helped me up and got me to my room."

I lean forward and lower my voice. "Well, if he ever puts his hands on you or any other woman in this house, I will kill him and not think twice about it."

"Women need to know their place. There are strict laws to keep women safe. If they don't follow them, there are consequences." Isaad's voice leaves no room for discussion. He doesn't make eye contact and continues to eat.

"Your country, your women. But where we come from, women have the freedom to do what they want. There was a time when that was true in Afghanistan before the Taliban took over. Don't you remember? Are you trying to tell me you go along with their philosophy?" My anger is going to get the better of this situation if I don't get a handle on it.

"Not all of it. But many of my men do." He turns to Jess. "You need to be careful or you could get hurt."

Isaad is cold and distant, not a temperament I'm used to from him. I know after last night, he has a lot on his mind.

"I've suddenly lost my appetite. Daphne, I would like to inspect the welt on your face, if you don't mind."

"Not at all." She turns to Isaad. "Thank you for dinner and the warning."

Isaad nods but keeps eating.

We get into the hallway. "Let's go back to my room. I've covered the cameras and disabled the bugs."

"You need to play nice because we're in deep shit." She twirls her hair with her fingers.

The door closes behind her. "Since when do you swear?"

She cuts me off before I continue. "Since you haven't seen me in ten years and I'm a big girl now."

She doesn't understand that I needed to get away from her, so I wouldn't destroy her. I've tried so hard to stay away from her. It hurts.

I ignore her comment. "Let me see your face." I grab her hand and lead her to the bathroom, our meeting place.

I put my hand on her shoulder, and she winces. "What's wrong?" My anger kicks up imagining what happened with Rakesh.

She shrugs away from me. "Nothing."

"Take your shirt off," I demand.

She puts her hands on her hips. "You're going to demand that I take my shirt off? Bossy much?"

"I know you have on a sleeveless shirt underneath. You wouldn't react like that if something wasn't wrong."

For years, I studied her, filled with admiration because of her struggles. I know her minute tells.

She pulls her top off, and it drifts to the ground. There are nail marks on each shoulder. Staggered welts cover the side of her face, not like she took a fall. My anger ignites with high octane.

"What happened?" Her eyes get big, and she blinks several times. "Out with it."

She tells me the details of what happened with Rakesh, then looks down.

"And? Because I know that's not all there is. You're a beautiful woman. He would not pass up an opportunity to hit on you."

I hold her face in my hands, tilting her face up to mine. Her eyes are glassy, with tears ready to fall. This is new because she was never a crier, but I don't think it's because she's hurt.

"He took his belt off—"

"I will fucking kill him!" I move toward the door.

She tugs at my shirt and puts her hands on my chest. My blood fires up, but for a whole other reason.

"Calm down. Nothing happened." She fiddles with the buttons on my shirt. "I reminded him who I am to Isaad and the article I'm writing. His job would be on the line."

She grabs my shirt. "You've got to use your head in this game because there's more."

I lean my forehead on hers, breathing her air for strength and peace. "You know I lose my shit when someone hurts you. It's an automatic reaction. Some things never change. But you need to be more careful."

My hands move to her lower back, and my thumbs rub up and down along the ridge of her spine. Her body is that of a woman with the curves a man could want and more. Her breath hitches. I fought so hard years ago to keep from feeling this fire, but the flames are winning.

She explains the panel in the wall, which is something I'm going to investigate since we haven't found Pippa yet. We decide to come up with a strategy tomorrow.

My thumb skims her smooth skin. "Do you want me to get you some ice?"

"No. I'm fine." She closes her eyes, melting into my touch. I suck in my breath.

I close my eyes and hug her to me. "Will you stay with me tonight, and we'll sleep just like we did when we needed to block out the world?"

Her body relaxes into mine. "Are you sure that's a good idea?"

"Only if you want to. Just like when we were younger. I don't care what anyone thinks. We need to stay safe." I choke out the last few words.

"I'd like that. Things got real in the last twenty-four hours. I'm so glad you're here. I wouldn't want to be here with anyone else."

We walk into the bedroom, and I throw her one of my T-shirts. She comes back from the bathroom with my T-shirt down to mid-thigh and scampers to the bed, throwing herself under the covers.

From what I can see, she's a knockout. She's not a little

girl anymore, but still hides her body. Her foster father always made her feel ugly and self-conscious with cutting comments. I wanted to knock him out every time she held her head down with shame.

There's a knock at the door that stops us cold.

"Who is it?" I'm tired and looking forward to time with Jess without interruption.

"Isaad wants Ms. Wilder back in her room. I will escort her, now," Rakesh bellows.

Jess puts her hands out in a sign to calm down. "I'm coming." She puts her clothes back on and heads for the door.

Before she opens the door, she mouths the words "Email me." And then she's gone, away from where I can protect her.

"Shit!" I'm beyond pissed. My need to know she's okay outweighs everything else, but keeping my head on straight is imperative. I search for the paper where she wrote the information about the website and begin contacting her. It's going to be a long night without her with me.

ELEVEN

Jess

THEIR NEED TO keep everyone separate unsettles me. I haven't been a model citizen, but their hosting skills need an upgrade.

My nerves got the better of me as I tried to stay with Sean. I always feel more secure and safe around him. Isaad's definition of safety is skewed and without reason. If it weren't for Rakesh running loose, he wouldn't need to keep the women safe.

I fire up my laptop and enter the dark web address to talk to Pippa. If Sean can read lips, maybe he got my message to email me.

Hey,

I wanted to see how you're doing and to let you know that SK is here. Do you remember him? He's doing something for IS that has to do with mining, but that's all I know.

How are you doing? Can you tell me any more about where you are in the house?

Love you,

J

Before I get her response, an email comes in from Sean.

Jess,

I hope this is the right address and email. Some letters were smudged with balsamic vinaigrette ;) Respond as soon as you get this.

Sean

I get a return email from Pippa with another address for us to meet in a chat room. I send it to Sean and tell him we only use the first initial of our names.

We meet up in the chat room on the dark web. It's called "the dark web" for a reason. It's sketchy. I'm eager for Sean to hear from Pippa, so we can locate her and get her out.

> Pippa: Hi S, Glad you showed up. I need a little help here.

> Sean: I heard. What can you tell me about where you are?

> Pippa: I know that I'm underground. There's no sunlight. I'm chained to the floor with an ankle cuff.

> Sean: That seems to be the running theme here. There is a maze of tunnels. Can you get me any other markers, like sounds you hear?

> Pippa: I don't know where I am underground, and it's quiet, for the most part. They put a bag over my head when I got here, and we went down a set of stairs.

> Sean: Is there anyone else with you or near you?

> Pippa: No, not that I know of.

Sean: What are you doing here for Isaad?

Pippa: I got hired to do a job, but once I got here, it turned into something else. Gotta go, someone's here.

Sean: J, are you still here?

Me: Yeah, I'm here. What's going on? Is she going to be okay?

I panic. Who's with her? What's happening?

Sean: Do you know the details of what she's doing here?

Me: No, why is that so important? We just need to get her out.

Sean: I'm not here only for the mining. I'm here on a rescue mission. I thought she might have had some details I need. Are you okay?

Me: For now. I wish I could have stayed with you, but I don't want to raise any suspicion. I don't want to miss a meal again.

Sean: What are you talking about?

Me: As punishment for leaving my room last night, I wasn't let out of my room until dinnertime. I stole some food to put in my room just in case it happens again. I've been on a lot of tough assignments, but this one scares me.

I wait for Sean to reply as I watch the three dots on the screen. He may be cursing up a blue streak at my recent information.

> Sean: I need to talk to Isaad. I'm going to get you and Pippa out. It's going to take some time. Bear with me.

> Me: That sounds good. I'll be fine. Talk soon.

I watch as his name disappears from the chat. The screen goes blank, and I'm alone again.

The isolation of being in this house is getting to me. This is the most bizarre assignment I've ever been on. I need it to end soon so I can get out of here. Sean is our only answer. But I have other questions that need answers.

TWELVE

Jess
_____

AS SOON AS the door unlocks in the morning, I look both ways and sneak down the hall to Sean's room. I knock on the door, hoping he opens it soon.

What appears on the other side of the door is a half-dressed man with bed head and red eyes, signs of someone who hasn't slept well. My eyes scan his torso with keen interest. I don't think I've ever seen a man this close-up in such great shape. He must work out for hours a day.

I step past him into the room. The door shuts with a soft click. "I see you got as much sleep as I did."

"Yeah, like not much. I'm trying to wrap my head around what's going on." He sits on the edge of the bed.

"You said you're not just here for the mining. What are you—"

There's one knock at the door and the buzz of a keycard gaining access to the room. Sean shoots off the bed and heads for the door. Rakesh stands in the doorway.

"What. The. Fuck?" Sean says as Rakesh peeks around Sean to see who's in the room.

"Isaad wants to meet with you to discuss moving

forward with the mining." He looks at me. "What are you doing here?" he sneers.

Sean hauls him up by his shirt and throws him across the hallway. Rakesh jumps back up and goes after him, swinging. Sean meets him with a kick and an uppercut. He straddles Rakesh, ready to wail on him.

I make it to the hallway in time to grab his arm in midair. "Stop. This won't solve anything."

Sean pulls his arm away and gets in Rakesh's face. "If you ever touch her again, I won't think twice about making sure you make it to a special hell."

"If I don't kill you first, American scum." Rakesh throws Sean off him, brushes himself off, and walks away.

We go back into his room, realizing they have caught it on video. Sean sits next to me on the bed and puts his arm around my shoulder. "He never should have been allowed to get away with that."

I turn to look up at him. "You need to do less talking with your fists and more thinking with your brain. We've got to figure out a way to get to Pippa and get out of here. It won't be easy."

He takes my hand in his and rubs his thumb across the top of it. "Why did we lose touch?" There's sorrow and questions in his eyes that haven't been there before.

I shrug. "I don't know. Things change. People change. And life goes on whether or not we want it to."

He pushes a curl behind my ear. We're in a moment that could go either way, and I concede to him. He pulls me toward him and kisses my forehead.

"And what about you? Who has captured your heart?"

I crumble inside. You. You captured my heart from the moment you rescued me from Brady. When you protected me from bullies. Even when you got married to the wrong woman. It's always been you. But I don't say what's really in my heart. I can't take that chance. Pushing away from him, I'm out of his grasp and stand, needing the physical space.

"What's our plan?"

His arms hang empty at his sides as he sits on the bed. "So, you're single?"

I clasp my hands in front of me. "Maybe. But we don't have time to discuss that."

A piece of hair hangs over his forehead, and he smiles. He looks like he did back in high school, fresh and charming with a glint in his eye. It brings back my heartache to see him with other girls in the hall between classes, putting his arm around their shoulders, and glancing back at me with something akin to a look of fear. His commitment to them was half-hearted and more for show than anything else. I didn't understand the purpose. He had nothing to fear from me.

He gets up and stands in front of me. The heat rolls off him like waves off a summer pavement. My hands come up, but don't touch him. We're frozen, staring at each other in our own worlds.

"You look like the cat that ate the canary. Hmmm? We'll revisit my last question at a later time." He bends down and opens the drawer of the nightstand. "I have something I need you to keep for me." There is a silver piece of metal in his palm.

I reach for it and tumble it around in my hand. "What is it? It looks like a piece of silver."

"It's not silver. But the even odder part is, I don't know what it is." He raises his eyebrows.

My head snaps up. "What do you mean, you don't know what it is? You're the mining expert."

"I've never seen anything like it. It has some strange qualities. I need you to always keep it with you, like in your bra or underwear. I've got to get this back to Neil so he can analyze it."

He bites his lower lip, resisting the urge to smile. It looks sexy as hell and is doing things to my sex drive.

Heat rises to my cheeks, and I change my focus to the piece of metal in my hand. "Not a problem. I'll keep it safe."

"That's what best friends are for." The words rumble in his chest.

"Yep," I say without making eye contact.

He's only ever going to see me as his best friend, and I'm not sure I dare to push for anything more. Time is not on my side. We need to keep our heads clear.

"I'm going to get dressed and see what Isaad wants. We'll probably return to the mine today, so you must stay low and out of sight." His eyes pin me.

I won't. I'll go in search of Pippa again and try to find where she's being held prisoner here because that seems to be the other theme in this house.

On my way back to my room, I'm stopped by Isaad. He tilts his head. "You seem very comfortable with him for having just met him." He says it as if he knows more than he's letting on.

I choose my words carefully. "He seems like a good man. We've formed a friendship, but it's not stronger than your friendship with him."

"Are you sure you're just friends? I can't imagine any man wanting to be just friends with a beautiful woman like yourself." He holds my upper arm and strokes his thumb up and down. His touch gives me the creeps.

I tug my arm away from him. The men around here have a possessiveness about them that's irritating. "Oh, I'm sure we're just friends." There's no lie in my answer.

His eyes narrow as he frowns. "I'll see you later for dinner?"

"Yes. Have a good day." A smile forces its way to my lips.

He stuffs his hands in his pockets. "I'm looking forward to reading your article."

"I'm working on it. You'll be the first to read the final draft when I have completed it."

I have a notebook full of notes on everything that won't be in the article, including observations on my stay at the House Made From Hills.

I hurry back to my room, close the door, and lock it. Xanax is calling my name from my suitcase, but I should only use it during my panic attacks, and I need to keep my wits about me.

I do my daily yoga routine, ending with a short meditative moment. Yoga helps ground me, and I need all the grounding I can get. I wasn't much into sports, so yoga keeps me limber and strong.

A hot shower is in order as I step under the spray. When I was younger, I used to think I could burn away my skin color. Then I would be like the other kids, and they would like me, along with my foster parents. But my skin turned red and angry in the shower and dried out, leaving a whitish film, only to itch enough to need moisturizer. Coconut oil was the only thing that gave me relief. I still use it on my face and hair, but it deepens the tone of my skin that I've come to accept over the years.

Acceptance is too strong a word. Tolerate describes it better. It's a blessing and a curse. My skin has aged well, but the color triggers anger in those people who focus on it.

Feeling fresh for the day ahead, I slip into a pair of shorts and a T-shirt. My suite is the only place I can dress comfortably. Outside my room, dressing in traditional clothing makes sense. I can blend in and stay out of sight. I've learned it's the best way to gather important information and details that otherwise might not present themselves if I was overt about my appearance.

There's a level of comfort hiding behind flowing, draped clothing. I don't have to worry if anyone is looking at me and judging me.

My first order of business is to cover the cameras around the room. Sean gave me some black tape to put over the holes in the walls and ceiling, which I can reach from my bed, desk, and chair. The security and scrutiny are unnerving.

I open my laptop and continue to write the article I started on Isaad. Many things have changed since I first came here about a week ago. Sean is a complication I didn't see coming.

My emotions stretch from one end to another, from terrified one minute to having my libido turned up to ten around Sean. Not a place I like to be, especially in the middle of finding my sister. The intensity seems to have a life of its own in this house and grows each day. It vibrates around me, and I'm not sure why.

I get up to stretch and wander to the immense windows overlooking a small garden in the middle of a circle of trees. At first, I see a flash of red, the back of a woman's head. I crane my neck to see beyond the trees to get a better look at her.

She's not wearing traditional clothing of any kind. She's with someone I can't see. As they turn back in my direction, I can see who it is because I would recognize that face anywhere.

THIRTEEN

Pippa

A STEEL CUFF binds my ankle, and I'm chained to the floor like an animal. This is not what I signed on for. Okay, so my line of work, operating on the dark web, isn't exactly clean and wholesome, but I deserve some human rights. I'm struggling with bouts of depression that I need to put on ice to survive and get out of here. It's a battle I'm not winning.

Most wouldn't complain about the decked-out suite with a master bedroom and bathroom that could fit a party of five. This room has all the modern conveniences except a window with a view of the one thing I treasure most, the outdoors. The chain allows me to travel to every corner of the suite, but it's cold and heavy.

The three square meals a day are five-star quality. They're delivered on time and fully garnished. I'm given two hours a day to work out in a gym so I can keep up with my bodybuilding, my requirement when I took the job. Little did I know a guard would accompany me to the gym and stand outside the door. Routine is good in some ways, but I'm itching to get out. My inner free spirit screams for release.

My freckled fair skin misses the sun even without sunscreen. There's nothing like the sun's warmth to make you feel refreshed and alive, seeping into you like a cozy blanket. Today, I will beg him again to go outside.

I hear the lock to the door click open, and he walks in, taking up the air in my cell. His arrival is on the early side. I'm not used to seeing him during the day. He usually visits me late at night. Something has changed.

"How are you today, my pet?" He runs his finger through my hair. He knows the word pet irritates me. "I'm always amazed at how red your hair is. It's so beautiful and unique."

"I'd be better if I weren't chained up like a dog." This gets me a scowl. I remove his finger and put on my dejected look. "I would love to see the sun. It's been two weeks. Please. Just for a little while."

I take his hand in mine and suck on one of his fingers. The fastest way to a man's heart is knowing how well to suck.

"You're not giving up, are you?" He smiles.

It's a rare gift from the worried man who usually comes to visit me. I think I might have Stockholm syndrome at this point. I'm lusting after one of my captors.

He bends down and swipes his keycard across the cuff as it falls off. I get up and stretch. Sitting for hours on end is not for a body that's used to being in motion.

I kiss him and put my arms around his neck. He's a handsome bastard with some kink I enjoy.

"Thank you. I hope you're going with me instead of sending me with one of those goons."

He pulls me to him and taps my nose with his finger. "Yes, I want to take you to the garden."

We've gotten to know each other over the month that I've been here. He's my primary contact since I hardly see Isaad unless he needs an update on my progress, which is slow.

Unlike before, he doesn't cover my head. I try not to look around too much, but I take in the clues where I can. We walk to an elevator I've never seen and take it up to ground level. I can see the garden from the window at the end of the hall. My pace quickens, and I drag him with me.

"Come on. I can't wait." He grins at my childlike behavior.

I push through the door and face the sky. A crystal-clear blue-sky ceiling greets me. My hands stretch out to my sides while I spin around. This is my slice of heaven. The sun warms my skin and soaks into my soul. My lungs breathe as I gulp in fresh air so I can store it for later. If only that were possible.

Rakesh has been kind and patient with me. Isaad assigned him to me, and I'm trying to use it to my advantage. I doubt Isaad knows what's going on between us; otherwise, he would have Rakesh's head. So far, we've kept it hidden, but if Isaad sees us today, it may be a different story.

Isaad hired me to steal digital currency for him so he can finance his dream, as he calls it. I don't have the details, and nor do I want them. It's not my concern. My goal is to get paid and get out of here, but we seem to have different opinions about my departure date. I had to call Jess. I'm operating in the dark, and I can't contact Neil.

Things went south about three days into the job. He wants me to rewrite the entire code for a program called White Raven. When I completed it, I sent it to a couple of friends around the world for safekeeping. The program is valuable beyond measure because of what it can do, and it took a year for me to complete. The problem is, I can't remember the details from the beginning, so I may be in this dungeon for a while. I'm hoping Jess's lover boy can get us out.

Rakesh is smitten, or it may be I'm something new and different for him to play with. Some women would be happy to be spoiled by his charm and money for the rest of their lives. I can't be tied down. The world calls to me, and I have so much more to see and do.

I sent out my SOS to Jess about a week ago. She was to be my only contact while I was dark. Thank God for our email to communicate. I don't know what I would do without her. If she knew why I was here, she would blow a gasket. I was supposed to be taking the high road and using my skills for good, which I did, kind of. I'm deep in thought when Rakesh nudges me with his elbow.

He keeps his hands in his pockets. "How's it going down there?"

"Okay, but it's slow going." I keep my response brief because I have an NDA with Isaad, and I'm not sure how much Rakesh knows about my work.

We walk farther out into the woods. "What exactly are you working on?"

I'm about to get my answer, but I know where my bread is buttered. "You'll have to ask Isaad. He told me it's top secret. I'm not allowed to discuss it." I keep my focus straight ahead.

Rakesh's voice is tight. "But you and I have a secret no one knows about either."

In another time and place, Rakesh and I would be perfect together, but we both know the score and where our loyalties lie, even though he keeps asking me to stay. A relationship is impossible for many reasons.

We take our time strolling from the garden into the woods, talking and laughing. He's a smart man with a quick wit. I'm hungry for human contact, which keeps me tied to him. He plays the game well, as if he's done it before.

I stop to look at a unique flower, and the hair stands up on the back of my neck. I look around and up at the windows of the house, but I only see the woods reflecting in the glass.

"Are you okay?" Rakesh follows my line of sight to the windows.

I shrug. "Yeah." I could swear someone is watching us. Maybe Isaad is keeping tabs on me.

The outdoor visit is over way too soon. We're back in the dungeon and not the fun dungeon I'm usually into. My energy deflates, but I grab enough of the outdoors to sustain me until the next outing.

He puts my cuff back in place. "Is that necessary?" I sigh.

"You are a most precious asset, and I can't have you leaving me before Isaad gets what he needs." He runs his finger along the tattoos on my arm. "You are a unique woman. I hope you will reconsider my offer. You need to be by my side." He kisses my forehead. "I'll see you tonight."

The door shuts behind him with a soft click. Every time he leaves me, the walls close in. I must meditate every day just to keep my sanity. Making the most of any situation is my strength, but I have my limits. I need Jess more than ever to find a way out of here. I might be looking at a death sentence.

FOURTEEN

Jess

MY HAND BANGS on the window once, and I freeze, realizing what I've done. Bringing attention to Pippa wouldn't be good for anyone. I crouch down on the floor, shaking, and then peek over the bottom edge of the window frame, careful not to be seen.

Pippa laughs and carries on like she's on vacation. The man next to her is Rakesh, who is also smiling, something I've never seen him do. Her survival skills surpass mine. I know she's being kept against her will, and yet she looks to have the enemy by the nose. She should make a run for it or try fighting for her life. Maybe she has a plan I haven't figured out yet.

The good news is I know she's here and okay. The bad news is I don't know how to get to her or where he's keeping her. I watch them head back inside as I try to form a plan. There's not much to it, and Sean won't be too happy. I'm going to go back to scout out things behind the panel to see if I can find her, but I'm worried about the repercussions if I get caught again. Pain or death are not my thing.

My suitcase has a full burka outfit that will cover me from head to toe. I figure I can wander around the halls without being detected, and it sounds like most of the men will be at the mine today.

I get dressed with the mesh mask covering my face. There is a strange sense of security and peace that comes over me when wearing these clothes. I can hide in here, away from the world, and view it as an outsider looking in, like I've always done. I feel like no one can touch me. Delusion is a powerful force.

I'm used to this role, hiding behind a mask with large clothing to cover my body. Years of yoga have made my body lean and strong, but I lack the self-confidence to show it off.

Over the years, men see something in me I don't see in myself. Their looks and comments are unsettling and foreign. The whole vibe of this house is uncomfortable. I can't tell if the women are here by choice or if they are being held against their will.

During the day, the doors are unlocked as I pull mine closed behind me. I walk down the hallway without being hurried, so I don't draw attention to myself. But inside, my nerves are running like a bi-turbo engine on jet fuel.

Above me is the thumping sound of helicopter blades. I look out the window in time to see Isaad's profile sitting next to the pilot in a small chopper. It'll make it easier to find my way around without Isaad here. I'm hoping Rakesh has left with him. My opportunity has presented itself.

I wander around the halls without direction, hoping the people on the other side of the cameras, if there are any, get bored. I stop in front of the table with the vase. Oddly, there are no cameras here.

There's a painting on the wall above the table, and I

pretend to admire it. My sleeves cover my hands, giving me the perfect opportunity to reach out and turn the vase. I turn it and quickly sneak in behind the panel. Once I get on the other side, I notice a handle. I tug on it to close the panel and look around. A low mechanical hum comes from somewhere down the tunnel. Intuition tells me Pippa is not on this level. If Isaad wanted to hide someone, he would go deeper.

There's a stairwell that takes me to a lower floor. The basement is where Rakesh put Sean and me in a room to wait for Isaad. I don't see anyone down the hall, and I check for cameras. There don't appear to be any in the stone walls.

I jiggle the handle of each door and call Pippa's name in a low voice. My nerves are on high alert as sweat drips down my back. I move farther and farther away from the stairwell, away from the safety of my room. Safety? I need to remind myself that there is no safety here, only suspicion and watching over my shoulder.

I come to the end of the hall at the last door, cast in darkness. The light above it is out. "Pippa?"

Chains scrape across the floor as if they are being dragged, and I step back from the door as my heart pounds in my chest.

"Jess, is that you?" The door muffles her voice.

I lay my hands on the door. "Yes, oh my God! Are you okay? And why do I hear chains?"

"I'm fine. Isaad has me chained up at the ankle so I won't escape. Fat chance. How the hell would I ever get out of here?" Her sadness travels in waves and hits me.

Tears well in my eyes, and I dab them at the corners. "I've been looking for you for a week. Why does Isaad have you chained up? I saw you through the window. You and Rakesh looked cozy."

"Have you seen him? Not bad on the eyes. I figured I'd make the most of the situation. He and I disagree about my freedom. He wants me to stay. I want to go, as in tomorrow would be good."

"Does he have orders to keep you as a prisoner?" I'm afraid of the answer, and the chains add another layer to get through to get to her.

"Well… yes." She sniffles. "What about Sean?"

"He told me he's here to do mining and rescue someone, but that's all I got from him."

"Jess, put your hand above the door handle, and I'll put mine up on this side." I do as she asks. "I need you to listen to me. Isaad is a very dangerous man, and he's in with some dangerous people."

"How do you know? What exactly are you doing for him?" I know the answer because it means she's doing something illegal.

"It's complicated, but in short, I started by stealing cryptocurrency for him. How do you think he's financing everything? But he has money coming in from some other sources I can't trace. He has me doing some other things for him that could keep me here for a long time."

Silence hangs in the air between us. We both understand the danger, and it seems to follow us, but this is out of both our leagues.

"God, Jess. What have I gotten myself into?" she mumbles.

I sigh. "I knew there were some things that didn't add up. How did you get tangled up in this?"

"There's no time to explain. Go back to your boyfriend and be super careful. Because to be honest, I don't know how we're going to get out of here." There's desperation in her voice, resigned to the fact that she may be here for a very long time.

Wait. "Boyfriend?"

"Oh, please, girl. You've had it bad for him ever since I can remember. You'd better go after him while you have his undivided attention." I sense her smile on the other side of the door.

My fingers curl on the door. "I think he only sees me as a friend."

There's a pit in my stomach just saying the words I don't want to be true. I hate that he only sees me as a friend.

The fire comes back to her voice, if only for a moment. "Yeah, right. You need to open your eyes. There are a lot of reasons he left. Get out from under your baggy-ass clothes and turn on the sex appeal."

"Easy for you—" I hear voices at the other end of the hall. Beyond the door is a space carved out of stone. I squeeze myself into it, hoping the black clothing and darkness of the hall are enough to conceal me.

The men go into another room and shut the door. I tiptoe to her door. "That's my sign to go back. We'll be back to get you out."

"Be careful. I love you." Pippa's voice breaks, and it shreds me.

"I love you too." I choke out the words, hoping this isn't my last contact with her.

I run down the hall and make my way up the stairs. I go into the hallway, closing the panel behind me. I resist the urge to run down the hall to my room. Rakesh is up ahead. I thought he might have left with Isaad.

"Hey, where are you coming from?" He grabs my arm.

My pulse pounds in my throat. "It's me, Daphne. I was going for a walk. Is that a crime in this house?"

His face is against my burka. "No, but I'm going to look at the tapes, and if you're lying, I will punish you without Isaad's permission. Remember your place here, Ms. Wilder." He releases my arm.

Without a word, I turn and walk to my room. Once I get there, I rip off my clothes and strip down to the T-shirt and shorts underneath. I stow the burka away out of sight. I let out the breath I'd been holding in. The security I felt hiding in my clothes vanishes because no one ever really sees you, and isn't that the point? Instead, it suffocates me, hemming me in as claustrophobia sets in, and my skin feels more comfortable than ever before.

Rakesh's words rattle me. I know he will make good on his promise to hurt me. He has two very distinct sides to him, the lover and the punisher. I pray he doesn't see anything on the tapes. I have to warn Sean. He's my only defense.

My breath is uneven as my head spins on how we are going to escape. Between the cameras and security guards, it will take a magic trick to get us out of here. From where I'm sitting, it's a no-win situation for us.

FIFTEEN

Sean
_____

MY HEAD IS NOT in the game, and that makes me weak. I'm distracted by thoughts of a beautiful woman with skin smooth as silk, violet eyes, and a full body. If I think about her much longer, I'm gonna give myself a hard-on, which would not be good among a group of men.

She ties me up inside. She's always had that effect on me. The urge to be with her strengthens, now that I see the woman she's become, smart and patient.

For the first time in many years, I slept through the night. I didn't wake up once. I realize how broken I am from war and life. The deck of cards life dealt me was the road less traveled, as in no one would want to travel on my rutted path. What's clean on the outside hides the dirt on the inside. I've seen and done some things I'm not proud of out of necessity. I forgot how much Jess keeps me grounded. My compass always points back to her.

When we were kids, I was her superhero, coming to her rescue when she was being bullied by some insecure asshole. We grew up together and then grew apart.

Hormones can be a blessing and a curse. I started

seeing her in a different light, one where I wanted to smell her, touch her, feel her, and be inside her. But I couldn't do that to her. I wouldn't do to her what my father did to my mother. The less time I spent with her, the better off both of us would be. At least, that's what my sixteen-year-old self thought.

Time should make me forget the scent of wild roses, the softness of her hair, and the sparkle in her eye. I convinced myself that getting married would make it go away. Thoughts of her went away for a little while, but she was never completely gone. Even my time in hell didn't distract me from thoughts of her.

Here we are, single and fighting for our lives, not so far away from where we came from. Two kids from broken homes, only she doesn't know how broken mine had become.

We've been at the mine for a couple of hours. Isaad joined us later by helicopter. The miners work with heavy machinery to move dirt and rocks to the trommel, but they also pick up the odd pieces of silver metal and put them in buckets. They transfer the buckets to a truck. If they are junk, why have your workers spend time picking them up?

I survey the mine for hours and decide to take a break. I follow the road out to another area that's been written off as a barren spot, which makes no sense because it has the perfect geography for gold. The soil holds the clues.

The road ends as I trek on an uneven path, climbing over rocks, and finding a spot to sit down. Something in the dirt catches my eye. My fingers rub off the loose dirt. The smooth, rounded surface tells me what I need to know. It's a good-sized gold nugget, oblong with no actual shape, taking up the palm of my hand. It resembles a bug.

Bug. She is the most beautiful bug on the planet. I place the nugget in my sock because I have plans for it.

The odd shape presses between my ankle and my boot, reminding me it's there. Jess presses on my soul, never letting me forget she's always there. Under different circumstances, I would never take a piece of gold. This goes against the gold mining code of ethics. I don't feel bad because there's plenty of gold in that mine.

"There you are. I've been looking for you."

Isaad makes his way over the rocks. "Needed a break. The mine has excellent potential, by the way, from everything that I've seen."

He nods as if he doesn't care. "I'm sure it does."

Are we here for the gold or something else, like the silver-colored metal?

I use my hand as a visor. "You said you could only mine at night." From this angle, Isaad is a dark silhouette.

"There have been some recent developments allowing us to mine anytime we want to. Let's just say I have the government's blessing, whether they like it or not." He takes a drag of his cigarette without elaborating on how this has come about. "I wanted to talk to you about Ms. Wilder. I understand she likes to snoop around my house." He keeps his focus on the horizon.

"What are you talking about?" I act as if I don't care about it.

"Rakesh caught her coming from an area she shouldn't have been in. He's looking at the tapes now." I stand to face him. He looks in my direction. "Don't underestimate him. He's well-educated and a well-trained soldier. He has my permission to take care of things that need to be taken care of."

His words rev my engine. "And you're telling me this because?"

He crushes his cigarette under his boot. "You seem to have taken a liking to my houseguest."

"You told me to find someone to keep me warm." Let's see where this goes.

He chuckles. "I did, didn't I? You need to warn her to stick to writing the article and stop looking for another story that's not there."

"Typical reporter. Always looking for the next story. If you have nothing to hide, then it shouldn't be a problem." I put my hands in my pockets.

He adjusts his large brim hat to shade his face. "We all have our secrets."

"Since I need to keep her safe, especially from Rakesh, I'll have her stay in my room until I leave, or she leaves with me." I'm not offering a discussion. I'm giving him a courtesy by letting him know.

He grimaces. "I also noticed you blocked the cameras in your room, and so did she."

I put the ball back in his court. "The better question is, why do you feel the need to spy on me or anyone else?"

He turns to look at me with his mouth turned down. "You're overreacting. It's not spying. I simply keep track of what's going on under my roof."

"Why bring me here if you don't trust me?"

He lights another cigarette. "I trust you, but things have changed in my life. I'm not the same man I used to be. The world is not a safe place anymore. She needs to stay in her room." For the first time, he raises his voice.

From my point of view, the world was never a safe place. I take a couple of steps toward him so I'm inches away from his face. "From what I understand, Rakesh was less than a gentleman when he found her. May the best man win." I smile. "I'll let her decide what she wants to do."

Isaad frowns as if it's new information, but doesn't ask

me to clarify. "Rakesh has old-world views about women. He just wants to keep her safe."

I don't want to get into a pissing contest with him. "If that's what you want to believe."

"We have a bird to catch. I assume you want to take the chopper back with me."

The urgency to get back to Jess is overwhelming. "Sounds good. Those mountain roads are like riding a rollercoaster without the adrenaline rush." He slaps me on the back and smiles.

These days, he seems to smile less. He's elusive, staying in a restricted section of the house that requires a keycard. Jess has done a tour of the house and filled me in on the layout.

The time back on the chopper goes by fast, and I'm eager to see Jess. Leaving her alone for too long is never a good idea for many reasons. The first that comes to mind is Rakesh. The second is her curiosity, which always gets her into trouble.

We land on the roof, and Isaad uses his keycard to gain access to the elevator that takes us to the lower levels. The button panel is in Arabic numbers, and there appear to be six levels.

"How far down does this house go?" I stare at the display panel above the doors.

"There are many levels for different things I'm working on."

My head turns in his direction, and we're in a stare-off. He's not willing to tell me what's on the other floors. Something imperceptible passes between us. Distrust and anger radiate off him. I'm unclear why. He called me here. I didn't just show up to say hi.

The doors open, and I resist the urge to sprint down

the hall to get to Jess. I knock on her door. What I want to do is throw it open and hold her to me.

"Come in." Her voice is thready.

I come through the door, close it, and lock it behind me. "Don't you think you should ask who it is before you just let anyone in?"

She shrugs. "I knew it was you."

"Really? How did you know it was me?"

"I heard the helicopter. Besides, I don't have time for guessing games. I have a lot to tell you. So have a seat."

SIXTEEN

Jess
___

"WHO'S BOSSY NOW?" he says with a smirk.

I reach up to push his shoulders down. The bed creaks as he sits on it. His size makes him intimidating. He is about six foot five, easily a foot taller than me.

Something is off, and he's flustered. "What's wrong?" I pull up a chair to sit in front of him.

"Isaad called me out about us blocking the security cameras and then told me you needed to stay in your room. Wait." He grabs my hand and takes me to the bathroom. His touch spreads through my arm, warming me from the inside out.

"What?" I follow him to our usual meeting spot. "We've got to stop meeting like this." I giggle.

He stares at me without expression, sits on the toilet seat cover, and continues.

"It gets better. Isaad told me Rakesh is looking into the tapes of where you were in the house. He gave permission for Rakesh to do what he wants to you. Isaad told me to warn you about snooping around for another story." His eyes darkened, and his mouth became a taunt line.

I stop breathing. My heart hammers in my chest. "Well, that's interesting."

I tell him about my undercover operation to find Pippa, where she's located, and how to get there.

Then he loses his shit. He projects off the seat cover as if it's on fire.

"You did what?!" His hands pull at his hair. "Have you lost your damn mind?"

I cross my arms and face him, standing my ground. "I was out of sight under the burka."

"You were in plain sight. You could've been caught, and then what? Are you trying to get yourself killed?" His face contorts with pain. He puts his hands on his hips as his fingers curl into his hipbones. He's acting like an overbearing alpha boyfriend, which he is not.

"No one could see me, and I stayed out of sight. I'm an investigative journalist. I go on dangerous assignments all the time. You don't have the right to tell me what to do and what not to do. I haven't seen you in years. You can't come in here and boss me around."

His hands fall by his sides, and he looks up at the ceiling, breathing through his nose. When he looks at me, it's with the most intensity I've ever experienced from anyone.

His eyes cut into my soul, and I know what he's about to say may change us forever. My fingers twist together. I'm not sure which way this conversation will go.

He bends down to eye level. "Let me be clear. This is my territory. I understand the culture, the geography, and the dangers. You are out of your depth here. We," —he waves his finger between the two of us— "are in danger. I'm trying to come up with a way to get us out. As a highly trained former Navy SEAL, I know about danger and risk. This is right up there at level eleven. I will not lose you again."

What registers is as a trained SEAL, he feels he's in danger too, which doesn't bode well. But I'm stuck on the last comment.

"I'm confused. You won't lose me, as if I was the one who left you behind? Besides, you never had me to begin with." My words slice through the air. I want this out in the open.

He stands up, but his body sags. He hangs his head so I can't see his eyes. When he turns to me, it's there etched on his face, the pain, angst, and loss.

"There is so much I need to tell you and so much you don't know. Things at home were not great. While you hid in baggy clothes, I hid behind my star quarterback status. We lost touch with who we are to one another. You're right, I never had you, and that was my fault."

He puts his hands on my shoulders. "I didn't want to leave. I had to leave. There was no other choice."

I'm at a loss, but I know there is more. I won't press him. My mind tries to catch up with his words. I whisper. "I had no idea."

My arms circle his neck, and I hold him to me. His big forearms wrap around me, covering my entire back. He buries his nose in my neck and breathes me in, sending a quiver down my spine.

Our energy shifts. As two kids who grew up together, we see each other in a very different light. We're adults with unresolved issues from our childhood. Those issues had us make decisions we didn't understand.

I gather his sadness into my body and hold him tight. His head moves slightly as his lips brush my neck. I let out a soft moan and clear my throat to cover it up. I'm sure it was a mistake on his part.

He pulls away from me, and his large hands hold my face. We touch foreheads.

"I will not lose you again. This time it's going to be different, but you need to listen to me."

I'm too shocked by his honesty to jump into this emotional pool with him. "Okay," is my only response.

His thumb brushes my lower lip, sending a shock wave between my legs. "Let's get you packed up so you can move into my room."

I pull his hands away from my face to quell the pulse between us and to give me space.

"Slow your roll. Why do I need to move in with you? Are you sure that's a good idea?"

Panic rises. I'm not ready for this. It's too much, too soon. I won't be able to control my emotions or keep them from springing out after being buried for so long.

"It's either that or Rakesh can come to your room anytime he wants to pay you a visit with his all-access keycard." He shrugs.

I stare at him for a millisecond. "I'm going to pack my things up and room with you."

"That's what I thought." The heat of our encounter follows me out, warming my back. I've got to keep it together.

There's not much to pack up, which we do in silence, trying to process what is going on between us and where it's going. More than ever, we need to be on the same page as danger swirls around us.

We get to his room and I haul the suitcase up on the baggage stand.

"Feel free to unpack and put your stuff in the drawer and closet. There's plenty of room." He motions toward the dresser.

I can't resist and open the drawers. His shirts and underwear are neatly folded and piled up. I laugh. He's still a neat freak.

"Some things never change," I murmur to myself.

He digs in his suitcase and unzips a panel at the bottom. "The military only added to my OCD tendencies. There are very few things you can control in life." There's a hitch in his voice.

I know about not having control, but I've learned to embrace it and problem-solve my way through things.

"Your wife must have been happy not to be living with a slob." The comment falls out before I can grab it back. I twist my fingers and look over my shoulder at him.

"I wouldn't know. I was never home long enough to find out if she was happy. She was happier with one of my friends. They're married with two kids and another one on the way." He doesn't look at me, and there's no emotion attached to his words.

"I'm sorry." The pain of betrayal is something I've experienced, just not in a marriage, which has to be ten times worse.

"Don't be. It takes two, Jess. She wasn't right for me, she never was." There's finality in his eyes as they look up and focus on me. He's come to terms with it.

I ease the moment with a deflection. "It looks like you have a lot of toys in your suitcase."

"I always come prepared. I have a feeling they replaced the bugs with new ones. I'll do a sweep, find the bugs, and rip the cameras out of the wall. That should send a clear message." The action hero gives me his heart-stopping smile.

After he does a sweep and finds the bugs, he uses his fist to punch a hole in the wall and rips out the cameras to cut the wires. There are four that he throws into the trash from across the room.

"That was a three-pointer for sure." He picks up the trash can and sets it outside in the hallway.

In these moments, I remember how he used to be and why opposites attract. He finds two more bugs, cuts the wires, and crushes them under his foot before adding them to the collection in the hall.

"That takes care of that. Now, let's go have some dinner because when we come back, we have a lot to talk about." He's a man on a mission coming straight for me. I'd better hold on. This is going to be a bumpy ride.

SEVENTEEN

Sean

THROUGH DINNER, my thoughts are on what I want to say to Jess and how I want to say it. My mind is foggy. I'm not sure what came over me. My feelings for her have been at a simmer for years, but seeing her portrait flipped a switch I haven't been able to turn off.

I want to tell her everything and nothing at the same time. Sheer terror results in the loss of my appetite. Being raw and open feels out of control for me, not a place I'm used to being. Precision and control are my modus operandi. If we're going to be together, she has a right to know the truth.

Dinner is a tense event with few words spoken and unsaid accusations. The trust between Isaad and me shreds before us. Suspicion on both sides settles in as my imagination runs amok with what he's hiding.

I'm ready for the battle I know is coming. A couple of things need to come together before I can make my next move. The first thing is finding and getting to Pippa, which will be no easy feat. Then there is the real mission of finding Red Enigma.

In the distance, I hear Jess laugh. "What do you think, Sean?" Isaad asks me something.

"What? I'm sorry. My mind was somewhere else." I try to cover up by stuffing food in my mouth.

Isaad puts his utensils down and stares at me with intensity. "What's on your mind?"

"I was thinking about your offer and how long I'm going to stay on for. What about you, Daphne? How much longer do you think you'll be here?" I'm a master of deflection.

She stops mid-chew, looking like a deer in headlights. "I don't know. I want this article to be perfect before I send it to my editor and leave."

"Don't forget, I want to read it before you send it." Isaad picks up his knife and fork and eats again.

"Of course." She gives him a faint smile.

"You are considering my offer. Money is not an issue. Name your price. I need to know soon." He doesn't look at me, seeming so sure I will want to stay here.

"I'll let you know as soon as I figure out the logistics." I need to gain his trust to find the cracks in the foundation and a way to escape. "Oh, and Ms. Wilder will stay with me from now on. She'll be safe with me."

Isaad takes a swig of his drink. "Hmmm. I noticed you ripped out all the feeds in your room. Setting them out in the hall was a nice touch." This doesn't seem to concern him.

"Including the bugs," I retort. "I don't like being spied on, so stop replacing them." What was a crack in the earth between us is turning into a crevasse.

"Fair enough. I can understand that, especially with a beautiful woman in your room. You'll want to keep her out of harm's way and make sure she doesn't roam around too much." More like out of Rakesh's way. He turns to look at Jess.

Smoke circles his head like a crown, but he's no king. He said there were things I wouldn't like. I think I've just scratched the surface. Something more sinister festers here.

Jess and I excuse ourselves to go back to my room.

"You were quiet at dinner." Her tone is low but knowing.

I take her hand in mine. "I have a lot on my mind."

She nods and gives me a weak smile.

We get in the room, and I double lock the door and shove a chair under the doorknob. I don't want any surprises.

I turn to her. "Let's build a bed fort like we used to."

"Really? I had forgotten about the bed fort. I used to love that." Her face lights up with a tinge of forlornness lingering in her eyes.

A girl after my own heart, hopefully, even after I tell her my reasons for leaving.

I pull the comforter down and grab a small lamp to stick under the sheet. The flashlight on my cell phone gives us some lighting and makes the bed tent glow. I play some music from my '90s playlist.

She comes out of the bathroom in pajamas and stops at the end of the bed. "Wow, music too."

Without hesitation, she crawls under and props a pillow under her head. The light reflects off the sheets, giving her face a soft glow. Seeing her like this puts me right back to where we started when we were kids. But we're not kids. We're adults with secrets and wounds, changing how we view life.

I crawl in from the other side in my T-shirt and boxers. I stuff a pillow under my head, and we lie face-to-face.

My mouth goes dry. I've never shared this with anyone,

but of all people I should have shared it with, it should've been her. Peace settles over me like it always does with her. My heart beats faster, unsure of the outcome of this conversation.

"Do you remember when you used to call me late at night to come over, and I was there in a flash? And then there were those nights I showed up on my own." A lump lodges in my throat. I want her to understand why I did what I had to do.

"Yes." She frowns.

I squeeze the pillow under my head. "Things were not a bed of roses at my house."

"I figured something was going on." Her voice is soft, but her eyes never leave mine.

I must have a look of shock on my face because she laughs. "I have known you since we were ten. You have a terrible fake smile, and you would always wear it when you crawled into my window late at night."

I steel myself, getting ready to confess. "What I'm about to tell you, I have told no one, not even my ex-wife." Her eyes widen. I know her mind is spinning about what my story might be. "My father may have been a cop and a good one at that, but he was a violent drunk. He took out his anger on my mother, who protected me at all costs. There were many times she shoved me out of harm's way."

Her hand covers mine, and I grip her fingers. "That's hard on a little boy." Her voice doesn't have pity; it holds understanding.

"I would come back in the morning, and bruises covered her body. She would moan in pain when she moved." The pressure builds behind my eyes as I will my tears to stay away. "I couldn't save or protect her," I whisper.

My voice is that of a broken child. The hardness of those memories has lessened over the years, but putting them into words brings the emotions back to the surface.

The pain in Jess's eyes comes with the strength and determination that she'll be here for me. She'll be the wall I need to lean on.

I force myself to look at her as I continue my story. "When she died of cancer, he blamed me. He said I was the reason she died, and then he came after me. Sometimes I was lucky enough not to be home, and he would destroy the house. I came home less and less. I wasn't big enough to defend myself. That's why I started going to the gym when I was thirteen."

"I remember your dedication." Her thumb caresses the top of my hand.

"I lifted weights until my body gave out. I may not have been able to defend my mom, but I sure as shit was going to defend myself. My body hadn't matured yet, but I got stronger every day. I just kept working out and kept telling myself, 'Today, I will be the strongest.' Did you know I became the quarterback by accident? The coach saw me throwing the ball around with another player. I was as big as a linebacker and had an arm to go with it. That was my escape from my father, even as I tried to be the best for him." The memories I've held at bay come screaming back.

The pain bites at the surface as I struggle to push it down. I've come this far. As I tell her, it's like a movie reel before my eyes. I can step back there in an instant. The terror, anger, and sadness live inside of me, clawing to get out. I take a moment to compose myself and draw circles on her hand with my thumb. My lip trembles as I fight back tears, sucking it into my mouth to stop it.

"My senior year of high school, we came to blows. He

came home drunk and started hitting me with a piece of rusty metal. It lit a fire in me that I've been trying to put out ever since. We punched each other and rolled around until I was on top of him with my fingers around his throat. I pinned his arms under my legs, and his face turned blue." I swallow the emotions of the moment.

"I rolled off him and crawled across the floor, realizing I could have killed him that night and not thought twice about it. He grabbed his gun and aimed it at me, told me to get out and not to come back."

The pain of being beaten with a piece of rusty metal was nothing compared to the fear I had of myself and what I was capable of. I let out a deep sigh. The tightness in my body gives way. There's a relief in telling my story as little pieces of it fly away like paper burning into ash.

"But you didn't kill him, and that says a lot about you." She strokes my face with her hand, and I kiss the center of her palm. She lets out a small gasp.

"I spent the rest of my senior year at a friend's house. When I came home, it was to pack up and tell him I was going to college; that I had enlisted in the Navy to become a SEAL. He said I was leaving him like my mother left him. That was the last time I talked to him. He died last year of cirrhosis of the liver and left me the house, but I haven't had the courage to go back." I let out a short laugh that sounds hoarse. "Imagine a Navy SEAL without courage."

"There's bravery and then there's emotional courage, and you have both. I understand why you left. It's part of the reason I left, to get away from the emotional and psychological abuse. Therapy helped me a lot." She gives me a slight smile.

I hear her words, but I'm too focused on telling her the

rest of my story. "Do you remember when we kissed at the junior prom?"

She looks away from me. I use my finger to tilt her head up so I can see her beautiful eyes. "Yes," she says painfully. "You ran away from me like I was poison."

I wrap my hand around her back and pull her toward me with the lamp between our shins.

"You were the sweetest thing I had ever tasted. I was the poison." Forcing myself to look into her eyes, I tell her. "I was so afraid I would grow up and be like… him. I didn't want you to be in a violent situation. The last thing I wanted was to hurt you. You are so special to me. I always felt I wasn't good enough for you, like you could do better than the guy who came from a broken home. I can be myself with you more than with anyone on the planet. There's nothing to hide from you."

She moves her head away from mine. "Do you think you had the corner market on broken homes? There's no way you would physically hurt me. You were always protecting me."

"What if I got drunk and violent? What if I got angry and hurt you in a rage? I couldn't take that chance. After that night, I promised myself to stay away from you." I beg her to understand.

Her eyes flutter down. "I was so angry with you and felt so alone, like there was something wrong with me. You didn't even give me a choice; you cut yourself off from me without an explanation."

When she looks up, there's anger and hurt written on her face, but it morphs into compassion. "For years, none of it made any sense, until now. I was so hurt that I shut myself off from being hurt by a man. You would have ever hurt me."

My fingers skim her face, pushing the hair from her

cheek. "I'm so sorry, but I didn't want to hurt you anymore or chance it. I was dying inside. You were my rock, my other half that calmed me down." Tears shine in her eyes. "I never have more than one drink. Control over myself is all I have. But something changed when I saw your portrait."

"What portrait?" She stiffens.

EIGHTEEN

Jess

I DIGEST his confession about what was happening behind closed doors in his life. There was nothing easy about the damage his father caused him. He grew up not understanding that we have control over our actions, but he hadn't seen it differently from what was in front of him. How could he?

He left me in the dark to make assumptions about us, teetering between being angry and hurt. I blamed myself for not understanding teenage boys. They are fickle at best. The lines blurred between feeling what we had together and being best friends. I thought he didn't know how to navigate his feelings.

The teenage years weren't kind to me, and without knowing it, he made it worse. I understand his reasons, but it doesn't erase his abandonment.

The incident with his father rings a bell as I remember him coming to school with a black eye. He said he had gotten into a fight; he didn't say with who. My head spins when he tells me about the portrait, capturing my attention.

"The portrait Raquelle painted of you in the field." He frowns.

I stare at him in disbelief. "How do you know Raquelle?" I prop myself up on my elbow.

"It's a long story, but I'm friends with her fiancé, Misha." He looks at me as if I should know this.

My jaw drops. "Raquelle is getting married? In what parallel universe?" Raquelle was always about her career. She went through men like candy and never entertained the idea of settling down.

He smiles. "In a universe where people find their soul mates and spend the rest of their lives together." His eyes penetrate me.

I don't want to know what he's insinuating. I'm on information overload and not ready to deal with this.

"Are you talking about the photo she took of me in the lavender field in France?"

"Yes, she painted you, and it's incredible. It has a home above my fireplace." He lights up from inside, with a sparkle in his eye.

My eyes focus on my finger, making circles on his chest. "You have a portrait of me? That couldn't have been cheap. Raquelle's work is expensive."

He lifts my chin. "Money isn't an issue for me. Best investment I ever made. It reminds me of what I left behind, but you never left me. You've always had a place in my heart. I tried to tuck you away out of sight, but you were always there." His thumb strokes my cheek. "I've been rambling on and haven't asked you what's been going on in your life."

"What if I told you I have a boyfriend?" I lift my chin defiantly.

"What if I told you I don't care? Besides, I don't see a

ring on your finger." He holds the ring finger of my left hand and kisses the tip.

I snatch it away. "Maybe I left my ring at home so I wouldn't lose it." I move away from him to my side of the bed.

He takes the lamp out from under the covers and turns off the flashlight on his cell phone. It's pitch black in the room, but I know exactly where he is. The song playing from his phone is *I Knew I Loved You* by Savage Garden.

Heat rolls off his body, seeping into my skin. He puts his arm under me and pulls me to him so my head is on his shoulder. I'm thrown back to the time before the kiss, when we held each other innocently and out of need. We were two friends who were there for each other without judgment.

"I don't think you're engaged or have a boyfriend. You're an easy read for me. I will fight for you, not just against others, but for us. I know there's an us. Even if I have to convince you, there's an us."

My body tenses as my mind and heart tilt to a place I haven't visited in some time. The tsunami of emotions takes me under. I need time to process what's going on between us. Going from zero to sixty breaks my speed barrier. He doesn't know about my letters to him, and I never want him to find out.

He kisses my forehead. "Good night, Bug. We'll talk more tomorrow."

His smell fills my senses with clean Jersey ocean air and pine. Even amid the turmoil of recent information, I find comfort in him. No one has ever brought me so much peace.

"Good night, Mr. Knight," I say, emphasizing the sound of the silent K. The last thing I remember is the smile on my face and in my heart.

My morning wake-up call starts with a large hard-on wedged against my back. Torn between wanting to turn over and see it or lying still until he wakes up, I suppress a giggle.

"I can hear you thinking. It's too early for thinking," he mumbles.

Heat rises to my cheeks. I flip over. The pillow buries half his face and musses his hair. I push the hair off his forehead, and he grabs my hand in midair. I jerk back.

There is something in his face I've never seen before aimed at me. Lust is heavy between my thighs, and the electricity in the air arcs between us. My breath stalls, waiting for his next move.

"I want to kiss you and make it count this time. It's for real. No more running. Are you okay with that, or am I moving too fast?" His grip softens.

He's asking for permission. I melt on the inside, wanting to know what it would feel like to have his lips on mine again, this time as adults. A nod is what I'm capable of at this point. The man who's had a piece of my heart since age ten has told me he wants me as much as I want him, only he doesn't know I want him because I'm not brave enough to tell him. Fear holds me back.

He laces his fingers in my hair and pulls me toward him. His kiss is tender and tentative at first. He explores my lips with nibbles, sucks, and licks. "Jess, these lips are a delicacy."

Heat starts at my core and works its way between my legs, adding to the wetness. I've never been this affected by a kiss. He pushes me down on the pillow and teases my mouth with his tongue, asking to be let in.

My focus is on his lips and the warmth they're creating as my body becomes flush with desire I didn't know was possible. I invite him in and don't hold back. His tongue explores my mouth, darting in and out. But I give as good as I get. I suck on his tongue hard to let him know what I'm capable of and what I can do to him. It elicits a moan from him. He stops and stares at me for a moment. His eyes glaze over with wonder and confusion.

His hand moves down my shoulder and over my breast. He squeezes it, playing with my nipple through the fabric. I close my eyes and make a squeaking sound, arching my back, and wanting more when suddenly he's off the bed.

"God, Jess. You are so perfect and beautiful in every way. Am I moving too fast for you? I am, aren't I?" he pants. I don't know if his questions are for me or for him.

I'm lost in an adrenaline-induced haze, mesmerized by his cock tenting his briefs and the T-shirt stretched across his pecs. It hits me. He wants me. Not just a fling or a one-nighter or just because I'm there, but all of me, inside and out. Tears form in my eyes.

He crawls over the bed and sits on his heels next to me. "Why are you crying?" His hands grip together in his lap. Fear coats his eyes. He doesn't know what to do.

"No one has ever thought I was beautiful, let alone perfect. You try growing up in a home where you're told you're less than daily. I guess you would know." I try to sniff the tears back into my eyes and fail. They trail down my cheeks.

He dabs the wetness with a tissue. He leans up against the headboard and puts me between his legs.

"You don't see how men look at you when you walk into a room. You're beautiful because you don't know it and you don't use it to manipulate them." He wraps his arms around my waist.

His head rests on top of mine. "This isn't the best time to bring this up, but we need to get the keycard away from Rakesh."

I look over my shoulder at him. "That won't be easy. What do you suggest?"

"I'm not sure. We need that keycard if you want to get Pippa out of here with us. I could probably tackle Rakesh to the ground and take it from him, but that might get too much attention and get me killed," he says deadpan.

I turn my body to face him. "Good point. Can I help?"

"Yes, it's the oldest trick in the book. But it works every time. We're going to do some practice runs. The traditional clothing you've been hiding under will work to our advantage." His statement is mysterious but confident.

He lifts me so I'm straddling him. My center is directly over his raging hard-on, which has not gone away. I wonder if a significant amount of blood has left his head with this scheme of his. I put my hands on his shoulders and try to rub up and down on his hardness.

He grins, knowing what I want from him. "No, you cannot rub up on me because I can't control myself." He pushes my hips away from him. "We need to keep our heads on straight for right now."

I cross my arms. "Hey, that's my line."

He grins at his play on words. I get the feeling I'm not going to like his plan.

NINETEEN

Jess

HE HAS COME up with the most harebrained scheme to get the keycard that I've ever heard. Sean excuses himself from a day at the mine, claiming he ate something that didn't agree with him.

We spend the time in his room going over the plan and ordering food from the kitchen. I practice how to get the keycard from Rakesh. Sean teaches me how to lift it. I'm a pickpocket in training.

"I can't do this." My frustration makes me nervous. "I'm not a spy or secret agent." I punch the bed with my fists.

He grabs my shoulders. "Listen to me. You've got this. Have faith."

"Besides, I can't stand Rakesh." My heart races talking about the next step in our plan. "I don't get my sister's attraction to him." I make a gagging sound.

He chuckles. "She's smart and playing him to her advantage." He brushes his fingers down my face, and I lean into him. "Use your hatred to our advantage. You are beautiful, sexy, and a brainiac. Just know that if Rakesh was gay, I would do this. It's the only way to get the key and save Pippa."

"Are you saying you'd take one for the team?" I bust out laughing.

Without batting an eyelash, he says, "Yes, because I know how much she means to you."

His sincerity blows me away. I understand he would do anything for me. "When you put it that way, I don't have a choice. You'd do that for her?"

He nods. "I would do that for you." His eyes fill with intensity.

"I'm going to put on my big girl panties and do what's necessary." I face him with my shoulders back, looking way more confident than I feel.

"For future reference, I prefer no panties." He smacks my ass like he owns it.

"Hey!" I rub where he smacked it. He wiggles his brows.

We go over the plan one more time. "Maybe I should get drunk so I can loosen up."

His eyes darken. "Pick pocketing and alcohol never go together." He takes a step closer. "Trust me, everything is better without alcohol."

Given his upbringing, I'm not surprised by his words, but I'm incredibly turned on by his ability to take control of himself. Everything I've ever dreamed of stands in front of me, and I'm scared to death. He could leave me again, decide I'm not good enough, or I'm not the one for him, or… the list goes on.

"You're in your head again, Bug. Take a couple of deep breaths and relax. You need to use your head and get him to touch you." He gives me a tight smile.

I stick my tongue out with a yucky face at the thought, but it's game time. I pick the pink outfit with a hijab. The pink will accent my eyes, which is where I want his attention to be, instead of my hands. The looseness of the garment will help hide what I do with my hands.

There are a couple of things I've observed in my time here. One, the men always drink after dinner. Two, they drink a lot unless they are on duty. If my memory serves me correctly, Rakesh is off duty tonight, so he will be drinking. Since drinking is on the forbidden list outside of the glass house, these men get their fill while they are here.

In my search to find Rakesh, I decide on a different plan. My plan is better than me faking it, and I can sense Sean is right behind me.

My heart pounds in my throat, and my palms are sweaty. I've never had a reason to do anything like this before. But I agree with Sean; there's no other way to get to Pippa and get us out of here.

Rakesh walks toward me. He's dressed in black and wears a turban on his head. I smile at him. It's showtime. He scowls.

I bow my head like a good submissive woman. "Good evening, Rakesh."

"Why are you out of your room at this time of night?" His voice is tight, but his eyes are unfocused, compliments of the alcohol.

"What is with you, anyway? Can't a woman roam freely around here? Besides, you're not my boss." I step closer to him, invading his space with my hands on my hips.

He bends his head down. I hear him inhale and exhale through his nose. "Some of my men have never had American pussy before. They would enjoy your company. They might even share you or fight for you, whichever comes first. I don't care because I don't like you or that piece of American shit you're with. You're too nosy and don't know your place." He sways and then regains his stance.

Okay, so I wasn't expecting this response. My blood boils. He's hit every one of my triggers in a couple of sentences. My foster father's voice comes back to me.

"You're a sick bastard." I raise my hand back to slap him in the face. He catches my wrist midair and tightens his grip. His smile is pure evil. I can feel it in my bones. "Get your hands off me!" Where is Sean?

He grabs both my upper arms. "You're coming with me. My men need some entertainment." He sneers.

Out of nowhere, Sean comes from behind me and sucker punches Rakesh in the face. He lets go of my arms as he flies backward. I'm so flustered that I forget what my assignment is in this staged event.

He and Sean exchange punches, holding each other by the shirt. I get between them and grab Rakesh's keycard off his shirt.

"Stop, just stop it! Enough," I yell.

Rakesh wobbles on his feet, swaying from side to side. Sean gets in his face. "Don't you ever touch her, understand?"

"You American men with your big egos and little dicks." He laughs at his joke, wiping the blood from his nose. "I will do what I want when I want in my country. I've got my eye on you and I watch everything you do." He points his two fingers from his eyes to Sean. "Isaad will know your true intentions."

Sean pushes him in the chest. "Isaad and I are old friends. He knows my intentions."

"We'll see." Rakesh smiles, turns, and walks down the hall.

When Sean and I get back to the room, I close the door behind me and lean up against it. I'm breathing heavily, my heart continues to hammer in my chest, and my palms are slick with sweat. I look up at the ceiling.

"You didn't need to go so overboard." I take the keycard out and hold it out to Sean. "Mission accomplished." What greets me is not what I expect.

He stands with his back to me, hands on his hips. "You'll stay in your room for the rest of our time here. It's the only way I can keep you safe." He stares at the floor without focusing on anything.

"Your job is to rescue us. I can take care of myself. I've been doing it a long time." He needs to stay focused on the plan and not on me.

He continues as if he hasn't heard a word I've said. "I couldn't even keep her safe. I can't put you in danger."

I stand next to him and put my hand on his arm to get his attention. "You couldn't have saved her. You were so young, and as an adult, she had choices too. Not everyone can be saved or wants to be saved. You had no control over that."

The pain in his eyes is that of the little boy who grew up feeling out of control, lost, and angry. He sits on the bed and I sit in his lap, holding his head to my shoulder.

"I would have you sit in my lap, but you're too big." A small bubble of laughter comes from him.

"This is just what I needed. Feeling out of control weighs on my chest." His body lets go of some of its tension.

"That's what best friends are for. They understand what you need. Most things in life are out of your control."

I thread my fingers through his hair and want to kiss him, but resist. With each kiss, each touch, my heart falls farther into his safety net, getting caught in the process. I don't think I've been this deeply in love before. Now is not the time to find out.

"What's the plan to get to Pippa?"

He holds up the keycard. "First, we need to get this back to Rakesh before he discovers it's gone. I need to make a copy."

"You can do that?" We're out in the middle of nowhere, and he's got more gadgets than 007.

"You'd be amazed at what's hidden in my suitcase."

He seems to have returned from his time travel to a damaged past. It's what resilient soldiers do to survive.

He takes out a small machine along with several other tools. I watch him work to copy the key code and transfer it to another card. He puts everything back together and puts a small dot on the back of the keycard he made.

"There." He holds it up. "Let's hope it works. This is not my area of expertise. That would be my partner, Peter Bryan, but it looks damn good. We won't know if it works until we get to her room, and then we'll pray."

He puts it in his pocket and hands me Rakesh's keycard. "As fate would have it, Isaad is requesting our presence for drinks and dessert. It's a great opportunity to set up the return of the keycard."

I nudge him with my shoulder. "We're a talented team."

"You're the brains and I'm the brawn. Kind of like Beauty and the Beast." He has a sheepish grin on his face, looking like a ten-year-old.

"You're definitely the Beast with brains. When did you get this big? Please tell me you're not as hairy." I squeeze his shoulders.

"The military will do that to you. Working out helps me keep the demons away. And it's all about the manscaping." He takes his hands in mine. "Let's get ready. We have a keycard to return."

What demons is he talking about? The thought that he

has PTSD crosses my mind. SEALS are a tough group, but they're still human. I can't imagine the things he has seen and heard. Gut-wrenching and soul-searing pain of human life, some of which I'm sure he had to end to save the mission or his life. My heart breaks knowing his demons may not leave him soon.

We make it to the dining room, and everything goes as planned until it doesn't.

Rakesh comes into the room and points at me. "You American bitch! You stole my keycard when I fought with that piece of shit." His face flushes red as he points at Sean.

I turn to Isaad for some support. "I have no idea what he's talking about."

"Rakesh, calm yourself and apologize to Ms. Wilder." He frowns at Rakesh's behavior.

Rakesh puts his hands on his hips and yells, "I will not. Let's go back to their room and see if we can find it."

I sit calmly even as my nerves take a dive, but I keep my head in the game. "Is it possible you dropped it?"

"No. I've never dropped it before," he says through gritted teeth.

I place my napkin on the table and walk over to Rakesh. "Let's retrace your steps." I stand in front of him, shaking on the inside.

Everything goes according to plan, except for Rakesh's accusations. Everyone in the dining room, including Sean and Isaad, is looking for the keycard.

Rakesh bends down where I dropped it earlier. "I found it. I don't know how it fell off." He looks at it quizzically and then gives me a look that could kill.

"It could have easily fallen off." I shrug.

"It's never happened before until you showed up.

There are a lot of things happening since you've come here."

Heated words pass between Isaad and Rakesh in an argument I can't understand. Sean catches my eye with a silent message not to respond.

Dessert resumes, but the conversation quiets between the three of us. Sean and I excuse ourselves and head for his bedroom.

We enter the room, and Sean turns to me. "That was close. But now I need to make plans to find Pippa."

"Not without me, you're not."

TWENTY

Sean
_____

"YOU'RE NOT GOING." She needs to do what I tell her to do, even though that will never happen in my lifetime. I have to remember that I don't need to protect her like we are still kids.

She steps closer to me, inches from my face. It takes everything I have not to grab her and consume her with a kiss, letting her know she's mine.

"Nope, I'm going with you whether or not you like it. I want to see if she's okay. I'm a grown woman able to make my own decisions, and I've been in danger that would make your hair curl. If I'm with you, I'm safer. Besides, I can be your guide. I know where her room is and can get us there faster. This is the end of the discussion."

I let out a deep exhale and stare at her. "You're still stubborn beyond belief."

This takes away from my search for Red Enigma, but she's worth it. Nothing has come up on my radar about where Isaad is hiding the hacker.

"Thank you for noticing. Now what do we need to do?" She puts her hands on her hips.

I rub the back of my neck. "I'm hoping you can help me get dressed. I'm going to need a disguise. The cameras have facial recognition. Isaad is not stupid."

She walks over to her luggage and pulls out a blue and white striped cloth. "I can use this to make a turban."

"You mean a lungee." I smile.

She tilts her head in my direction. "Yes, smarty pants. You're going to need to change into a black shirt and pants. There's only one problem: you're a little too white and stick out like a sore thumb. I'll be right back."

While she disappears into the bathroom, I change into black jeans and a stretched black polo shirt. She comes back into the room, her eyes go wide, and she stops dead in her tracks.

"Oh." Comes out of her mouth.

I flash her a charming smile. "See something you like?"

She clears her throat. "Maybe. I never thought I'd be using my color foundation on a man, but here goes nothing."

As she applies her tinted foundation to my face, up to the hairline, and down my throat, I rub her leg above her knees. "You're distracting me." She brushes my hand away.

"That's the idea."

I've opened a floodgate I can't close, no matter how hard I try. When we were younger, this is what I was afraid of: this depth of longing, wanting, and heat. We swirl around each other with an insatiable hunger. When I'm this close to her, I'm lost in her. The chemistry is like being hit with endorphins after a long run, but I'm tired of running.

With each rub, a blush comes into her cheeks, and she squirms. I'm enjoying every minute of turning her on. I'm one step closer to the intimacy I long for with her. The need to be inside her overwhelms me.

The blue and white striped cloth is a loose fit around my head. A piece comes down on one shoulder.

She stands back to admire her creation. "There you go. Now, you look more the part. Keep your head down."

I look at myself in the mirror. "You did a magnificent job. I don't even recognize myself."

My skin is a couple of shades darker from the neck up. I have an odd realization of what life must be like for her. Her skin color was never what I saw. I craved what was inside. Her soul sang to me, and we connected on a different level.

She dresses in the deep blue traditional garment with a full burka, hiding her beauty.

I bend down in front of her and talk into the screen. "How do you feel in there?"

"When I arrived here and first put it on, I felt secure. Now I feel claustrophobic. They don't want their women out in the open. It's sad because some of them are incredibly beautiful." Her voice is small in the burka.

"Feeling safe is an illusion anyway," I mumble.

She looks down at where her fingers are playing with the hem of her top. "Yeah, I know."

I fold her hand in mine before we head out. "Let's get going. I have no idea what to expect, but I always try to anticipate surprises."

We make our way through the hallway, down to the movable panel. She follows behind me with her head down. She shows me how the vase works by turning it. The device seems silly to me, like something you would see in a movie, but maybe that's the idea. It's so cliché that no one would think to look for it.

The tight spiral stairs descend to the lower level, and

the hallway is dark. I grab her by the elbow as we pass other men in the hall, who nod and smile. They must think I'm taking her down here for entertainment or as a prisoner.

She stops at the last door at the end of the hall. "Here's her door."

"Pippa?" I call out.

She replies, "Yes?"

"I need you to go to your closet."

"Okay. Why?" Her voice fades away.

I should rename them "The Sisters with Questions." I ignore her question and turn to Jess.

"When we get in there, I need you to keep your head down and go for the closet. Got it?"

She nods.

I take out my keycard and pray to the keycard gods, if they exist, that it works on this door. The light on the pad goes from red to green, and I blow out the breath I was holding in. The chain on the floor leads from the center of the floor to the closet. My heart sinks. One more layer I have to get through to get her out.

Jess throws off her burka and runs to her. She holds her as soft murmurs come from them to comfort each other. When Jess steps aside, I hug Pippa.

I check her over from head to toe for bruising or other injuries. "Are you okay?"

Her eyes are glassy, and they hold a plea for help. "Yes. Isaad treats me well. Rakesh is another story. He wants me to stay, but I can't. I've got to get out of here. Why are we in the closet?"

I lower my voice. "Isaad has the entire house bugged except for the bathrooms and closets. We're safe to talk here."

"My room's not bugged," she says matter-of-factly.

I narrow my eyes at her. "How would you know?"

"I looked for them when I got put in the room. Maybe it's because I'm underground."

There's confidence in her words. I don't understand why she would search for them in the first place. I have questions that need answers. There's a tingle at the back of my neck. She may be the hacker I'm here to rescue.

The center of the room has a table with three monitors. Each one shows something different on the screens.

"What are you doing for him?"

She glances at Jess. "Well, he hired me to steal from Bitcoin accounts for a short time, and when my contract was up, I would go home. But it was a ruse to get me here because of the program I wrote." Worry covers her eyes as she shifts her gaze between me and Jess.

"What program?" I'm afraid to ask.

She looks down at her hands and then looks up at Jess. "You're not going to like this. I wrote a program called White Raven. The program can infiltrate any internet system around the world through a series of backdoors using complex coding. That's the simplest way to explain it. The owner has access to anything and everything."

Something niggles at the back of my brain. "He wants you to hand it over?"

"When he questioned me, I told him I have it on a computer at home that requires several biometrics to access. I sent it to a friend, and I don't have the original. I don't even know how he found out about it. He's keeping me so I can write it from scratch. I don't have it memorized. It's going to take a very long time to write again, time I don't have. But either way, he's not getting it. It's too dangerous in the wrong hands." Her words catch in her throat.

"I see you wear the black hat in the world of hackers."

I refer to the fact that she's on the wrong side of hacking. Jess looks confused, but Pippa gets my meaning.

She crosses her arms in front of her. "More like a gray hat. I move funds around to charities, too. I'm not all bad."

Jess turns to her. "We talked about this. I thought you were going legit?"

Pippa puts her hands in the air. "The offer was too good to pass up. The money is insane. White Raven was a program that came out of nowhere. I was screwing around with it until it turned into something much more. I could sell it for billions, but I'm not willing to sell it or rewrite it for Isaad."

"But what's he using the cryptocurrency for?" They both turn and look at me. "What? Who doesn't know about cryptocurrency?"

"I don't know. But soon it won't be so easy to steal it as cell phones get the security in place, so I guess he's going for as much as he can get." Pippa shrugs.

Her bright red hair rests on her shoulders. "Do you know anyone named Red Enigma, by chance?"

TWENTY-ONE

Sean

"YES." She looks away.

This narrows things down. "That would be you, wouldn't it?"

She nods.

"When did you become a world-renowned hacker?" I'm in awe and curious about the brainiac in front of me.

Her eyes have a faraway gaze. "Immersing myself in programming is what I did to escape from my home from hell. Thank God, I have enough money. I'll never go back."

"Trust me, I know all about escape," I reply without thinking.

Pippa stares at me with questions floating in her eyes and then says, "Things were not as they seemed."

I glance at Jess, staring at the floor.

Pippa lifts her chin and closes her eyes. I'm not sure what she knows. She could have easily hacked into government files to find out about me over the years. Maybe she was Jess's contact.

Jess gives me a soft smile and holds Pippa's hand.

"Well, Neil sent me here to get you home in one piece. Many people are looking for you, and now I know why. You're a valuable asset."

My mind spins, trying to grab hold of a plan to get us out of here. There are several that come to my mind.

There is a soft buzz, and Pippa's eyes go wide. She puts her fingers over her lips and leaves the closet, shutting the door behind her.

"Hello, my love. How are you today?" Rakesh says.

Pippa clasps her hands in front of her. "Good. You know, I decided I can tell you a bit about what I'm doing for Isaad. I'm stealing Bitcoin for him, like a shit ton. But I can't figure out what he's using it for. Do you know?"

His face is impassive, and he stares at her, trying to gauge her question. "It's not for you to worry about." He steps closer. "I find it interesting that you would tell me now. Especially since we have two other Americans staying in the house."

Jess stands in front of me as we watch from behind the slats in the closet door.

Rakesh closes in on Pippa and grabs her arm. "Tell me, have you had any unexpected visitors lately? Or contacted them some other way?"

She struggles to get free as he holds her tight. I put my hand over Jess's mouth to keep us from being detected. Even from here, I can see the coldness in his eyes.

Pippa pulls away from him, and he drops her arm. "If I had someone to rescue me, do you think I'd be standing here talking to you? I would have been long gone. Just to be clear, you're the only one who visits me." Her words choke out, and she holds her head in her hands.

Rakesh frowns and seems surprised. He stands there for a minute trying to figure out what to do. Well played,

Pippa. He wraps his arms around her as she calms down. He grabs her by the back of her hair.

His words hold a threat. "If you're lying to me, I will find out. As much as I enjoy being with you, I will not betray our mission."

Pippa nods without asking about the mission. If I didn't know better, I would say she's a seasoned spy. That may be the other reason Neil is desperate to get her back.

Rakesh lets go of her hair, and something passes between them, an understanding. She cups his jaw in her hand.

"I would never ask you to betray your beliefs or cause. In a lot of ways, we're playing for the same team." Her words ooze with sincerity. She's good.

A small smile forms on Rakesh's lips, but his eyes scream suspicion. She kisses him like an old lover who has traveled this roadway many times.

He nuzzles Pippa's neck and kisses up to her ear. Holding her face in his hands, he looks at her with affection. This is a side I haven't seen of him.

I remove my hand from Jess's mouth and wrap my arm around her, waiting for her reaction. Her body stiffens but then relaxes into me.

Rakesh caresses Pippa's breast and takes down one side of her blouse. His lips make their way to her nipple, and he sucks on it, teasing it. Jess gasps and tries to turn around to face me. I clamp my hand over her mouth again.

Rakesh stops what he's doing. "Did you hear that? I think it came from the closet."

Pippa grabs him by the arm. "Baby, sometimes you need to give that suspicious mind of yours a rest. Let me give you something to focus your energy on." She kisses him with passion.

Jess and I hold our breaths. That was too close.

Rakesh unbuckles his pants and says, "I need your mouth on me tonight. Take off your clothes." There's a strain in his voice.

Pippa strips in front of him, one piece of clothing at a time, and falls to her knees. He looks at her adoringly. She enjoys every minute of being with him, even as his prisoner.

Jess watches, transfixed by what's going on.

"Haven't you ever seen two people get it on before?" I whisper in her ear.

"I've seen Pippa naked before, just not like this."

Jess's skin is flushed. Her breath is shallow, and her eyes are wide, but she doesn't look away.

I bury my nose in her hair and inhale her wild rose scent. "Do you like what you see?"

She shakes her head.

"I think you're lying. If I dipped my fingers in your panties, what do you think I would find?" I feel the warmth of her skin under my hand.

Pippa is bent over the computer chair, facing us, and Rakesh slowly enters her from behind. Her face is in ecstasy, and her moans get louder and more provocative.

I pull Jess to the back of the walk-in closet and slide my hand down the outside of her pants.

"I don't need to feel you. I can smell you." Her eyes close, and she lets out a soft mewl.

I spin her toward me. I want her to focus on what's happening on this side of the door. The electricity crackles between us.

"It's always been you. No matter where I was or who I was with. You were always there, but you scared me with that kiss. There's a fear in loving so deeply that I could lose myself. I know what you're thinking. Why now? Some of the best things happen at the wrong time."

I've said it before, I can take it back. Her chest heaves with eyes dilated. I grab her ass and pull her toward me so she can feel what she does to me. There is a look of awe and fear on her face. "What's holding you back from us?"

She shakes her head. "I'm…I'm not sure. This seems like some sort of dream, and one I never expected."

"I'm not hard because of what's going on in the next room. You make me this way. I'm just sorry it took me so long to realize that it's always been you. Give me a chance, Jess." I swallow the lump in my throat. I've never put myself out there like this.

She kisses me tentatively at first, but it escalates into passion in a matter of seconds. Grabbing my hair, she takes over. Our tongues play together, biting lips, and sucking on everything. My lips skim her smooth neck and tug on her earlobe. This is what I want from her. What I've always known has been underneath the quiet exterior.

We break our kiss as we notice it's gotten quiet in the other room. We hear Pippa say, "I'm exhausted. I kind of want to sleep alone tonight if you don't mind. It's been a long day."

"Of course." He kisses her and leaves with a soft click of the door to the hall, but not before he takes one more look at the closet door.

She puts her clothes back on and opens the closet door. "Enjoy the show?" Nothing modest about her.

Jess turns on her. "I can't believe you. You're sleeping with the enemy."

"You get more with honey than with vinegar. Besides, he's hot. Did you see how big—"

Jess holds up her hand. "Stop. No, I did not see."

"Why? What were you two up to? You look a little flushed, Jess. Are you finally going to let yourself be with the man of your dreams?"

"Shut. Up." Jess's jaw muscles flex. She reaches down to put her burka back on.

"You can't hide forever, sis," Pippa taunts.

"I think we should leave you here. You two seem like a good… fit." She pushes past Pippa and toward the door.

On my way out the door, I turn to Pippa, "We'll figure this out and plan our escape. Try to think of anything else you might know. You seem like you might have some experience with the spy game."

She does not react, but the slight lift of her brow gives her away.

The walk back to our room is silent. Anger radiates off Jess. I've never seen this side of her, and it's a little scary.

TWENTY-TWO

Jess
———

I'M FLIPPIN' pissed right now. The burka flies across the room as I rip it from my head. How could Pippa out me like that in front of Sean? How could my body betray me?

My emotions scream on the downslope of a roller-coaster. He left me and abandoned me just like my parents. I won't go through that again. I don't know if I can let it go. He had his reasons, but I need to wrap my head around them. My fingers clutch the front of my blouse.

No man has ever made me hot and wet in the space of two minutes like he does. The way he talked to me and about me had me tied up in knots. I loved it, and I don't know what to do with it. I need to hide my feelings from him until I can figure this out. My lust is snowballing, gaining strength and speed.

He closes the door behind him and leans up against it with his arms and legs crossed in front of him. "Out with it. Why are you so mad?"

"I'm going to take a bath and regroup. We'll talk about this later." I avoid looking at him.

I rifle through my suitcase, search for my pajamas, and

march to the bathroom. He knows enough to give me space.

The bathroom is the size of a basketball court. There's a rain shower, a private toilet area, and my favorite part, the enormous clawfoot bathtub with jets and a waterfall faucet.

I'm obsessed with bathrooms. They were my hideaway growing up. I could escape from the tyranny of verbal abuse, soaking my hurt and sadness away. I'm hoping to soak my anger away.

I fill the bath with bubbles as I slip into the water up to my neck with jets blasting and mountains of bubbles covering the top. The warm water surrounds my body and fills me with a sense of comfort and security. I breathe in through my nose and out of my mouth.

If I'm being truthful with myself, I fell in love with Sean years ago. The kiss we shared changed us. We were over as friends, and I wanted more, but he refused to have much to do with me. I never understood why until he revealed what was happening behind the curtain. His father was a drunk, but I didn't know how bad it got for Sean. My heart breaks for him, and that's where I'm conflicted.

My thoughts take me back to happier times between us when we were kids and there for each other no matter what. Hormones can be your best friend or worst enemy. They were my enemy because I wanted something I couldn't have with him.

Being the only girl of color in the school didn't help. I was an outcast, bullied, and made to feel like I would never measure up to anyone's standards. Home life didn't help, and I turned inward, creating stories in my head.

Anger dissipates as jets pummel my body, but my body remembers what happened earlier in the evening. I close my eyes as relaxation takes over. How am I ever going to get that out of my head? He held me differently than before, securing me to him in a stance of protection and lust. I crumbled under the idea of being wanted, possessed by him.

The relaxing moment breaks when the door flies open. My eyes pop wide, and my hands instinctively cover my bare breasts. Sean stands with narrow eyes with one of my letters clenched in his hand.

A staring contest begins, but his eyes are wild. I look at the papers in his hand and realize what they are. No. This can't be happening. Not now. I shake my head.

"Don't say a word." He stalks toward me and pulls up a stool. "Allow me to read this to you because this is only the second time I'm reading it, but oddly, every letter is addressed to me." He puts his finger up. I dread what's coming next.

Dear Sean,

Once again, I'm writing this letter to tell you what I want you to know, to tell you what's really in my heart.

You're embedded in my soul. You've always been there, and the kiss when we were sixteen sealed it for me. We were always there for each other, but that kiss changed everything between us. I wish it had never happened. I don't know why you turned away from me, but it cut me like a razor. There were no stitches to sew me up. I wish you weren't still the man I want every single day. No one has touched me the way you do without ever being intimate.

In my emails to you, I try to stay upbeat, writing about frivolous things going on in my life, trying to distract you from the hell going on around you. I know you will come back damaged, maybe irreparably. Most soldiers, let alone SEALs, will return with scars. The wounds are deeper on the inside.

I still want you, scars and all, with your sleepless nights, bloody nightmares, and night sweats. I will take your tears, fears, and self-

doubt about whether you did the right thing. Never second-guess your-self. It leaves voids that can't be filled.

Your heart and soul are what I'm after, and that I will always want. You've carved your place in my soul that can never be replaced by anyone else. But that's not true for you. I guess my love affair with you was a one-way street.

This will be my last letter and email because you're getting married. She deserves every piece of you without your childhood crush lurking in the background. I don't think she's right for you, but I'm biased.

I have a hard time not feeling around you. You brought out the best in me. You're part of the reason I became an investigative jour-nalist. I need to make the world a better place, too. Bring the darkness, kicking and screaming, into the light, no matter how ugly it is.

Wishing you the best in your marriage. You'll understand why I can't be there, or maybe you won't. It's just too much for my heart to bear.

I love you now and forever. I don't think that will ever change.

You'll always be my best friend.

Yours forever,

Bug

With each word he reads, I sink farther into the luke-warm water. Tears spring to my eyes of their own volition. Hearing him read my words, thoughts, and wishes is more than I can bear, but I don't stop him.

This is self-torture. Death would be an easy out. My heart cracks for him to know the truth. I could slip under and let my lungs fill with water. I've been holding my breath for too long anyway. He knows everything. There's nothing left to hide, bare in every way.

The bubbles dissipate, leaving the water clear. My arms gather as many as I can to my chest, the place where he lives. I peek up. His eyes hold unshed tears.

His mouth is a taunt line. He whispers, "Why didn't

you tell me? I read every one of these. Each one talks about how you felt about me at different times, except for this one. This one is your last goodbye."

My anger roars back to the surface. "Don't you stand there and tell me I should have told you. You tossed me aside. You were the star quarterback with the cute girl-friends, and what was I to you anymore? Nothing. I didn't fit some preconceived mold. Then you left without saying goodbye. That was the end for me, but the ache never went away. I don't do well with abandonment, remember?" Hot tears stream down my pulsing face, dispersing the few bubbles below.

He tosses the letters on the floor and gets on his knees. "No, that's where you're wrong. You were the mold. There is only one of you in the world, and I didn't want to destroy you. You were the perfect butterfly. You needed to be saved from me, so I pushed you away." He hits himself on the chest. "I didn't know who I was, but I knew you were strong enough to make it on your own. I had to get away. There was no other choice. You deserved the best life even without me."

I smack the water with my hands, splashing him. "That wasn't your decision to make. You never asked me what I wanted. As Mr. Control, you thought you had all the answers. I only ever wanted you just the way you are." I choke on my words because I've never said them out loud.

The water clears. I'm naked to him, but his eyes stay focused on my face. He takes my hands in his hands and holds them underwater.

"We've wasted so much time. Please forgive me." His voice cracks, and the plea in his eyes kills me.

I whisper, "Maybe things are meant to be this way."

"We're together. I feel like our connection is stronger

than ever. Maybe we needed time to grow up to get to this place," he bargains with me.

"Sean?" I sniffle.

"Yeah, Bug?"

I let go of his hands. "The water's getting cold."

He reaches down, lets some water drain out, and turns on the hot water. My heart pounds in my chest at what's transpired, but I'm relieved he knows how I feel about him. He ripped the aluminum foil off my heart, letting in his energy, and my soul feels freer. I'm still afraid of what he might do with it.

He leans on the edge of the tub. "There's smoke coming out of your ears again. What are you thinking about?"

He stands and turns his back to me and takes off his clothes. He strips off his pants and lets them fall to the floor. His glorious ass is better than my imagination.

"Ummm." I'm at a loss for words.

He looks over his shoulder and smiles. "Cat got your tongue?"

He pulls his shirt over his head, and I see the three large stripes across his back.

I gasp out loud. "He did that to his only son? He was an animal." I'm enraged that anyone would hurt their child.

He turns around, unashamed of his nakedness. His body is a work of art, with rippling muscles, cut abs, and intricate tattoos. He's any woman's erotic dream.

He shrugs. "I'm over it, to some extent. I forgave him years ago. He got wasted that night. I doubt he even remembers what he did. It's in the past, and that's where it needs to stay. Move up." He motions with two fingers.

I move up as he slides in behind me. The water flows over the side and makes me laugh. I lean back with my head on his shoulder. He's taking us to the next level, and my heart thumps in my chest.

He pushes my hair to the side. "It looks like there is nothing left between us. Everything is out in the open. Why do you carry the letters with you?"

"They remind me of where I came from, how much I've grown, and in an odd way, the kind of love I want with a man. I've never quite found it." The waves lap against the side of the tub.

"I know where this man wants to go from here with you. I hope we're on the same page."

TWENTY-THREE

Sean

IF I DIDN'T MAKE a move, we would still be talking about what could have been or what I should have done. I'm done talking about it. I need to claim her before she lives in her head and analyzes everything to death. The only man for her is me.

Her body is stunning, with full breasts and fuller hips. I bring my hands around her waist and cup her breasts, holding them out of the water. Her nipples pebble in the cold air. Perfect. I roll them between my fingers and thumb as they get harder. They're a gorgeous shade of bronze, and I can't wait to get my lips around them.

Her eyes are closed, and she moans. I scoot down and move her up, wedging my rock-hard cock between her ass cheeks.

"Oh," she says without opening her eyes.

"Bug, I have one last secret." Her body becomes tense.

"You have a secret love child here in Afghanistan." She turns her smirk toward me.

"No, but that would have been a good one, considering

how beautiful the women are here. I control things in the bedroom." Words hang between us.

She turns around and faces me with a smirk. "I can't imagine. Are you going to control how many orgasms I have?" Sarcasm drips from her words.

I splash her, and her laugh bounces off the tile walls. "Not quite that dramatic. I like to experiment, but not without your consent and trust."

"Someone likes to get naughty." She bats her eyelashes.

I bite her earlobe. "Naughty is my middle name."

"No, your middle name is Bradshaw because your dad loved the Steelers."

"He hoped I would be good enough to play for the Steelers. As I recall, I swore you to secrecy."

"And look who has the control now." Her smile is seductive, but I'm not sure she realizes what it does to me. "I'm good with the trust. You're going to have to slow down with the experimentation. I'm not what you would call super experienced." Her finger swirls the few bubbles floating on the surface of the water.

I hold her chin in my hand, tilting her head. "Good. It makes things a lot easier. I want to do many firsts with you."

She gives me a faint smile. "Okay."

"Now, I need your hands on me before I lose it completely. It's taking everything I have not to thrust into you, so you understand we belong together." I bring her lips to mine, holding her behind her neck.

She grabs my cock, which is hard to the point of pain, and slowly moves her hands up and down. I place my arms on the sides of the tub and let her explore. Then, she does something unexpected. She dunks her head underwater and wraps her full lips around my cock. My eyes roll back as my head rests on the edge of the tub.

The mix of the warm water and her mouth is going to make me come in seconds. Her hair floats in the water, and she pops to the surface with a smile on her face.

"Oh my God! I've never done anything like that before. How was that for experimental?"

Water streams down her face, and her matted hair clings to the side of her head. The girl who was my BFF is still there, waiting to come out and play. This is what I love about us.

In an instant, we've flipped everything from our friendship into a sexual relationship. She brings trust, humor, fun, and openness into this new experience, making it seamless as if we were always like this.

"It felt fucking amazing. Come here." I growl, grasping her upper arms and having her straddle me.

Our eyes lock. Time freezes as we realize where we are going, and we can never come back. Once we cross the bridge to lovers, there's no return.

She has a worried look on her face. "Mr. Knight, I think it's too big."

"Trust me, it'll fit. In this position, you can control the movement, but understand from now on, I call the shots." I give her half a smile.

She splashes me. "Is that what you think? You always were a control freak."

I wipe my face. "That's what I know." Although I'm doubting how much control I'll have over her. "I see your smart mouth even makes an appearance during sex. Let's see if I can't fix that." I reach up to caress her face and push her wet locks away.

I pull her toward me and kiss her tenderly. Then with more urgency, pushing my tongue in, taking over, sucking on her plump lips and tongue, waiting for the moment I can taste between her legs.

My cock nestles between our stomachs. I kiss down her neck to her nipple, sucking and biting, getting strangled moans, small screams, and panting. She's right on the edge. I ease my finger in her and fuck, she's tight. She's slick as I feel her squeeze me.

"You're ready, sweetheart. Ease yourself down onto me. Take your time, but eyes on me." I want to see her as we become one, feeling each other for the first time.

She nods with her eyes focused on me. The intensity of the moment reaches into my heart. She's the one I'm meant to be with. She's my other half, my better half. I never would have survived my childhood without her. There's much more to learn about her from her smell, touch, and vegetarian ways. I'll plant a garden for her, take up yoga… well, maybe. Our story is coming full circle.

Her tight pussy grips me as she eases onto me, and I see her grimace. I am still inside her and then take over, pulling out and easing back in. "Breathe out each time I push in." I'm bigger than average, but not too big for her to take me.

We're finding our rhythm as water splashes over the side. She throws her head back and pushes her chest forward as I bite her nipple hard enough to create a spark. She gasps.

"Eyes on me, sweetheart." She's made for me. Her eyes snap back to mine. "I don't want to miss a minute of one of our firsts."

She smiles. "This feels way different from anything else I've ever experienced."

"It should. It's been a lifetime in the making. I won't last much longer."

My orgasm coils at the base of my cock, ready to explode, but I won't go without her, not now, not ever.

She's close, and I thrust into her a couple more times.

She screams my name as she has the first of many orgasms I will give her. Music to my ears as I follow her in ecstasy. She falls forward, panting as if she's running for her life. We'll have to work on her stamina. I have plans for us.

In this moment, I know I love her more than I'd ever loved anyone in my life, but she was not ready to hear that from me. I kiss her cheeks, eyes, and lips.

I pull her away from me. "You okay?"

My body stiffens. She notices.

"What?" She asks.

"No condom. I'm so sorry. I got so damn caught up in you." Our foreheads meet. "I lost focus. It's not like me."

She smiles like she has a secret. "It's okay. There's nothing to forgive. I'm on birth control. Besides, I can't imagine anything being between us for our first time. This is the way it should be."

She lifts off on wobbly legs. I step out of the tub and hold her hand to help her out. I dry her from head to toe and swing her up into my arms, surrounded by her giggles.

After tucking her in bed, I dry myself off before joining her. She puts her leg across my thigh, her head on my shoulder, and closes her eyes.

Her sigh is deep. "I never imagined it could be like this. It wasn't like this with anyone else."

I chuckle. "One, I'm glad this is how we came together, pun intended. Two, let's not talk about past lovers because I could lose my mind thinking about it." I can feel her smile.

We both slept for a while, but my body craves more. Later, in the wee hours of the morning, I take her from behind as she lies next to me; her legs curled up slightly. She is my perfect fit, the way her body curves into mine. I let her come before me, and we lay there spent.

She falls back to sleep, but my mind is spinning. I

hoped this much sex would wipe me out, but my survival instincts kick in. I toss and turn during another sleepless night.

In my mind, I've gone over twenty different ways to get us out of here alive. I know I can't do it alone, which means I need to call for backup. At daylight, I'll call Mac and the boys, especially his brother Declan, the chemical explosives and hurt locker expert. I've kept him on the sidelines because of his memory loss, among other things, but he's been doing better, and we need him in the field.

I pray they can make it here in time. Mac won't be happy to leave Mara, his pregnant wife.

TWENTY-FOUR

Sean
_____

SOMETIMES I THINK that if I don't sleep, the nightmares will never haunt me. Each one has a recurring theme, me covered in blood. How I get covered in blood changes with each nightmare. The blood comes from a child, a woman, or a young man.

Plenty of young boys take up arms to fight because it's what they know. Their innocent eyes stare at me until they pull the trigger of an AK-47. The kill-or-be-killed mentality is not for everyone.

It was a calling for me, but the damage has been done. I'm still fighting the war inside my head almost every night while I'm here. If I'm going to be my best for Jess and stay in the field, I'm going to need help with the trauma this place caused years ago.

The light peeks from behind the blackout curtains, and a ray shines on Jess. The scene reminds me of when I would come into my mom's room with the early morning light and find her beaten and bruised. I would crawl under the covers and snuggle up next to her. She said it always made her feel better.

My mom must be watching over me and sent me to Jess. I can't think of a crazier circumstance to be reconnecting with each other. I had every intention of looking for her when I got back stateside. My next challenge is to get us out of here in one piece.

Jess rolls over with a smile that lights up her face, and her brown curly hair mussed up around her head. Waking up every morning like this would make me a lucky man. She's all I've ever wanted, bringing a sense of peace I don't feel with anyone else.

"Good morning, Mr. Knight," she says with a groggy voice.

I roll toward her. "Good morning, Bug. How did you sleep?"

She props herself on her elbow. "Good. But you look like you didn't sleep a wink." She reaches out to stroke my forearm. "Talk to me."

My eyes focus on where her heat warms me. "I have nightmares left over from my time here in Afghanistan. They have gotten worse since I arrived here."

"PTSD." There's no judgment in her reply.

"Yeah, I try not to sleep so I won't see them. They come and go. Since I've been back, they're stronger than ever." I stoke her fingers on my arm.

"Um. It sounds like you could use a distraction."

She was always good at knowing when to end a conversation and moving on to another topic.

She pulls me down to her and kisses me deeply, spearing my mouth with her tongue, teasing me to come out and play. My hands find her C-cup breasts as I pinch and stroke them to peaks. I latch onto one with my mouth, sucking and biting as she bucks her hips.

"More, please," she moans.

"You only get what I give you. Remember? I'm the one

in control." Reaching over, I press the play button as Faith Hill sings "Breathe." I can finally breathe with her.

"That's what you think." She's going to be a lot to handle.

I lick my way down her smooth, flat belly, the result of yoga. I kiss the inside of her thighs, teasing her by blowing on her pussy. Then I feast, biting and licking her lips and swirling around her clit. She tastes better than I could have imagined. I hold her hips still with my hands as I bring her close to orgasm and then hold back.

"Please, I need to come." She looks down at me.

"Good things come to those who wait." I suck on her clit as I pump my fingers in and out of her. She detonates within seconds, thrashing her head and chanting my name.

I climb up her body and lean on my elbows. She spreads herself for me. As much as we know each other from our past together, we're in unfamiliar territory. There is something in her face I've never been privy to before: sheer lust, passion, and confidence. She feels the soul-baring intimacy as much as I do.

The pace needs to be slow so I can savor every minute, every movement as I inch my way in. I bend her knee up to her chest, sinking in deeper. This is the closest I've ever been to anyone in my life.

"Tell me what you feel?" I say in between thrusts.

"You! You're big." She bites her lower lip with a smile. "I'm full with you. You end and I begin. I imagined this moment so many times, but real life stole the show. I don't want to be without you. Please don't leave." Her words break with emotion.

"I'm not going anywhere." I thrust into her and we touch foreheads, breathing heavily, taking up each other's air.

Backing away, I want to see everything on her face. No

words pass between us, but the web of fate spins us together as if this was always the way it was meant to be.

I pick up the pace so we can finish together. I want her to feel me for the rest of the day. Sweat beads on our bodies, and her skin blushes a beautiful rose color. She's close and so am I.

"Come for me, Jess."

She does in all the glory a man could ever want. I'm right there with her, and we crumble into a heap of orgasmic bliss. This is a different high, one where the person knows you better than anyone else and accepts you for who you are and aren't.

She's the most beautiful woman I've ever been with and the last woman I'll ever be with, whether or not she knows it. I wipe the sweat from her brow.

"You should rest up. I have to make a phone call." I wink.

"What are you doing, making up for lost time? I'm going to be sore for the rest of the day." She turns her head away sheepishly.

"You bet your sweet ass I am. Sore is good." I kiss her nose and get my SAT phone.

The phone rings, and Mac picks up. "What's up, Wild?"

"I need an extraction with a full team. Three people, including myself. Can't talk long. They could intercept this call." My words are stilted and short.

There's a long sigh at the other end. "Yeah, I'm on it, mate. This needs to be short and sweet. I've got to be back for our baby, or Mara will kill me from across the Atlantic. Trust me, she has that ability."

"I need Declan. It involves explosives. We need to get him on board. He's too talented to be sitting behind a desk," I order as a partner of the firm.

"Might be just what the doctor ordered. He needs to get back in the field." Mac knows his brother's abilities need to be used for the mission.

The next ten seconds are spent giving him the coordinates and speaking in code. This operation is off-book. Mac has got to call in some chips because we need air power.

The specifications will be in a shared email of what I need and what to expect. This is going to turn into more than an extraction.

I click off, so the call won't be intercepted. I put the phone away and look up to find Jess perched on the edge of the bed, staring at me.

"What's going on?" I had to pick a smart one with ultrasonic ears.

I sit on the bed next to her and hold her to me.

She looks up at me. "You can't go walking around naked all the time. My libido gets going every time I look at you."

"That's a good thing." I kiss the top of her head. "I can't get us out on my own. My team is coming for backup. They'll be here in two days."

There's fear in her eyes. "Two days?"

"I've got some loose ends I need to tie up before we go." There are more loose ends than I know about.

I hold her gaze. "Is Pippa a spy?"

She has a puzzled look on her face. "I don't know, but I don't think so. She's been hacking for a while. I don't think spy games would interest her. Why?"

"Some things aren't adding up. She has skills that require training." My frustration shows.

I hold her face in my hands; my thumbs caress her cheeks. "I need you to listen to me. You must stay in this room for the rest of the day. I'm going to the mine today, and I don't want anything to happen while I'm gone. No, you cannot visit Pippa. It's way too dangerous, especially since we've breached her room. I don't know if they're on to us yet. I guess I'll find out today. Promise me you won't leave."

She nods her head.

"Say it."

"I promise, but I'm scared for the first time on any assignment I've been on. I'm afraid for all of us. Are we going to make it out alive?" Tears crest in her eyes.

My eyes penetrated hers. "I'm going to make sure of it. My teammates are some of the best in the world."

"Sometimes even the best get killed. I don't think I could handle it if something happens to you now that I've found you." She clasps my hands in hers.

For the first time since I left the military, I'm more determined than ever to get everyone out safely. I will calculate everything down to the last detail, but there's no guarantee. I've got to bury my doubts if we're going to make it out of here without losing anyone.

TWENTY-FIVE

Sean
_____

I MEET up with Isaad for a late breakfast. He's eating and reading the paper. Even though he's only eight years older than me, he is an old soul. A plume of smoke hovers over the table as the morning light tries to pierce it.

"Are you ever going to give those things up?"

I sit across from him and order enough food for two men. Keeping up my stamina is a necessity. Between Jess and this mission, I need to stay on my game.

He looks over the paper at me. "Probably not. Tell me, did you have a good evening?"

I'm in a mood. "Yes, I did. Did you have a satisfying evening?" My eyes dare him to guess the meaning of my statement.

He takes off his glasses and smiles at me. "I did. It looks like you've won the heart of Ms. Wilder." He leans back in his chair.

"I wouldn't say that. We're still in the getting-to-know-you phase." My food arrives, and I eat as if it's my last meal.

He rests his chin on his hands. "Even sleeping in the same bed together?"

"Who says we're sleeping in the same bed?" I say with a mouthful of food.

He looks away. "Fair enough. You and I are going to fly out to the mine today. But I want to take a slight detour into Kabul."

I stop chewing. "Why?"

"I've got some investors from China I want you to meet."

Bells go off as I remember Jess saying she heard Chinese spoken in the house. This may be the break I've been looking for in what's going on here.

"I thought you didn't want investors." I continue eating. Keeping the atmosphere casual works in my favor.

"Things have changed," he mutters.

I put down my fork and glare at him. "Things seem to change at a rapid rate around here. You want to tell me what's going on?"

"All in good time. Have you thought any more about my offer?" He straightens a knife on the table.

I need to play my cards close to get to the bottom of what's happening here. "Yeah, we need to talk numbers, conditions, and benefits. I have a few demands." I look him in the eye and smile.

He stares at me for a minute, judging if I'm telling him the truth. "Well then, let's get going. We have quite a day ahead of us."

I've gone undercover plenty of times before, but this is at another level. My vibrations tell me I'm at the edge of something big, and excitement pumps through my veins. If this goes south, I don't want to take down my friend, but if he's on the wrong side of this, I'll do what's right.

We take the elevator to the rooftop as a helicopter flies

in from the north. This isn't the stripped-down chopper we took from the mine, but a luxurious Airbus Eurocopter worth about ten million dollars. Layered pieces point to the fact that there's more going on here than meets the eye.

The flight to Kabul is short, but my heart is racing, worried about getting shot down by a SAM, a surface-to-air missile. As we enter the Kabul airspace, the firing has ceased on the ground and in the air. It's as if they have suspended everything. Isaad looks over at me and gives me the thumbs up.

Only someone with a hell of a lot of money and power could pull this off. There's no way stolen Bitcoin pays for this. I doubt he bought the helicopter with cryptocurrency. But from the little I know about cryptocurrency, it's a possibility.

I'm questioning why Neil wanted me for this assignment. This seems like an op more up the CIA's alley than a former SEAL. Spooks always slither into these situations. Their forte is making contacts and infiltration. What is Neil's game?

We land north of the city at a warehouse. Parked next to us is a Gulfstream G500, not the bottom of the barrel in the class of private jets. My gut tells me the big guns have arrived, and trouble isn't far behind.

Isaad turns to me. "You must leave your weapon on the chopper."

I take my M17 out of its holster and lay it on the seat. I'm not giving up the one on my ankle. In a survival situation, I want to be the one doing the killing.

The Chinese contingent file off their plane dressed in black suits with black ties and a white shirt. I identify the bodyguards in this group, and they are carrying weapons.

Isaad approaches them and shakes hands with the three of them.

He pulls his shoulders back and gives his sales pitch. "This is Sean Knight. He's helping with the mining efforts and will be on board soon for the rest of the plan. He's one of the best and a former Navy SEAL."

I shake hands with the three men. They are introduced as Chen, Fan, and Ling. Ling seems to be the leader. The air fills with distrust as soon as Isaad mentions my credentials. It might be because I'm ex-military or an American or both. Americans aren't trusted in various parts of the world for several reasons. They nod in my direction.

Ling folds his hands in front of him. "It's good to have an American on our side. It makes things easier. Isaad has praised you for a while. When it comes together, this will be a global coup."

If I wasn't looking at him, I would think he was an American. His English is spot-on, without a trace of an Asian accent. My mind sticks to the words *global coup*.

My face remains impassive as I nod, but I don't look in Isaad's direction. Maybe he wants it to look like I'm in on their plans.

"Sean hasn't been brought up to speed, but we're getting there." He smiles at them.

Ling smiles. "Once he sees the benefits, will there be any question? He'll have to prove himself first. We'll see."

The other Chinese nod, and Isaad leads the way inside the warehouse. He punches in a code and uses his thumbprint and a retinal scan. Security is tight, much like his house.

After my eyes adjust to the light in the warehouse, they land on the floor-to-ceiling arsenal. I keep an ear to their conversation, but I can't put anything concrete together.

They have every weapon known to man in here. The only thing I don't see is uranium, which doesn't mean they don't have it.

The Helmand Province, south of here, holds uranium. With their money flow, they could easily extract it and use it for nuclear warfare. They have enough firepower to take over a small country. A big red flag waves in my head. Maybe this is what Neil wanted me to find out about.

I haven't identified the connection between Isaad and the Chinese. I pick up on the name of something called Stellarium, and I'm not clear on what it is, but it's pivotal to their entire program.

The Chinese guards shadow me as I walk around and look at the operation. They're not very subtle. I want to take out my phone and snap some photos, but there's no way to do it without attracting attention.

Isaad walks toward me. "What do you think?"

"It's extremely impressive. What country were you planning to overtake?" I put my hands in my pockets.

He laughs, something I haven't seen him do during my trip. "You still have a sense of humor I enjoy." He never answers the question.

I bait him. "How did things go with the Chinese?"

"It feels good to have a world power behind you and ready to take the next steps." His face lights up, and he seems more relaxed.

"And those would be?" I push.

He slaps my back. "All in good time, my friend."

We board the luxury chopper. The first thing I do is grab my gun and check the clip. There's a brief calm that comes over me, knowing I can defend myself.

Heading toward the mine, we fly over some of the lushest landscapes of Afghanistan. The countryside is beautiful with beautiful people, and yet it can't heal itself. Oppression has become the norm. War, hunger, and displacement are part of day-to-day living. If they could get it together, they would be one of the richest countries in this part of the world based on mining alone.

The cabin is quiet as the chopper touches down at the mining site. The day has become overcast, and there are dark clouds to the west. It feels like a sign of things to come. I'm not a superstitious person, but nothing about this assignment has held true.

Isaad comes up behind me. "You're thinking about the uranium, aren't you?"

He's smart, which is not to my advantage. "Yellowcake. Comes with high risks. Are you thinking about mining it?"

Isaad stands with his hands on his hips and stares at me as if he's trying to decide if he wants to continue the conversation.

"That's where you come in. I have access to every mine in Afghanistan, and I want you to head them up. We can talk about a percentage of the profits after the first six months. I'll make you a millionaire in your first year, a billionaire in no time." He doesn't know that I don't need his money or anyone else's.

I had learned at an early age to keep my face neutral to not set off my dad, who warned me, "I'll punch that look off your face permanently." Little did he know, it helped me keep my ass out of trouble.

I pull off my Aviator sunglasses. "What's with the reference to a global coup?"

"We've discovered a mineral that burns at a very high temperature, but never burns away. It seems to feed on itself. The implications for an energy source are infinite."

He has to be talking about the silver-like mineral I found in the mine. "You discovered a new mineral? I find that highly unlikely."

He continues. "It's only found here in Afghanistan as far as we know. It's a game-changer." He looks off to the horizon. "There are many things that need to be in place and many that need to be brought to their knees before we can change the world."

He's exited the highway on a road I'm not sure I can follow. Things are adding up to world domination, which is ridiculous, but he hasn't given me the complete picture.

From what I've seen, he has enough cash flow to do whatever he wants, especially in this country, and with the Chinese backing him, the sky's the limit. I'm not comfortable in the role of a spy. It's not my thing, but if I'm going to sort this out, I need to play the part.

"You've piqued my curiosity. Care to fill me in on your plan for world domination?"

He rests his hand on my shoulder. "One step at a time. I need to know you're fully invested in being my right-hand man."

I must have given him a look of surprise because he chuckles. "I don't think Rakesh will be too happy about that."

He waves his hand with the cigarette in it. "He'll be fine, and he is well taken care of. His loyalty is unmatched. However, you're the wild card."

He gives my code name, Wild, a whole new meaning.

He gets a call, talks quickly, and turns to me. "We have to go. There's been a shooting at the house."

My nerves light up, praying Jess kept her word about not leaving the room, but I have a bad feeling.

TWENTY-SIX

Jess

THE NIGHT with Sean was beyond any fantasy I've ever had about him. He reached inside me and took control, which was a relief. I trust him with my life and would follow him to the ends of the earth to be with him, accepting his scars inside and out, no questions asked.

I can't help but feel I may be returning the favor to my savior. He needs someone to save him. I want to be the one he can lean on and depend on.

Although I didn't count on him finding those letters ever. My feelings are out in the open, and I'm not sorry. How many nights did I cry myself to sleep after he left without a word to anyone? Too many to count. I read him better than anyone else, even today. He's hiding his PTSD and is going to need support. But if we're going to be together, I've got to work on getting us out of here.

I may have agreed not to visit Pippa, but I didn't agree to no snooping. Two heads are better than one. Maybe I can scope things out and get more information about this place.

The first thing I look for is a gun. I pull Sean's suitcase out of the closet and unlatch the panel hiding all his firearms. There's a lot to choose from as my eyes land on a short-barreled gun. I have no clue what it is. Guns aren't my specialty, but I want to defend myself. My hairspray may come in handy to cover up any cameras and give me time to investigate.

The dark blue garment with a burka taunts me from the bed. The more I'm with Sean, the more comfortable I feel in my body. I need to own who I am and what I look like.

The fullness of the outfit used to feel like protection. People couldn't see me. I need to be invisible for another reason, to find out what's going on in this house.

Slipping into the garment for what I hope is the last time feels uncomfortable and suffocating. Sean has helped me feel like I belong in my skin. I'm slow to accept that he sees me in a beautiful light, but his adoration feels incredible. I wouldn't feel this way if I had worn this my entire life. The women here live under constant oppression, which, on some level, is normal for them. I don't want to live not being able to be seen.

I tuck the gun into the back of my waistband with the keycard in hand. The small pocket in the front of my pants holds my phone, and the other side holds the small can of hairspray.

The hall seems clear until I see a group of women heading toward Isaad's personal quarters. I fall in line behind them with my head down. The group is a mix of women wearing burkas and hijabs. We pass several guards as they look down and away to avoid eye contact. The group hangs a left as I go straight ahead. I look over my shoulder to see if I'm being followed. It's clear. I move quickly, looking for security cameras along the way.

There are several locked rooms with the same door, but I need to use my keycard wisely. There's a faint hum that gets louder as I walk farther down the hall. I pass the only door labeled in Arabic letters. A loud hum comes from behind this door. Across the hall is a hidden camera. I continue down the hall and circle back, flattening myself against the wall to avoid detection.

Reaching up, I spray the camera with hairspray and know I only have minutes, maybe less, to get what I need in the room. I jiggle the handle, but it doesn't budge. I swipe the keycard as the light turns from red to green, unlocking the door.

I step inside, closing the door behind me with a click. The chilly air gives me goosebumps. Banks of computers fill the room. Most go from floor to ceiling with blinking red and orange lights. I've got to lose the hairspray and roll it under the edge of one of the computers.

Beyond the computers is an empty room with a glass wall. The door leading to the room has several scanners, but I can't make out the purpose of the room. I take out my phone and take pictures of the scanners.

Monitors cover the entire wall inside the room. Clusters of them are marked with the various continents, North America, South America, and Antarctica. The monitors show things like hospitals, mines, and banks. I take as many pictures as I can of everything in the room.

The click of the door to the hallway alerts me as someone enters. I stuff my phone in my pocket with the keycard in my underwear and duck down behind a row of computers.

My heart thunders so loud that I fight to hear over the buzz of the computers. Fear seizes me like it did when I would hide from my foster father. He would call my name over and over, but I never came out until he had left or fallen asleep. Pushing through, I crawl along the floor to the door, hoping whoever is in here heads to the glass room.

A man stands outside the glass room with his hands on his hips, staring at what's inside. I think it might be Rakesh, but I can't be certain.

He doesn't go into the room. I can barely make out his face in the reflection of the glass. The risk is too high for me to try to leave because he might see the reflection of the door opening.

I creep closer to the middle of the bank of computers, in case the man leaves, he won't see me. My knees are tucked under my chin as I huddle on the floor, waiting for him to leave. I lock down my nerves as I try to control my breathing. Sweat drips down the valley of my spine despite how cold it is in here.

He leaves as I breathe out a sigh of relief. I use my yoga breathing to calm down and head for the door. It closes with a soft click. I head back in the direction I came from, walking as fast as I can to the main hallway away from Isaad's private quarters.

Up ahead in the hallway, I see Rakesh texting on his phone. Guards run in his direction, yelling at him in Kati. They run past me toward the hall I just came from. I stop in the middle of the hall and look around as if I'm lost.

"Hey, what are you doing in this part of the house? It's off-limits." Anger reddens his face. His cell phone rings.

I shrug my shoulders, and he walks toward me while listening to someone on the other end. He grabs my arm before I can remove my burka.

"Wait, Rakesh. It's me." He stops, and I pull off the burka. "Thanks for finding me. I got turned around. I have no idea where I am." I'm not sure my attempt at playing dumb works on him.

He ends the call and gives me a suspicious look, and then smiles with malice. "Let's go for a walk, Ms. Wilder."

He squeezes my upper arm and drags me down the hall. I'm running to keep up with him. We get to the door that leads outside, and I stop walking as he jerks to a stop.

"Where are we going?" I struggle against his punishing grip.

"I thought we would go for a walk in the woods. Give you a personal tour of those cabins you were so interested in." His face is inches from mine. "Or I tell Isaad you were in his private area. No one is permitted there."

"I told you, I got lost." I look away and try to keep my face from showing any emotion, but I know there's fear in my eyes.

"That's what a spy would say. You're not as innocent as you look. Let's go." He grits his teeth.

I try to pull away from him as his fingers dig harder into my arm. My breath becomes shallow as I realize why he wants to go to the woods. I sort through the options in my head. There aren't many, and this won't end well for me.

He knows where the cameras are out here and can do anything he wants to me. No one will hear me scream. We come to a clearing between the trees. My body propels forward when he throws me to the ground face-first. I roll over onto my back as the gun presses into my spine. He pins me with his body and bares his teeth. His smoky breath enters my nose, making me gag.

"Let's see if I can find a can of spray on you, maybe even a copy of my keycard."

He grabs my blouse and rips it from my shoulder. I try to roll away from him. He slaps me hard across the face, making my ears ring.

I try to get my head together. Fighting him is not the

answer. It'll make it impossible to get to the gun, that digs into my back. He can't find the keycard, or I'm a dead woman. Maybe I'm a dead woman, anyway.

His hand raises again, and I still my body. "Stop," I say loud enough to get his attention. "All I have is my cell phone. Here." I reach into my waistband and pull out my phone.

He rips the rest of my top off me and looks to see if I have the keycard in my bra.

"I see what the American piece of shit likes about you." His eyes follow my body from head to toe. "You will be naked and scarred when they find your body. I want to see the American lose his mind."

A scream rips out of my lungs as his fist meets my jaw, and the side of my face slams into the ground. My head fights to stay clear and conscious as his hands tear at my blouse. I open my eyes to see my top in shreds on the ground. He stands up and grabs hold of the waistband of my pants. It's now or never.

I reach behind me, take out the gun, sit up, and fire. It kicks back, throwing me down. He falls to the ground, holding his leg, screaming in pain. My hands shake so badly that the gun falls to the ground. Our eyes lock. His eyes scream death. Adrenaline spikes in my bloodstream. My eyes scream to survive.

The gun is my only lifeline. Picking it up off the ground, I run into the woods looking for somewhere to hide. Sweat pours from my body as my heart pounds in my chest, but my feet get me going as I keep running. I don't look back, but I keep waiting for the shot in my back. He shouts in Kati.

Climbing up the hill past the cabins, I see a small cave on the side of the hill. I squeeze myself in there, hoping my dark pants will help camouflage me. A shiver runs through my bones as my adrenaline drops and the cool air of the cave seeps into my skin.

It's not long before I hear the thumping of helicopter blades above me, praying it's Sean. If Rakesh's men find me first, I'm dead.

TWENTY-SEVEN

Sean

"WHAT HAPPENED?" If this has anything to do with Jess, I'll lose my shit.

Isaad's face turns serious. "I'm not sure." He doesn't look in my direction.

"Who's involved?"

I'm trained to remain calm in difficult situations, but none of my missions had emotional ties.

His head turns in my direction as his eyes bore into me. "It seems Ms. Wilder may have had an encounter with Rakesh, again."

My fists pound on the seat. "Fuck! She better not have a scratch on her, or he won't live to tell about it."

"I thought you said you were just getting to know Daphne. Seems like a pretty serious reaction to have for someone you just met." His smile holds a secret I'm not sure I like.

"Just so we're clear, it's about respecting women."

As we fly over a clearing, Rakesh rolls on the ground holding his leg. Guards run toward him from the house. My only thought is good girl.

"You'd better call off your dogs from looking for her. I'll find her myself," I yell over the thumping of the chopper blades. Isaad nods.

I flip into fight mode, and Rakesh will be at the receiving end of it.

Before the bird fully lands, I open my door, and we race out to the woods. Rakesh's arm is slung over the shoulder of one of the other guards being led back to the house.

I grab his shirt. "Where is she?"

He tries to push me off him. "I don't know. That bitch shot me."

I punch him in the face and kick his injured leg out from under him as he crumbles to the ground, screaming in pain.

Running ahead to find her, I stop to get my bearings. Where would she go to protect herself? The cabins. I follow the trail up the hillside and start calling her name. As dusk settles in, the consuming darkness won't be far behind. I've got to get to her before the bears, wolves, or wildcats come out for a meal. Even in this war-torn part of Afghanistan, they roam the land in healthy numbers.

The rocky terrain gets steep behind the cabins, and I call for her again. There's a slight movement coming from under the outcropping of rocks. She emerges from inside the rock cave, her lower half dressed in a dark color, making it difficult to see her. He tore away her top, leaving her in a bra. She's shaking and holding her arms in front of her.

I climb up the rocks to help her down. Blind fury propels me. I want to kill him, but I don't let her see that side of me. When we get to a flat surface, I take off my shirt and wrap her in it, hugging her to me.

"Are you okay? Do we need to get a medic?" I see red

welts across her face and scratches on her shoulders and chest.

"I'm fine, just a little shaken." Her cheek bleeds as she holds her head.

He will pay for laying a hand on her. "How did you get his weapon away from him? That was a brave move."

She stands and stares at me. "Well..." Her body language says there's another spin.

"Why do I think this is about to go in a different direction?"

She reaches behind her back, pulls out my 9mm, and hands it to me. "It's got some power to it."

"I know. Now that I know you're okay, I want to spank your ass for defying my orders." The weapon gets secured in my waistband.

She blushes. "He was going to kill me. As he stripped off my clothes, he said he wanted you to find me naked. By the time he got off me to rip off my pants, I had seconds to get to my... your gun, and then I shot him."

I hold her to me and kiss her nose, cheeks, forehead, and lips. "You are so brave, but we need to have a serious talk about what it means to follow orders."

"There's more, but we can talk later. I'm hungry, tired, and in pain. He almost punched me unconscious." Her body crumbles as I hold her up.

My jaw clicks from clenching my teeth. "Do I want to know what the more is?" There's always more where she's concerned as she looks for the next big story.

She stops for a minute and breathes. "Oh, yeah, you do. The photos are on my phone."

Even with my tours of duty, she might be the one to send me to an early grave.

I hold her to me, walking back to the house and enter the kitchen to get some food to go. I turn to the chef. "Give

Isaad my apologies. We'll be eating in our room tonight." He nods as he continues to work.

Jess orders enough food to feed an army. She'll only eat half of it. When she's stressed out, she orders lots of food, only to put half of it away for later. Old habits die hard. I go in the opposite direction; I don't eat when I'm under stress, but I have to keep up my strength for this mission.

She locks the door behind us and strips down to her short shorts. No complaints from me, but this isn't the time.

I get a washcloth and antiseptic to wash her wounds. "You need to start at the beginning and tell me what happened today because I've got plenty of my shit to share."

She hands me her phone as she munches on a celery stick and smirks. She knows I hate the sound of crunchy food. It's too noisy.

"Look for yourself."

Pulling one of my shirts from the drawer, I wrap her up in it. "What's the code to unlock it?"

She hesitates. "0602."

Her written letters are one thing, her heart poured out into words, but having my birthdate as her lock code is her daily reminder of me. My heart gallops in my chest. I never knew she felt this way. Maybe things were meant to play out this way. We both might be ready to discover each other as adults.

I don't look at her as I punch the code into the phone and open the picture gallery. "Where is this and what is this?"

"I went to Isaad's part of the house to see what I could find, which is why I had to take your gun." She shrugs one shoulder. Dark circles form under her eyes as the day has caught up with her.

I'm bewildered. "You did fucking what?" My blood

boils for the wrong reasons. "How could you take a chance like that? Rakesh could have killed you on sight. You're lucky he took the time to drag you into the woods."

She needs to understand how things happen in this part of the world without warning or necessity.

"He's too busy thinking about how to kill people than to think about who is snooping around. I made it look like I was lost. It worked for about half a second until he saw an opportunity to get rid of me for good." She's fierce, which is what makes her such a tenacious reporter.

She tells me about everything she saw, and none of it makes sense. There are many missing pieces, and the ones we have don't fit together.

"I finished the article on Isaad. I emailed it to him, and then I'll send it to my editor." She hugs her knees to her chest.

Things are ending here, but I'm not sure what it's going to look like.

"I'm sure he'll love it. His ego's bigger than it used to be." He's a shell of the man I once knew.

I share the events of my day to compare notes, only they don't add up. "I'm calling Neil. It can't wait until morning."

I get out the SAT phone. He picks up on the first ring. "I hope I didn't wake you, Sleeping Beauty, but we have a problem."

I tell him the short version of my meeting with the Chinese and Jess's discoveries.

Silence greets me on the other end. "Shit. This is bigger than I thought. I'm sending my best team to see what they can find and help get you out."

My team is who I need to get out. "What the hell is—"

He clicks off. I'm more convinced than ever that he set

me up in a covert assignment other than the one I think I'm on. It's time to call it a night as I stow away the SAT phone.

She's fading fast. "Bug, let's go take a shower and wash this day away."

She stops chewing. "Okay." Her eyes look lost.

I take her by the hand and lead her to the bathroom. The scrapes around her face and chest need to be cleaned, which I gladly do for her. I strip off her shorts as I kiss every part of her body. I take off my clothes and huddle with her in the shower.

Her back is flush against my front. The minute I undress her, I stand at attention, and there is no backing down. My back protects her from the shower spray. I'll protect her until the day I die. Today confirmed that I never want to be without her again. My arms wrap around her waist, and her head rests under my chin.

Our bodies mold together. "I wanted to ask you about your tattoo."

"Which one?"

Her skin is the most beautiful mocha color I've ever seen. I love the feel of it under my fingers.

She looks up at me sideways. "The frog and the butterfly."

It doesn't surprise me that's the tattoo that catches her attention. "Do you remember the book *Frog and Toad Are Friends*?"

"Of course."

"I'm Frog and you're my best friend, but you're no toad. You were the beautiful butterfly just out of my reach." The frog's tongue doesn't quite reach the butterfly. She traces the images with her finger. "I'm going to get the frog's tongue re-inked to make it longer."

Her lips turn up in a sexy smile.

I reach down between her legs and dip my finger in her wet pussy. Her head falls back on my shoulder, and she moans. I kiss her neck and shoulder while working my finger in and out of her until she says my name.

"Bend over. Hands on the wall."

Her skin is smooth and unmarked. I run my hands down her back and push into her slowly. I hear her beg me for release, and I hold my pace until I can't anymore. The thrusts become faster and rougher, but she keeps begging me with her soft voice, like caramel for my ice cream, until we both come.

She stands up and turns to me while biting her lower lip. "Why do you have to get the tongue redone?"

"After incredible sex, that's what you have to ask me? Because now that I've caught you, you're mine, and I'm not letting you go." I grab her into a hug.

Her lips form an O. I have plans for those lips for a lifetime.

We're tucked in bed as exhaustion sets in. "When are we going to get Pippa? Maybe we can put her in the closet until your team comes to get us."

Her voice is innocent because she's in unfamiliar territory. She doesn't understand the finesse of war, the decisions that need to be handled at the last minute, and the lives that are lost. I'm hoping we can get to Pippa and get her out, but I know there are no guarantees.

"Listen to me carefully." I hold her chin in my fingers. "If something happens to me, you need to take my weapons and run into the woods. Go to the cave you were hiding in. My team will find you."

Tears form in her eyes. "Sean, I can't…"

"You will because you're strong and brave. I've seen you in action. You always have been. Trust me, you can do this. You will make it out alive." My stomach turns at the thought that I may not make it out. I finally have something to live for.

She nods and lays her head on my shoulder. I have a bad feeling about this op, but I don't share that with her.

TWENTY-EIGHT

Pippa

SEEING Jess relieves some of my anxiety, but it's been a couple of days. She doesn't understand why I would want to do the naked party dance with Rakesh. He's the only one I see regularly, and he's hot as hell. My ex-boyfriends pale in comparison. He knows how to please a woman, and this woman has needs.

I won't apologize for my sexual appetite. Most women are too uptight to enjoy what a man has to offer. My affair is a welcome distraction from my existence as his prisoner, as I lose myself and focus on the pleasure. I'm pretty sure I'm suffering from Stockholm syndrome at this point.

Even though I accepted the job, I'm a prisoner here. Dogs get treated better than this. I've been searching everywhere in the suite to find a way out, but have been unsuccessful. The room is solid with no windows or cracks for natural light to come through. Nothing gets in or out.

The ankle cuff has an electronic light on it that blinks red. The device reminds me of an electronic tag a criminal would wear when they're confined to their homes. Since it's an electronic device, I may have a shot at getting it off me, but I only have one shot at this.

Escape Rtist is one of my hacker friends online. Cute. I assume it's a he because most hackers are men, which is to my advantage. If no one suspects a woman, they won't look for a woman. He goes into several ways I can disable my cuff. The directions include materials I don't have without taking apart my computer. If I take apart my computer, I'd better be able to make a run for it. My guess is that once I disable the cuff, they will know and come for me.

I form a plan and pray. My food gets delivered by a guard, who hands it off to me as if it's nuclear. They give me plastic utensils. The phone on the wall has a direct line to someone who can help me twenty-four-seven. I break my plasticware and request a metal fork, spoon, and knife. Since they hate coming down here, they meet my request and hand over the metal utensils.

Excitement pumps through me. My plan comes together. Once I get out of here, I'll find Jess. I don't care if we end up in the forest for days; we'll be free, which is all I care about. Timing is everything, and I have to work fast.

I break one tine off the fork. The fatter end makes a great mini screwdriver to take apart my computer to get to the magnetic strip. I keep my computer plugged into the main server and work on prying off the back.

Escape Rtist gave me instructions on how to use the magnetic tape and my fork to get the ankle cuff disabled. I watched as Rakesh unlocked it with one of his keycards. The two things need to work together with precision, or it won't unlock. My back needs to be to the cameras, so it looks like I'm scratching my ankle.

The red blinking light turns green, and the cuff falls away. Tears spring to my eyes. My ankle feels light as I turn and twist it. The cuff weighed on me more than I thought. I want to run far, far away from here and never come back. My freedom means everything to me, and I wouldn't have given it up like this.

I drag the cuff to the closet with my foot and leave it there with the door shut. The black scarves from my wardrobe serve as a cover as I wrap them around my head.

I open the door using the magnetic tape and the knife, slipping into the hallway. There's one problem. I don't know where to go. The stairs at the end of the hall going up look like my best option. I keep my head down and move toward the stairs. They've already served me my dinner, so I'm thinking no one is down here because they are eating their dinner.

The second level looks almost the same as the lower level I just came from. There's an odd handle on the wall. I grab it, pull, and then push. The entire wall pushes open to an airy hallway with windows along the sides. I'm drawn to the windows as I watch the sunset spray the horizon with hues of red, orange, and yellow. Closing my eyes, I try to inhale it, warming my cold, lonely soul.

When I open my eyes, rows of closed doors fill my vision. I'll have to use trial and error to figure out which one is Jess's door. If I knock on every door, it's going to be a long night. I knock on the first door. A woman answers, showing half of her face between the door and the doorframe.

"Do you know where Jess is?" I plead with her.

She frowns, shakes her head, and closes the door.

I continue to the next couple of doors and get the same reaction. None of the women speaks, or they don't speak English. They don't know where Jess is.

The last door in the hall opens. A woman peeks out and pulls me in by my arm.

"What are you doing? Trying to get yourself killed?" Her words are punctuated with a thick accent.

I notice she's different from the other women. They are beautiful, but she is the only one who is blonde with blue eyes. She looks Swedish.

I'm desperate at this point. "I'm looking for my sister, Jess. Do you know where she is?"

"There's no one here by that name, and I know every woman here." Her brows pinch together.

It hits me. "Is there someone here named Daphne?"

"Ah, yes. She's writing an article about Isaad." She looks at me with suspicion.

There may be hope yet. "Yes, that's her. Do you know which room she's in?"

"I'm sorry. No, I do not. But you shouldn't go back out there. If the guards find you..." Pain etches the fine, porcelain features on her face.

"Are you being held prisoner here?" The answer is obvious.

Tears form in her eyes. "I want to go home, and I don't know how to get out of here without getting killed or raped. I was taken against my will and was told if I didn't cooperate, they would kill my family."

Her words hit me as if someone slapped me in the face. I hesitate, worried about telling her what I know, but I need to give her hope.

"People are coming here to rescue me." I grab her hand. "I'll make sure they come for you, all of you. Please don't tell anyone. If word gets out, it will be harder to get to everyone."

"Thank you." She holds my face in her hands and kisses me on both cheeks.

"I'm here to find my sister. I promise to get you out."

She hugs me as I hug her harder, willing her to believe

and trust me. She lets me out of her room, and I turn the corner, smacking right into a guard. He grabs my arm and starts speaking in a language I don't understand.

I try to pull away, and he grabs me harder. To avoid being captured, I bite hard into his shoulder. He yelps and lets go of me, allowing me to sprint down the hall.

Chaos ensues as guards come at me from every direction, caging me in at the end of a hall. They grab both my arms.

I struggle to get free and scream, "Let me go!"

They haul me back to the underground prison, but to an unfamiliar holding cell. There's a table in the middle of the room. They throw me into a chair and cuff my wrists to the table. My breaking point nears the surface as I pull at the cuffs but refuse to cry.

A large man limps into the room with his head down. He says something to the men, and they leave me alone with him. The hair raises on the back of my neck. When he looks up, his obsidian eyes hold anger as he sits on the edge of the table. I've never seen this side of Rakesh. I choose my words carefully.

"Tell me. What exactly are you doing for him?" His mouth forms a taunt line.

My life depends on not telling him what I'm working on. "I told you, I stole Bitcoin for him. How do you think he buys his toys? By the way, what happened to your leg?" I try for compassion to gain time as I think through a plan.

He leans down. "The American bitch writing the article on Isaad shot me."

Jess. "What is she, a super spy?" I laugh, but Rakesh remains quiet.

His eyes narrow. Two of his fingers run down my hair, and then he grabs it and pulls.

"Ouch! You're hurting me."

I grab his hand, holding my hair, and dig my nails into his skin, but he doesn't budge.

His face is inches from mine. "As much as I enjoy fucking you, I could kill you right now, but I won't because you're some precious asset to Isaad."

I try to back my head away from him. "Please, Rakesh, I thought you and I had something. The good news is I won't be going anywhere anytime soon. Isn't that what you wanted? Where's Isaad?"

"Liar!" He screams in my face. "You are all liars." He seethes. "I don't know where Isaad is, but it doesn't mean I can't beat you until you tell me what you're doing for him. I'm being kept in the dark ever since the American piece of shit arrived."

From the look in his eyes, the train has left the station, and I'm running out of options.

He lets go of my hair and backhands me across the face. Then he slams my head down on the table until I see stars.

"Tell me!" he roars.

The door flies open. Isaad stands there with a red face and teeth bared. He grabs Rakesh before he says a word and throws him against the wall. His words are rapid, and the only one I catch is American.

Rakesh stands in the opposite corner. He pulls himself together and sneers something at Isaad. Isaad spends no time unlocking my cuffs.

My ears are ringing, and my focus is blurry. Isaad sits down across from me.

"Is this what I have to look forward to? You trying to escape?" He taps a fresh box of cigarettes on the table.

"Yeah, this is what you have to look forward to because I want out. I don't know how long it will take to rewrite this code, and you can't keep me prisoner forever."

He pounds his fist on the table and stands up as his chair crashes to the floor. "You will stay here as long as it takes because I need that program. Maybe if you had a way to get to it, you wouldn't be here." He pulls his shoulders back. "Besides, no one knows you're here." He smiles and raises his brows.

This is the part where I bite my tongue and save my smart comment for later. He will take me back to my room and see the carnage.

When we return to the room, he sees what I have done to get free.

He sighs. "I will get you new equipment, and there will be a guard at your door." He turns to me. "The next time you try to escape, you may not be so lucky as to live. If I don't get that program, neither will anyone else."

I plead with him. "I will wilt here. Who can live like this? Please don't chain me up. I'm not an animal."

He makes a tsk sound and runs his thumb down my jaw. "I'm afraid I can't do that. We are animals chained to the events in our lives. They shape who we are and who we become. You will remain chained until I get the program." His eyes hold a sadness that's painful to watch.

He puts the ankle cuff back on me and leaves. There's a place in his soul where darkness resides and light may never shine. I know about darkness, but there is a black hole that consumes him.

TWENTY-NINE

Sean

MY REFLECTION SHOWS a man ravaged by war, fighting to survive, and madly in love. The odd combination leaves me restless.

Being madly in love in the middle of hell was something I hadn't planned for, and it confuses me. I scratch my four-day-old beard across my jaw. Blending in is the key to getting more information and escaping this place forever. I need to find the weak spot and use it to my advantage.

Isaad has been a mystery from day one, but he was unusually quiet at the mine today. The man who I considered my friend is buried in him somewhere. I'm not sure what happened to him along the way, but it wasn't good and changed him at his core. He doesn't trust me, and I trust him even less, especially given what Jess found out.

The bathroom door opens. Jess walks in with her hair mussed and naked.

"I see someone is getting comfortable with her body."

This woman makes me come undone with just her smile. Her naked body gets me hard every time.

She hugs me from behind and kisses my scars. "That's because of you. In your eyes, I'm beautiful."

"I got news for you. Every red-blooded man out there thinks you're beautiful. I have nothing to do with it. But understand, you are mine." Her fingers roam my skin and ink.

Her smiling eyes peek over my hunched shoulder. "And you're mine, Mr. Knight."

I turn around, running my hands up and down her back and over her ass. She rubs against me like a cat.

I whisper in her ear, "I bet you're wet."

I slip my fingers in her folds, and slickness coats them. Easing one finger in, I hear her moan my name. This will never get old. I stop, leaving her on the edge. Her eyes pop open, and her hands land on her hips.

"What?" I shrug.

She narrows her eyes. "Why are you stopping?"

"Because I'm going to scope things out tonight to find his command room and try to pull some info from the computers. I'm also going to get Pippa and bring her back here. Besides, I like to leave you on the edge." I kiss the tip of her button nose.

She crosses her arms and bites her lip to prevent a smile. "I never knew you had such a mean streak."

If she only knew the things I've done that would redefine the word mean, not because I wanted to, but because I had to take orders and survive.

"I don't know how easy it's going to be to download information without triggering something in the system."

"It's going to have to be a quick in and out, so I know what we're dealing with."

She leaves the bathroom and comes back with a zip drive.

"I have several backup zip drives. This has the most at

one terabyte, not nearly enough to get everything off those computers, but you may get something."

She's always using her head, analyzing things down to the last detail. I use a tactical strategy. We make a great team in and out of the bedroom.

I take her hand and lead her to the bed. "I need a couple of hours of sleep. It was a long day. I seem to sleep better with you next to me. You need to stay here tonight. This time, keep your promise."

She nods, knowing exactly what I mean. Satisfying her needs and mine might be the answer to getting her to stay here so I can get some sleep.

The intensity between us doesn't seem to lessen. I love looking into her eyes when she has an orgasm. I love seeing what I do to her. When I come with her, it's a quenching feeling, like finding water in the desert. We fall into a deep sleep.

My phone vibrates as the alarm goes off, so I don't wake her. I dress in black, wrapping the turban around my head the way she showed me. My beard has grown in, and I wrap the rest of the scarf around my face, covering everything but my eyes. I load myself down with several weapons and a knife because I don't know what's around the corner.

This house is full of mystery and surprises. I don't like either, but it's what I'm trained to do. I grab a zip drive in case I can download some information, but I doubt it.

I walk down the hallway leading to Isaad's part of the house. Recognizing me would not be easy for anyone. I'm well covered and walk with my head down, nodding at a guard now and then.

The command room is on the right, and I use my keycard to let myself in. There is no need to cover the camera since I look like a guard.

A chill hits me, and it's not from the air temperature. Before me is a room full of Cray supercomputers. There are enough here to run the NSA and the Pentagon. The blue light from a glass room at the other end grabs my attention.

A man is sitting in front of a wall of monitors. He's bald with round glasses and dressed in a white polo and khakis, definitely not from around here. I stay to the side so he doesn't see me. The monitors are grouped according to the targeted object. A live feed of the world banks has the words Phase 3, and hospitals have Phase 2, but there doesn't appear to be a Phase 1 unless we're already in it. There are also banks of monitors with codes on them.

I need to get in there to see if I can download anything, but it'll require a foolproof plan. This is my specialty. I can see the alarm button under the table, so I can't knock on the door and say, "Hey, can you let me in? I've got to download some stuff."

My best shot is to unplug one supercomputer and wait for him to come out. They must not be expecting visitors because these computers should be hard-wired to the wall.

I pull the plug and move to the other side of the room. The red blinking light goes out on one computer, and he comes out to see what happened. I grab him from behind in a chokehold and stick my weapon in his ribs.

"You yell, you die." I don't know if he speaks English.

He nods. "You're the American," he says with a British accent.

"The one and only. Nice to meet you. Now, I need to get in that room, which I can only access with your finger-print and retina. Are you going to be a good boy, or am I going to have to cut off your finger and rip your eyeball from its socket?"

He holds up his hands. "I'm good, I'm good."

His keycard, thumbprint, and retina unlock the door. I shove him into a chair and tie his hands behind him. I push the zip drive into one of the hard drives under the table.

He laughs. "You'll only be able to download a fraction, and it's heavily encrypted. Good luck."

"You're awfully confident for someone who could get shot in a matter of minutes." His face falls. "You ever hear of a hacker named Red Enigma?" His eyes go wide. "The joke's on you."

He's right. I'm running out of time. The longer I stay here, the more likely they'll find me. I pull the zip from the hard drive and put it in my pocket. I lift his trouser pant leg and secure a cuff on him with a blinking red light.

"Hey, what are you doing?" He tries to pull his leg away.

"Since you like to surround yourself with blinking red lights, here's one for your ankle. Did I mention it's a bomb, and I have the detonator?" My face is inches from his. "If you so much as whisper anything about our time together, I will know, and you will blow. Got it? I'm like the military version of Dr. Seuss."

He nods as beads of sweat trail from his forehead. I cut his wrists loose before I sneak out the door. It's not a real bomb, but what he doesn't know won't hurt him. Another one of Peter's toys. He's like our version of Q.

I need to get to Pippa and get her back to our room. Thinking of it as our room makes me think of our apartment in the city, our children, and our home. I want everything with Jess. I'll live wherever she wants to live as long as we are together.

As I make my way down the hall, I hear a scuffle down another hall with a woman's muffled voice telling someone to let her go. I'm torn between saving her and saving Pippa.

Pippa wins this round. I squeeze behind the panel and run down the stairs. I approach her room, the last one on the left, and use my keycard to open the door.

It's as if a tornado has blown through and she has torn apart the computer. The cuff sits empty, and she's nowhere to be found. Holy shit. Where the hell is she?

THIRTY

Jess

THE SHEETS MOVE, and his warm, hard body curls in behind me. His arm comes around my waist, pulling me tight to him in more of a death grip. He hasn't come back with Pippa. I would have heard her smart-ass comments by now. This is not good.

He buries his nose in my hair and whispers, "Wild roses, my favorite. I've never forgotten."

I'm afraid to turn over and look into his eyes. "What's going on, Sean? Did you find the computer room, and where's Pippa?" Panic sets in despite his romantic words.

He doesn't answer right away. His long exhale moves my hair. "I found the room full of supercomputers. I downloaded maybe one percent from the hard drive, but I don't know if it'll be enough to figure out what's going on. The tech guy laughed at me and told me everything is heavily encrypted."

I hold my breath, waiting for him to tell me about Pippa.

"I went to get Pippa, but she wasn't in her room. The computer was in pieces, and the cuff was empty. I think she tried to escape, but I doubt she got very far." He stiffens, waiting for my response.

I turn to face him, trying to hold back the tears. "Do you think they caught her and…" I hold my hand over my mouth.

I can't lose her. We need to make sure she's with us. She and I may not be sisters by blood, but we share an unbreakable bond. Sometimes family isn't who you're related to, but who you've bonded with. I'm not leaving anyone behind, not her and not Sean.

"I think Isaad needs her for his plan. It's probably the only thing saving her ass." His amber eyes darken, and I sense there's more to come.

He strokes my face with his fingers, running them over my brow, nose, lips, and jawline. "I need you to listen to me carefully. Remember what I told you. If we get separated, run for the cabins. That's where the team is going to make base camp."

My heart doesn't know what to do. What if something has happened to Pippa? Sean keeps mentioning that we might get separated. I'm not equipped to handle this. I knew I was in over my head, but I feel like I'm drowning without a life raft.

This might get worse before it gets better. Imagining not getting out alive is not an option. Dangerous situations on various assignments are nothing new, but none of them included the people I love and treasure.

They say there is a fine line between death and sex, that the adrenaline rush is equal. I never want to know what it feels like to kill someone, but I want to be as close to Sean as I can get before this goes sideways. I could tell him I love him a thousand times over, but he's an action guy, so showing him holds much more meaning.

I roll on top of him, straddling his hips. My eyes take in

everything about him. He says nothing, but his eyes look at me with the same intensity.

No words are needed between best friends, and even less between lovers. My fingertips memorize the face and body of my man as they slide down his cheeks, past his neck, to the nearest tattoo. A skull and an American flag are inked with other symbols that have no meaning to me.

"My SEAL team," he says.

His other shoulder is 3D, with a wolf howling at the moon as my fingers skate over it.

"Wolves are the symbol of the teacher. I've had many along the way. You were my first and most important."

My fingers rest on his lips. They trail down his abs as he gasps. I smile at him. No words. He remembers when I used to tickle him there. I reach for the hardness between his legs. I touch it and skim past it on the way to his thighs.

They are huge and hard as rocks with scars that tell the story of war. The pockmarks must be bullet wounds, but I don't ask. This is surface stuff. I want what's underneath.

His heart, soul, and nightmares.

My touch continues down his calves to his feet. He always had the cutest feet, but now they're handsome and perfectly shaped. I bite his big toe and suck it into my mouth.

He lifts his head. "Hey, Bug. You're at the wrong end."

I put my fingers to my lips, telling him to be quiet. He must see something in my eyes because suddenly, I'm flying up his body as he grabs my upper arms, bringing us face-to-face.

"This is not goodbye, so stop acting like you need to memorize every part of my body. We are in a new chapter, and this one is a helluva long story, so you better strap yourself in."

Passion blazes in his eyes like I've never seen before, a conviction of what we're meant to be.

"I've loved you for years, but I'm in love for the first time in my life." The words are out before I can pull them back.

"That makes two of us. The farther we drifted apart, the lonelier I felt. Life's ebbs and flows. I think we're flowing right now." He turns on that smile that sends me to my knees.

He flips us with him on top and kisses me as if he's going to suck out my soul so we can be one. His fingers find my core, teasing me and circling my clit. I rise higher and higher, lost in the sheer sensation of his touch.

He's panting as much as I am. "The only marks I want to see on your body are stretch marks. I will kiss every single one of them. Did I mention I was a ten-pounder when I was born?"

"Mr. Knight, —"

He cuts me off. "Yes, Mrs. Knight."

I narrow my eyes at him. "I didn't see you put a ring on it."

"You were always Mrs. Knight; I just didn't know it, and neither did you. And don't worry. I'm getting you the biggest ring I can find so everyone knows who you belong to."

Tears form in my eyes. "I don't need a big ring. I want a house in Jersey with a fence, flower gardens, a dog, and lots of kids. Having a house to call my own is what's important to me. I want to adopt children instead of fostering them. I want them to know they belong to us and are loved no matter what."

"We can make that happen, but I think we need to have lots of practice making babies, and you should only walk around the house naked." He wipes my saltwater teardrops with his thumb.

I laugh out loud. "Absolutely. I don't know about the naked part, though."

We make slow, exhausting love, exploring each other's bodies until they're seared into our memories. We're getting a second chance to make good on a kiss from when we were sixteen, the kiss that sealed our contract to be together.

Soul mates are so hard to find and even harder to hold on to if you don't understand who they are, who they've become, and who they can be.

After many orgasms, we fall asleep sated, looking forward to our life together. I say a prayer to a God I barely know, hoping this beginning doesn't have an abrupt end.

Through my sleepy fog, I hear a bang on the door and someone crashes through it. Sean grabs his gun from the nightstand and points it toward the offender. Rakesh appears in the doorway with guards behind him. We're outnumbered five to two.

He and his goons are pointing their guns at both of us. "Put your gun down slowly and put your hands in the air."

He smiles as if he's won the battle. But he doesn't know that Sean is bringing a war.

Sean puts his gun back on the nightstand and drags himself out of bed. A guard grabs hold of each of his arms with tentative eyes. He is buck-ass naked and twice their size.

Sean smiles at Rakesh. "See anything you like?"

That gets him a punch in the face, and I scream. Sean's head whips back, then comes back to the center like a boxer in a ring during the first round.

I'm still in bed, holding the sheet up to my chin, shaking. I need to do something, but if I make the wrong move, Sean might get killed. Sheer terror paralyzes me. Hopefully, Isaad still needs him, and I can come up with a plan.

Rakesh puts a gun to Sean's face and cocks it. "Maybe Isaad finally sees you for who you really are, an American spy. He wants to have a few words with you." He smiles.

Sean's hands are in the air. "Would you like me to go like this?"

"Put your pants on," Rakesh says through gritted teeth and swears in Kati.

Sean turns to me. "Remember what I said. I'll see you soon."

Rakesh leaves last, swiping the gun off the nightstand and pointing it at my forehead. "Your turn is coming." He limps toward the door and turns around. "See you after I break your boyfriend's bones."

I scoot away from him. This got more real, and I'm on my own. There's only one thing for me to do. I find one of Sean's other guns, a smaller one, and lay it on his pillow.

THIRTY-ONE

Jess
_____

SHAKING TAKES over my entire body. Sean wants me to leave him here and hide in the woods, waiting to be rescued by his team. As much as I'm not ready for this, I'm even less prepared to leave Sean behind.

I can't lose him now that I've found him. Otherwise, what was the point? Can fate be cruel enough to take him away from me twice? I know this house well enough to sneak back in and help Sean get out.

I take deep cleansing breaths to bring down my heart rate. I can do this. Firing a gun wasn't on my to-do list either, but I got the job done.

My charcoal gray outfit lies on the floor, calling to me. So far, these outfits have been good luck for me.

Sean keeps a complete arsenal of guns and knives in his suitcase. Grabbing a knife, I put the gun in my waistband behind me and the knife on the other side. The keycard slips into my bra. Covered from head to toe, I make my way to the hallway.

The first place I'm going back to is Pippa's room. Isaad

may have put her back there for the time being. A guard passes me and grabs me.

"No one is allowed in the halls. We're in a lockdown." He grimaces with anger. For a split second, I see fear.

I nod. "I'm going to my room now." He looks at me with doubt, not knowing who I am or where my room is.

He lets me go. I walk at first and then rush to the panel to get to the downstairs level to find Pippa. Men rush around in other hallways as I slip by them and down the hallway to Pippa's room.

I knock, keeping one eye down the hall. "It's me. Are you in there?"

"Yes." She sounds robotic. Fear skates over me.

I hurry to get the keycard and scan the door so it unlocks, and I let myself in. Pippa stands in the middle of the room, facing her monitors. Her beautiful red hair is a rat's nest, and her eyes are bloodshot. I know this look. She's been in her zone, working for hours on the computer without a break.

She shuffles toward me, and we embrace each other. "You're here. Thank God," she mumbles.

"What's going on? Sean came to get you, and you weren't here."

I pull back from her to inspect her state of mind, curious to know when she last ate or had anything to drink.

She gives me a crooked smile. "I did it. I created a virus to destroy his mainframe." Her face falls. "The amount of intelligence he has under this roof is enough to destroy a small country. It took everything I had, with some help from some friends. There's stuff on there I don't understand."

I take her face in my hands. "Where were you?"

"I escaped, and they caught me." She giggles. "Isaad

put me back in here. I begged him not to put the cuff back on."

She holds out her bound ankle as a tear leaves her eye. She's not a crier, so I know she's on the brink. "We've got to get out of here. I'm losing it. I never would have made it as a prisoner. Now, the only thing left is to release the virus." She wipes away her saltwater trail and moves toward her bank of computers.

"No!" I hold her hand. "They have Sean. If you destroy the mainframe, they might blame him. He downloaded some information from the supercomputers onto a zip drive."

She laughs like she's punch drunk. "That's not even going to skim the surface of this pile of shit. I hacked it and sent the information to another supercomputer where it is safe, for now."

My heart beats in my chest. "Where did you send it?"

"Don't worry. I got this. It's highly encrypted with code I've never seen before. I had a hacker friend of mine develop an app so I can release the virus remotely with a cell phone, just in case." She crosses her arms as if it's another day in the land of technology.

How big is her brain? The way she sees things amazes me. I've come up with a plan to get us out of here and get her to the cabins. But there's a glitch. There's always a glitch. I've got to get my cell phone so she can use the app, but I need to get her out of the ankle cuff. I pull the gun from behind me.

She puts her hands up as if I'm robbing her. "Whoa! Hold on there, Annie Oakley."

"Can you think of another way to get you out of here?" I hold the gun steady.

She shakes her head. I fire the gun and miss my target, the chain, and it sends me flying backward.

"Try it again, but loosen up your arms a little. Look over the top of the barrel." She instructs.

I lower my gun. "What do you know about shooting a gun?"

She grabs the gun from me and fires at the chain, hitting it with one shot. "Here." She hands it back to me.

"When did you learn to shoot?" I'm baffled.

"It's a long story. Let's get going."

Her eyes avert my gaze, making me question what else I don't know.

I reach for her clothes and hand them to her. "I need you to cover up. We're going back to our room to get my phone. We'll download the app and get you to the woods."

She covers up using several scarves. "Our room? Are you two fuck buddies now?"

I'm not in the mood for this. "We can't talk about this right now. Let's just say we took the leap"

We step into the hallway, and the house is quiet, way too quiet. Tension vibrates in the air. No guards are in the hallway. The doors are closed and possibly locked. The lockdown must have something to do with Sean. I say a silent prayer that Isaad needs him alive.

We enter the room undetected. "Ah, the sweet smell of sex." Pippa wears a huge smile.

"Shut. Up. We have to get my phone and get you out of here." I grab my cell phone and hand it to her.

"What's the password?"

I sigh, regretting I ever picked this password. "0602."

She frowns at me. "Sean's birthday."

"How would you know?" I stand with my hands on my hips.

She shrugs. "It might have something to do with your over-the-top celebration when we were younger."

"Good point." I stick my tongue out at her.

She laughs. "You've got it bad." Her fingers fly over the buttons. "Done. The app is downloaded, and it's ready on command. I need you to give me the go-ahead."

"Take the phone with you, and I'll figure it out with Sean. I'm getting you to the cabins, and then I'm coming back for him. He didn't plan on being taken prisoner." I head for the door but stop short.

His phone sits on the nightstand, but I don't have the passcode. A four-digit code is required because I've seen him use it. I start with his birth year, but it doesn't work. I have to be careful not to enter too many wrong codes, or it will lock me out. On a whim, I press the numbers that correspond to my name, 5377, and it unlocks.

That little devil. A smile forms, I can't hold back. I stow it away in my bra.

"Let me guess. His passcode is your name," Pippa says with a smile.

I make a face at her and head for the hall.

She grabs my arm. "You can't come back. It's too dangerous. This place is like something out of Mission Impossible, the dark side."

I pull my arm out of her grasp. "It's not up for discussion. I'm coming back for him because he's going to need someone, and it might as well be me." She nods, knowing she's in a losing battle.

The house has air conditioning, a high-end luxury for Afghanistan, but sweat drips down my back. I've got to get Pippa to the cabins and get back before they discover I'm gone. They'll beat Sean to force him to talk, which he won't because he's highly trained in interrogation techniques.

While he was away, I followed everything he did and

everything they trained him to do. The thought of what they could do to him in this situation makes my stomach turn.

We get to the glass door leading outside. I wedge the door open using a rock from the garden. The pitch black of the night surrounds us as we hold on to each other, stumbling over rocks and branches. As soon as we are far enough in the woods, I rip off the burka, which consumes me.

"Let's at least turn on the flashlight from the phone." I fumble around, trying to find the flashlight setting.

"No. They'll see us and then we'll be dead. Remember how we used to study the stars? We can use those to navigate. Help me find the North Star." Pippa tilts her head up to a sky filled with stars.

"Good point." I follow her lead.

I've never experienced the millions of beautiful gems the universe offers. They bear down on me, making me feel small and insignificant. The odds of us making it out alive are against us, but we may be that one in a million.

She points up to the sky, where the North Star shines brightly. "So, what's going on with you and Sean? Did you finally tell him you're madly in love with him?"

I squeeze her hand. "Yes, and he's madly in love with me too."

Pippa gives me a bear hug. "No, really? I'm so happy for you. I think he's been lonely since his divorce."

It strikes me I never told her about his divorce. I stop walking. "How would you know about his divorce?"

"I've been keeping tabs on him in case you wanted to find him. Jess, you need to know the military was rough for him." She has one surprise after another tonight.

I nod. "I know. He has nightmares, but I don't care. I want him the way he is."

"I guess you were right. She wasn't right for him."

We walk arm in arm up the side of the hill and find the first cabin. The door opens easily, and I use the flashlight to scope out the inside. It shines on the chains and ankle cuff bolted to the floor.

Pippa closes the door behind her. "My God, I'm cursed with chains and cuffs. They're haunting me."

I laugh. "Ghosts from the beyond. You have been a bad girl."

"Well, I'm about to make it right," she mutters.

I hand her the phone. "You need to stay here until Sean's team arrives. You'll know who they are because they speak English. Other than that, I don't know what to tell you. I think they may be here in the next twenty-four hours. There's a stream at the bottom of the hill for water."

"Who would have thought we would ever be here fighting for our lives?" I can't see her eyes, but I can feel her sadness coming at me in waves.

"Tell me about it. Please be safe. I'll let Sean know about the app. Wait for his call before you release the virus. I'm sure he's going to want you to release it. Love you." I hug her to me, kiss her on the cheek, and shut the door behind me.

I use the stars to guide me back to the glass house, where nothing is transparent. As I round the bend, the shadow of the house comes into sight, looking like a giant weapon, pointing at the sky.

I shiver and hesitate. There's only one thing getting me to go back into this house, and he's my lifeline. I put the burka back on and move ahead.

The rock kept the door open, allowing me to sneak back in. Tossing it back in the garden, I hurry to our room.

I expect to see Sean when I get there, but the room is empty.

My anxiety spikes. I take off my burka and start pacing the room. Where could he be? Are they torturing him, or did Isaad decide to kill him? If he doesn't come back soon, I'm going to look for him.

THIRTY-TWO

Sean

THEY HAUL me off to the bowels of the glasshouse house, aka Stalag 13. Rakesh limps along, which brings me joy. I smirk every time I look at him, which pisses him off.

I know what I'm about to face, and my SEAL training will kick in. If nothing else, I will have a better understanding of what's going on here. I may lose my life, but at least Jess is safe if she follows my directions.

We enter the metal room, which only reflects what's inside it, creating a barrier to the outside. The lights are dim, and a table sits in the middle of the room. Isaad puffs on a cigarette, legs crossed, head down. He's disappointed in me. My father would use guilt and shame to control me until that didn't work.

Rakesh slams me up against the wall and cuffs my wrists on each side of my head. The chains attached to them are short, limiting my movement. He punches me in the face and twice in my ribs, knocking the wind out of me. I may fall, but I always get back up.

"Enough," Isaad says dryly after the third punch.

Blood drips from my nose. "I assume it's soundproof

and has a technology barrier. Nothing in, nothing out. What happens in the metal room, stays in the metal room." I force a smile.

Isaad waves his hand as embers from the end of the cigarette fall to the floor. "Leave us." Rakesh leaves reluctantly.

I jerk my arms forward. "Is chaining me up necessary?"

His face doesn't hold the anger I thought it would. Dark brown eyes show sadness and regret.

"I thought you would be the one sure thing, but you've become unpredictable along with Ms. Wilder."

"Leave her out of this. Let me introduce you to the new me. Keeping people guessing is my new favorite hobby." I hold his stare, letting him know I will not back down.

He takes a long drag, looking toward the ceiling. "You've both been busy in my house. You were invited here as my guest and offered an opportunity."

"I like to know my options and what I'm up against." My back touches the cool wall as I relax, saving my energy for later.

He taps his cigarette on the edge of the ashtray. "Are you always against something? Is that an American thing? You against the world?"

I choose my next set of words with care. "I'm only against the enemy. The innocent who are in danger get protection."

"Am I the enemy?"

The air turns chilly as time grips the falling grains of sand, hoping to stop them. In the end, we lean toward our destiny. My stomach flips as he holds my stare with calculating eyes.

"I came here expecting to see my friend. I'm

wondering where he went. What happened along the way?"

He picks up his Cartier lighter and stares at it as he flips the top up and down. *Click, click, click.* The flame lights and extinguishes. His face glows, a face that's weary and worn beyond his years. Our souls are the same, living in different kinds of hell.

"Would you say we were close friends when you were here ten years ago?" He looks up, curious about my answer.

"Yes. We were close. As close as two people could be living in a war."

Because of Isaad, our SEAL team kept their heads in the game, tried to maintain some semblance of peace, and got ahead of the rebels.

"Then why did you leave me behind?" There's bitterness in his words.

His question catches me off guard. I stare at the floor, waiting for it to swallow me up. He's someone else who feels I've left them behind.

"My tour was over, and I went back and got out of the military. I had enough of war. Was I supposed to take you with me?" My answer has a sarcastic edge.

"You were supposed to be my friend and stay in touch, which you did, but infrequently and then not at all. Your team left one by one and never returned. I wanted to come to the United States to see what made it so great and what made its warriors so strong. Eventually, I got the opportunity, but under very different circumstances." That's the thing about war; you want to forget, so you leave everything behind.

He lights another cigarette, and I wait for him to continue. "I visited New York City with its skyscrapers and high-rises. Central Park was something to behold. I never imagined what awaited me when I got off the plane. It was like stepping into another world, the one you read about in books. At that moment, I understood why you left. There was nothing here to make you want to stay."

Holding the cigarette in his hand, he points the lit end up as the ash glows red. "I want what you have since you took my family from me."

Somewhere in the back of my mind, I know what's coming. It's the story that never makes the headlines because it happens too often. The blood stops dripping off my chin as sweat runs down my back.

"Your family?" The words force themselves out.

"You know, in the time that you have been here, you never asked." He lifts one shoulder.

"I didn't know to ask. I didn't know they existed." A lump forms in my throat as I try to swallow.

"I met Areebah shortly after you left. She was so beautiful. Her eyes were lighter than the sky with creamy beige skin, and full, melon red lips. There was a fire in her, but she only showed it to me because I allowed it. She defined love in a way I never knew, and she became my world."

His eyes become glassy, which creates more holes in my heart. I don't dare look away. I want to understand his hell.

"We got married and had two children, a girl and a boy. They were four and two, so innocent." Tears trail down his cheeks, but his eyes don't meet mine. "The Taliban had increased their bombings, killing hundreds. The Americans retaliated with their bombs, only they missed their target and hit my house with everyone in it but me."

He doesn't wipe his tears as I watch them fall from his cheeks, staining his shirt above his heart. "They didn't even see it coming. They were gone in an instant, like vapor. The pain eats at my soul and rips everything from me. I have nothing left. A lesser man would have wished death for himself. It only made me want more. The Americans took from me, and now I will take from them."

He looks up at me with fire in his eyes that comes with dark anger, full of twisted spite and revenge. I've worn that look and recognize it's an accelerant to more dangerous things.

But the emptiness in his heart serves a purpose. When I lost my mom years ago, I went to a dark place. The only thing I can relate to is losing Jess, which would be more than I can bear.

"I'm curious to know why you blame us and not the Taliban. Without the Taliban and ISIS, we wouldn't be here."

He stands up and pounds his fists on the table. "Because I lost twice. I loved you like a brother, and you left. The American missile took the last people I had left to love. If you had taken me with you, I never would have met her. I never would have known the depth of love so strong that you breathe one another, finish each other's sentences, and laugh until you cry. Thoughts of being without my family never crossed my mind. When you've lost everything, you run on revenge, and that's what I intend to get." His eyes lose focus as if he's gone somewhere else.

I picture my life without Jess, without our first kiss, and without dreams. My love for her can't be put into words. My feelings for her have always been there. Now, they are stronger than ever. I hang my head, unable to bear his pain.

The room goes quiet. He grabs my face and holds it in his hand. His face is red, but the tears disappear in an instant as if he's changed personalities.

"That's going to change. I have more than I ever imagined possible. I will get my revenge, but it will take some time. You think I'm on the wrong side of morality, but there are no morals where I come from. War is simply good politics." He pushes my face away as my head bounces off the wall.

He sits down and folds his hands on the table. "First, I need to know what you're doing here and who sent you. I will get it out of you. Your choice, of course." He inhales and exhales smoke through his nose, making him look like a dragon.

"I'm not working for anyone but me. It's my company, my rules. I came here to work for you, but I'm also here to extract a hacker named Red Enigma. She came here to steal Bitcoin. Instead, you've made her a prisoner. I can't imagine why."

Sarcasm is my go-to in times of stress and doesn't always work in my favor. I need to hold my cards close, not showing that I know Pippa.

"And what about your childhood friend, Jess Wilander? Yes, I did a full background check on both of you now that I have those resources at my disposal. How do you think I orchestrated this?" He waves his hands to the ceiling.

I should be surprised, but I'm not. Nothing felt right from the beginning.

"If you've known all along, why play the game?"

"Games are what it's about. We are either the puppets or the puppet masters of the world. Our goal is to have the world at our feet, begging for mercy. We will own everyone because we will have the antidotes, energy supply, and the banking system. Besides, I've enjoyed watching you fall in love with her before I kill her. It's very convenient that her foster sister is here too. Just one big happy family." His smile doesn't reach his dark brown eyes.

I strain against the chains. "You touch her, and I'll kill

WILD

you myself. Leave her out of this." I don't know what he's talking about. Puppet masters? Antidotes? Energy supply? "How did you become so twisted?"

"Living a life of war from the time you are old enough to walk will make you view the world in a much different way. The noise of missiles and gunfire becomes secondary to survival as you walk over dead bodies in your path to get water. It's not what you would call the American dream."

He gets closer, and his eyes narrow. "How did she contact you?"

I have to think fast based on how we communicated through the dark web. "Through email. Why?"

"I monitored her email. I never saw one to you." He's looking for my lie.

"We have a shared account and communicate in code on the dark web. She emailed herself, and then I can access it." I've got to keep Neil out of this.

"Interesting." His brows arch. "You're smarter than you look."

"Gee, thanks."

There's a knock at the door, and Rakesh enters. He leans down and whispers in Isaad's ear. Isaad's eyes bore into mine.

"Where's Pippa?"

THIRTY-THREE

Pippa

I'VE SPENT SO much time in my climate-controlled environment, I forgot how cold it can get in the forest. Even in the dead of summer, the mountains don't hold heat. Jess told me to stay here and wait for Sean's team. I hope I don't get shot by one of Isaad's maniacs.

The cabin lacks any creature comforts such as a bed, table, or chair. There are some pots, pans, and utensils. I grab a pot, a pan, and some knives for weapons. I'm guessing Isaad's men lurk out here on patrol. The fireplace is big enough to cook in, but I don't want to start a fire and draw attention to the cabin.

Ghosts linger here. Their presence adds to the chill in the air. Whatever happened was not good. The chains attached to the floor have the same configuration as the one in my room. Some are covered in blood. There's a cuff at the end, and the chain only extends the length of the cabin in each direction. Heavy despair runs through me at the thought of what might have happened here.

I lay on the floor. Waiting is not something I do well. If

I play a game on the phone, the battery will run out, and I won't be able to access the app for the virus.

My thoughts wander back to Rakesh, who won't be happy when he discovers I'm gone, which should be any minute. He'll report back to Isaad, who will raise hell to try to find me.

Rakesh is a man full of anger. I don't know what happened to him, but I sense it changed who he used to be. Over the past week, I got glimpses of a kind, gentle man full of love and understanding. Then there were those times when he was angry, almost punishing.

During sex, I could tell he was somewhere else; his face would grimace. He was silent during those times and left right after he was done. I never could have fallen in love with so much darkness and hatred. Being chained up was kinky at first, but it got old quickly when I realized I would be in them for a while.

I tuck my hands under my head, and my eyelids feel heavy. In the darkness, a lone owl calls out, breaking the eerie silence. There is no sound of any living creature. The door creaks open, and I scuttle to the corner. The cell phone in my hand gets secured in my pocket. I'm going to need my hands for the fight.

An enormous shadow enters the cabin, and a light shines on my face. I chuck what I have for weapons, the pot and pan to throw him off. My fingers curl around the knife.

He blocks my attempts with his arm. "We're the good guys." He moves the light away from my eyes and talks into his comm. "I've secured the package. Secure the perimeter," he says with an accent.

I'm praying he's with Sean. "Who the hell are you?"

"I'm Mac. Sean sent us to do an extraction." His r's roll, indicating a Scottish accent. "Roger that."

The door opens again, and three equally large men enter the cabin.

"Who do we have here?" This one speaks with an Australian accent.

"Let's get a fire going." Another voice says with an English accent.

The Aussie responds, "Have you turned soft? Do you need a fire to keep your feet warm?" One of them punches the other one.

"What is this, the international team of rescuers?" I'm hoping to have my pick. I prefer big men.

"Oh, look. She's got a sense of humor. This should be interesting," says the Aussie.

Mac speaks up. "No fire. Too much of a signal that we're here. Cover the windows and get out the lanterns. We'll stay here tonight and finalize the plan."

I stuff myself in the corner, watching huge shadows move around a small cabin in coordination.

Someone stumbles. "Shit! What the hell is that?"

"By the way, there's a bolt in the middle of the floor attached to a chain," I reply with sarcasm.

I hear a laugh. "Sounds kinky."

"Only you would come up with that, BP," Mac replies to the Aussie.

There's one over to the side, not moving. What's his story? The LED lanterns light up the dark room. The men stand in a semicircle in front of me, dressed in black from head to toe. Their faces are painted black with goggles on top of their heads, except for one. His skin is the color of my favorite dark chocolate, making me want to lick him. He's beautiful with scars on the side of his face.

They take off their night-vision goggles and hats and introduce themselves.

"I'm Dean." I recognize his Australian accent.

"I'm Beck," says the Brit I want to lick.

The one standing off to Mac's side says nothing at all. "That's my brother Declan. Don't mind him. He hasn't been on a mission for a while."

I remove the scarf from my head. Mac and Declan look at me as if they've seen a ghost. Declan gets a pained look on his face.

I stand up. "What's wrong?"

Mac clears his throat and turns to Declan. "You look a lot like our sister, Kendall. We lost her some years ago. We were very close."

"I'm sorry." My fingers braid my hair so it hangs behind my head.

Declan says, "It's a good omen. It means she's with us."

He almost smiles, and his shoulders come down from his ears. There's a darkness about him that intrigues me. His eyes are piercing hazel green, accented by wavy auburn hair, a striking combination.

Mac nods and turns back to me. "Where's the other one, Jess?"

"She went back to the house to help Sean."

"Fuck all! Sean will not be happy," Dean blurts out.

"There's more. The house is filled with women who are being kept there against their will. We need to save them." My voice breaks.

"Friggin' hell. We don't have a way to airlift them out." Mac runs his hand through his hair but doesn't question getting them out.

"It's not a problem. We'll get them to the woods and come back for them. They can hide out in the cabins." Beck's plan is the only one that will work.

I lock my fingers in front of me. "There's still more."

"How much more do you have?" Dean smirks.

"Enough to keep you busy for a while." I pull out Jess's

cell phone. "You see this." I point to the app that has a picture of a cartoon bomb. "This app will release a virus into Isaad's mainframe and destroy every piece of his information. I've backed up what I can and sent it to another place. I just don't know what will happen when I go to open the saved information again. His program may have a built-in Trojan that will destroy itself. I can't predict what will happen."

They stand with blank looks on their faces as if I've just said everything in Mandarin. "Let's not get stuck on the word Trojan. Does anyone here know anything about technology?" I slow down my words.

"I'm afraid not, love. That's Peter's area of expertise, and he's not here." Between Beck's accent and looks, I'm sure he could have any woman on the planet.

"My point is, if something happens to me or I can't get to the app, someone is going to need to click it to release the virus. There's a lot of crazy world-altering shit on Isaad's mainframe."

My focus jumps to each of them, looking for the one who can pull it together enough to know what I'm talking about.

They nod their heads in agreement. "We'll know what to do when the time comes. It's been a long day. Let's roll out our sleeping bags and get some shut-eye. Beck, you're on the first watch." Mac is clearly in charge, overseeing the operation.

"The lass can have my sleeping bag. I'll switch out in four hours with Dean." They nod and grumble at Beck. "Before I go, let me get the cuff off your ankle. It looks uncomfortable."

He pulls some gadgets from his backpack and works the cuff until it's off my ankle. I look up as his body casts a shadow around me.

"Thank you," I say while rubbing the chafed area. I think I'm in serious lust with him.

"What do we have for snacks?" Mac rubs his stomach.

"Is there ever a time when you're not hungry?" Dean says. "You're losing your shapely figure. Ever since Mara's been prego, you eat like a horse."

Mac shrugs. "What can I say? I have to keep up my energy until the baby comes. I hear we could be there a while, and sleepless nights are ahead."

"Better you than me, mate," Dean smirks.

Mac smiles. "Just wait. You're next."

"Leigha and I have a plan," Dean snaps.

"Everyone has a plan until someone gets pregnant. Then the plan is friggin' shot to hell in the best way possible. I can't wait." Mac's face lights up.

Everyone laughs. Their closeness comforts and calms my nerves, making me stop thinking I'm about one heartbeat away from losing my sister. But with this crew, we may have a chance.

I move my sleeping bag closer to Declan to get a closer look. He seems to shrink in the sleeping bag, which is hard to do when you're well over six feet. He looks at me with uncertainty.

"Will you hold my hand? I've been out here for some time, and I'm scared shitless." I reach out my hand to him like he's a long-lost brother.

His hand stretches out to me. My hand fits into his large, warm hand, and it brings me the comfort I crave. Let's hope tomorrow goes smoothly.

THIRTY-FOUR

Jess

MY BODY IS numb as I sit on the bed, frozen without a plan. If I try to find Sean, I'll get caught, but I can't wait here and do nothing.

My heart races, I'm light-headed, and there's a pain in the middle of my chest. Anxiety is going to kill me.

The ticking clock next to the bed isn't moving fast enough. A couple of hours ago, they took Sean away, and I got Pippa to safety. Where is he, and why isn't he back yet? My imagination runs wild, envisioning what they could do to him.

At some point, I fell asleep because I woke up to someone tugging at my arm.

"Get up, whore," a voice says with a heavy Kati accent I don't recognize.

I try to pull out of his grip. "Where's Sean?"

"You're about to find out."

The only thing visible is angry eyes surrounded by a black cloth.

He drags me down several flights of stairs. The farther down we go, the faster my heart rate picks up, and my hands sweat. I've learned to trust nothing inside this house. Each time I try to struggle to get free, his grip gets tighter.

He pushes me down an underground tunnel and stops at a door, swipes his keycard, and opens it. I step inside a dimly lit room.

Isaad sits at the table as cigarette smoke fills the air, making my eyes burn. Chains hold Sean to the other side of the wall. One eye is swollen shut, and blood streams from his nose and lip.

I move toward him. "Sean!"

Rakesh stops me, but I jerk away and reach for him. He's covered in sweat and splattered blood. Even chained up, Sean gave him a good fight.

"No." My word catches on a sob as I throw my arms around his neck. I whisper, "Pippa has an app on my phone to destroy the mainframe. She's in the woods."

As soon as the words are out of my mouth, Isaad pulls me away.

"Jessica, have a seat. We have much to talk about." Edginess replaces Isaad's usual calm temperament, which means he doesn't have Sean where he wants him.

I'm not surprised that he knows who I am. Things around here were weird from the beginning. Sean nods to the chair, letting me know it's okay to sit, but it's not.

My cover has been blown, and if he knows who I am, he might know my connection to Sean. I still have Sean's weapon, but this isn't the time to use it. My nerves try to get the better of me, but I push them down, giving me time to think things through.

"Why did you beat up Sean? I thought he was your friend." I swipe away the tears.

He sighs dramatically. "Yes, I thought so too until he took something that belongs to me."

"I don't know what you're talking about." He must be referring to the keycard.

"Tell me, why did you come here?" His face is hidden behind a blue veil of smoke.

I hold my chin up. "You know why I'm here, to write an article about you."

"You're not here to rescue Pippa?" His mouth forms a tight line.

I look over at Sean. "Just tell him why you're here," he mumbles.

He looks at me through his one good eye. My heart breaks knowing he's in pain. My mouth goes dry as I try to swallow.

"I came here to write the article, but I also came here to get Pippa. You know, the one you're holding prisoner like everyone else here." I want my words to get a reaction out of him, but he seems immune to anything caustic.

"Jess," Sean warns.

This isn't the time for my anger to be front and center. I need to hold it together and try to get us out of here.

"How did you know she was here?" He crosses his legs with one arm across his chest, supporting the one holding a cigarette.

Sean gives me a slight nod. "She sent me an email with a message that she needed help. The email included the coordinates, which I found out belonged to this house and you. I contacted you about the article to find her."

"Who helped you put it all together?" Isaad puts out his cigarette with force in the ashtray overflowing with smashed butts.

I look over at Sean for guidance. "Can I at least wipe his face?" I stall for time so I can think of something that won't implicate anyone.

"No. Sean got himself into this mess. He's a tough guy.

He can wait." Isaad's face is impassive. This hard side of him is one I've never seen in my time here.

Payback can be a real bitch. "Carter Maddox helped me put it all together. He's a—"

"I know who he is, but I doubt very much that you went to him to help you, especially after he burned you." Isaad's informants run deep.

Cold water freezes in my blood. He's too well-connected for a contractor.

Carter was a CIA operative working in China when I met him. I traveled to China to write a story about a bio-lab in Wuhan. There were rumors about genetically altered super viruses being engineered to wreak more havoc than the last pandemic. The story was an opportunity of a lifetime for any journalist. I couldn't turn it down.

The Chinese authorities caught up with me, but Carter was the only one who knew I was there. They ordered me to leave the country and never return, or they would send me to prison. They demanded my laptop and any external drives, which was fine. I backed everything up to a cloud and never returned to the hotel.

Chinese prisons are like a black hole. They suck you in, and you never come back. The evidence led back to Carter Maddox. I don't know why he wanted me out, but he can't be trusted.

"All's forgiven in love and war. We mended our fences." My eyes never leave his face.

"I believe the saying is all is *fair* in love and war, but have it your way." He spins his pack of smokes in his fingers, letting it hit the table, contemplating his next move.

"Where's Pippa? I need her." There's a quiet fury in his voice.

He doesn't need her. He needs her program, White Raven.

I cross my arms over my chest and ball my hands into fists. "She's safe." My brave front falls short.

He pounds his fist on the table and stands up. "I need to know where she is!"

I jump in my seat, startled by his reaction. "All you need to know is that she's safe. I'm not letting you near her." I'm not giving her up after coming this far.

Isaad pulls a knife from his pocket and hands it to Rakesh while staring at me. Anger pours off his face in waves.

"Go ahead. Torture him first, then make him bleed out. I know you've been looking forward to this."

Rakesh grabs the knife with a grin on his face and lunges at Sean.

"No!" The only word I get out as Sean lifts both legs and knocks Rakesh across the room as his head hits the wall, rendering him unconscious.

Isaad grabs the knife from Rakesh's limp hand, snatches me out of the chair, and holds the knife to my throat.

"Sean, do you think I won't take something of yours? Hmm? The Americans took something of mine, so it's only fair. Now, tell me what I want to know."

The sharp edge of the blade pushes against my skin. My hands curl around his arm, holding my neck. One wrong move may be my last.

THIRTY-FIVE

Sean

A SNAPSHOT of the life I once lived flashes before my eyes as Isaad holds a knife to Jess's throat. My eyes glaze over, becoming glassy. History is repeating itself. I see my father threatening my mother with bodily harm, and I'm frozen.

The little boy in me is tortured again by seeing a woman he loves threatened with death. I can't let this happen. I refuse to believe that life would be so cruel as to take two women I love from me in one lifetime.

"No, no, no. Not again. Please."

I hear my own words, but they are those of a boy who couldn't save his mother. The plea comes out as a voice from the past to who I am now.

"What's that? I couldn't hear you. The advantage is mine, so what's it going to be?" Isaad taunts me.

He pushes the knife against her skin enough to make her bleed. One drop of blood escapes, leaving a trail down her throat. I pull at my chains to get to her.

As if I can feel my mother, there's a whisper, "Use your head and your training." Being chained to the wall prohibits me from fighting my way out of this situation. I have no choice but to think this through. There's always a way out.

There's no hiding from the scene in front of me. He's crazy enough to cut her throat with the hatred that flows through his veins. I take a few deep breaths and figure out what I have to my advantage. The military trained me to use strategy and negotiation. Jess's violet eyes are my anchor to gain strength and plea with me to help her.

"You're missing some crucial information. One, your tech guy has an ankle band that's a bomb, and I have the detonator. My guess is he's in the command room right now. The good news, I don't have the detonator on me. Two, and there's always a two, Pippa will release a virus into your mainframe within a certain amount of time if she doesn't hear from one of us. Here is my counteroffer. You let us go, and I won't blow up your house, and Pippa doesn't release the virus."

My plan gives me time until my team is on site, which should be any minute if they haven't already landed. I have every intention of blowing this house up and releasing the virus. I keep eye contact with Isaad so he can decide if I'm bluffing or not.

Isaad curses in Kati and releases Jess. He doesn't say a word and unlocks my cuffs, letting my arms fall to my sides. The blood painfully flows back into my arms and fingers, replacing the sensation of pins and needles.

He grabs me by the throat. "You will go back with two guards outside your room. Jessica will stay with us as insurance until we resolve this matter."

He shoves me away. His anger is laced with the pain of a friendship destroyed by mistrust, war, and greed.

"If you or any of your men lays a hand on her, I will

slit your throat. Believe that." I wipe the blood from under my nose as it smears down my arm.

"I know she's your weakness. Too bad you showed your hand. In the meantime, I'm sending my men out to the woods to find Pippa. My guess is that's where she is."

I grin like the cat that ate the canary. "How do you know she's not hiding right under your nose? I wouldn't underestimate me, *friend*."

His eyes narrow. "We've become the best of enemies, which is too bad. I'm disappointed. I was hoping you would join Deep 8. Some prominent men have the power to control the world and make it what it needs to be." A blank stare comes across his face. He's convinced he has joined the right team.

"I'm sure you're familiar with the quote from Lord Acton, 'Power tends to corrupt, and absolute power corrupts absolutely. Great men are almost always bad men.' We will fight you to the end." I step closer, with my face inches from his. "My only allegiance is to my country."

I don't tell him my allegiance is also to the woman he holds captive. My gaze lands on Jess as I try to send her a secret message that I will always love her.

He grimaces. "You'd be surprised who is part of this elite group." His face switches to the smile of a madman. "You don't know what or who you're up against."

He waves in two guards who zip-tie my hands behind my back and haul me out of the room to stand in the hall.

Isaad grips Jess's arm as we walk behind them down the hall to the elevator. We squeeze into the elevator. The heavy air makes it hard to breathe.

He looks up at the numbers of the floors. "I know you finished the article about me. I saw the first draft you sent to your editor. Very nice, but it needs to be polished. I need to make a few changes." Someone has an ego.

The glasshouse is like a labyrinth; you can never find your way out. Everywhere you turn, Isaad is there and has eyes on everything you're doing.

"I'm sure you did," Jess replies.

"We're going to make sure your editor gets it tonight."

He turns to me with hard eyes. "She'll be underground, chained up. I want to make sure she stays safe."

Night turns into dawn. The windows in the hallway display a gloomy day full of gray clouds lying low in the sky at the top of the trees. The daytime scene seems à propos given how the night ended.

They cut the ties that bind my hands and throw me into my room. Two guards will never be enough to hold me back from getting to Jess. The minute Isaad held a knife to her throat, something changed in me.

I'm fighting for a different cause. This time I'm fighting for the woman I love. Given the significance of the situation, it seems like a small goal to have, but when a pebble hits the water, the ripple radiates out from the center.

I need her to be with me at the center. For once, I'll fight to heal the boy who didn't have choices, who cowered in the corner with no place to go. I'll get her back if it's the last breath I take.

THIRTY-SIX

Sean
_____

THE YOUNG AND inexperienced guards are no match for me. In the past, I would have tried to overpower them and make a run for it, but time is on my side. They need to get comfortable. Let them think I'm agreeable. My SEAL training kicks in and never leaves me.

Stumbling to the bathroom, I clean up and assess the wreckage. There's dried blood under my nose, and my lip needs stitches. Nothing I haven't dealt with before.

My first aid kit has the tools I need as I search for the syringe of morphine, needle, and thread. The morphine will numb the pain, and I can get some sleep.

I inject the morphine into my lip, saving the rest for later, and wait for it to take effect. Rakesh didn't do half the damage my father used to do to me. His abuse allowed me to tolerate pain better than most.

I close my eyes at the rationale. What child should have to tolerate pain? My father's beatings prepared me for the military, where you fight through the pain and ugliness. I've been to places that give me nightmares, but I came out on top in every situation. I wonder if my luck has run out.

The goal is to stall long enough to get my team here. Neil's team may not be far behind. If they aren't here already, they must be close. My strategy of throwing off Isaad needs to work to keep him out of the woods and away from Pippa.

And then there's Jess. No matter how hard I try, I can't stop thinking about her. I know Isaad won't lay a hand on her, and he will keep his word, at least I hope, but this has put a kink in my plan.

Damn her. She was supposed to be in the cabin with Pippa, but she knew I was in trouble. When she walked through the door, I was selfishly glad to see her. She helps keep my head screwed on straight. She still does that for me. Of all the places to search for her, Afghanistan wasn't on my list. She's a ray of hope in my eternal hell, making this op more bearable.

I stitch my lip like I've done in so many other places on my body. Time and patience are needed to bring the split pieces together. A smaller suture makes less of a scar. My team called me Dr. Stitch. Navy SEALs pride themselves on their battle wounds, but I don't want to look like Frankenstein.

Once I am done, I head for the shower to wipe away the day's grime, deception, and despair. I didn't want to give in to my suspicions about Isaad, but tonight confirmed my deepest fear.

He's in over his head with an organization I've never heard of, Deep 8. Neil will have a bead on this, and I can hand it over to him. This is more up the agency's alley than a global security company.

I find my cell phone, where I tucked it away, and turn it on. The chime lets me know there's a text, and I look at it through my one open eye. I'm hoping it's from my team.

Mac: 7+4+P=L

Music to my ears. We text in code using math, letters, and symbols. For our team, we try to steer away from military lingo in case we have unwanted visitors. His message tells me he has landed, his code name is 7, with four others, and Pippa.

Me: WILD - J

Mac:?

Me: DK

Mac: TM+NT

Me: #lvls+ungrd

My code lets him know I'm without Jess and that there are levels underground. He informs me they are ready for an ambush tomorrow night. I've got to find Jess before they get to the house.

I plug my phone in so the battery will be fully charged. Losing my bath towel, I slide into bed. The scent of wild roses floats my way from the pillow next to me. I grab her pillow and put it under my head, inhaling deeply to find some peace.

She doesn't know that I'm the one who took her pink Santana T-shirt years ago, so I could always have her with me. It doesn't hold her scent anymore, but that didn't stop me from keeping it. I would get it out after one of the beatings bestowed on me by my father. He never said it, but I knew he didn't like that I was friends with her. Instead of using his words, he used his fists to get his point across.

I drift off, unable to grip onto anything from the day. My nightmares never come as I wake up to the sun beating in the window, washing the room with the brightness of daylight. The morphine must have taken hold. I rarely sleep that long, but I'm going to need my strength for what's ahead.

The swelling in my eye has gone down, and the stitches in my lip are red but not very visible. I get dressed and turn on my phone.

There are no updates from the team. No news is good news. My focus will be on finding Jess somewhere in this maze of a house.

My stomach growls, signaling the need for food. I open the door to the hall, and the guards stop me.

"You're not allowed to leave your room." They're naïve and full of themselves.

I stand with my hands on my hips. "I need to eat."

One looks at the other. "We have our orders."

I pull my knife from behind my back and grab one guard. The other one pulls his weapon.

"I have two things going for me. I'm using your friend's body as a shield. You shoot, and he dies. I have a knife at his throat, which means I could kill him, anyway."

Sweat forms on the gunman's forehead, and his eyes flash with fear.

"Do yourself a favor and put your weapon down."

He lays it on the ground, and I pick it up, putting it in my waistband with the other one from the guard I'm holding.

"All this and I just want food." I walk backward with my hands up in a shrug.

I make my way to the kitchen. The chef gives me a wary look with a touch of fear.

"Can I help you, Mr. Knight?"

"Yes." I give him my long list of food.

"Is that all?" Isaad says from behind me.

I turn around. "Shouldn't you be thanking me for saving the lives of your men? God knows you have cameras everywhere."

"You still have a heart." His eyes are empty. "It's what I count on. I don't think I have one anymore. Please."

He moves his hand in the direction of the breakfast nook. His attitude is an about-face from the night before.

I sit between the curved windows and the wall, always prepared for an escape. I'll be able to scan for movement outside with the wall of windows behind Isaad.

"Where's Jess?" I lay my hands in my lap to appear casual, but I'm running in top gear.

Isaad sits down slowly as if his body has aged beyond his years. "She's safe. Nothing to worry about. No one can get to her." His words have a double meaning.

For once, he's not smoking a cigarette as he folds his hands on the table. "I wish you would reconsider my offer and join my team. A war is coming that you're not prepared for, and you need to be on the right side of things. You would have everything you could ever want, money, power, women, and luxuries beyond your wildest dreams."

"This is where you and I have parted ways. I'm not sure I understand why you would even consider me. I want to earn my money legit. There's only one woman I want, but I guess you've already figured that out. The power I need comes from the company I built from the ground up, where there is no price on loyalty. It has to be earned. Control of your life is an illusion. I'm living proof of that. War? I know war, and I will be ready." My words are more of an anthem, the ideals I live by.

Bitterness drives Isaad, and a need to think he has control over the outcome of events he orchestrates. He's about to find out how much he cannot control.

He leans back, thinking about my words. We're at an impasse.

"You don't see the bigger picture. We have the power to take over everything and bring the world to our door. We would wipe out the extremists and put an end to petty wars around the globe. They would be at our feet."

His use of the word takeover gets my attention. "It's not possible. Yin and yang. Where there is light, there will always be darkness. I've lived it. I know. How do you propose to do this?" My curiosity gets the better of me.

His eyes darken. "We have our ways. The wheels are already in motion and can't be stopped, but it doesn't sound like I have your commitment to the cause. It's a shame. I was hoping we would be on the same side again."

He's shrouded in quiet despair, living in his anger instead of letting it go. Anger is like a monkey on my back, hard to shake, but over the years, it's lessened its grip. That kind of hatred can eat you from the inside out. It consumes and colors everything you do, every decision you make, until it sucks out the last beam of light, and only darkness remains.

I make one last offer. "I can get you out of Afghanistan to make a fresh start."

He laughs. "It's too late for me. I'm on the path I need to be on to make a difference, to make them pay for what they did to my family." His fingers form a fist.

He's already bought into their rhetoric and the promises they made to him.

He watches me as I devour my food. My friend from the past has disappeared. Darkness has swallowed him, and I need to come to terms with that fact.

He's playing for an opposing team that doesn't seem to exist. They're in the wind. We can't even identify them, much less find them.

"We turned the house upside down, looking for Pippa. She's not here. So now we'll search the woods. Are you sure you want my men to find her?" His fingers tap on the table.

I need to play my cards right and beat him at his own game. I look up, stunned. "You would allow them to hurt her? She has the one thing you need, and there's a backup plan."

Confusion covers his face as he battles between his old self and new ideals. "She's only a pawn in this game. She served a purpose and came through with flying colors. I need her to finish what she started. Deep 8 is very interested in her program, and I can't allow her to destroy everything I've worked on."

"Yes, White Raven. Why couldn't she just give it to you?" I bait him to see what he knows about the program.

"Her original is a prototype and locked in her computer. She needs to improve the code to make it work the way we need it to work. It will change everything." He believes his own words.

The last thing the world needs is for the Deep 8 group to get hold of this program. Urgency hits me to get her out of here as soon as possible. My team doesn't realize how valuable she is, but they will protect her with their lives.

I need to buy more time, but I don't think he's willing to give up Jess. She's his royal flush in this poker game.

"I'll remove the ankle bomb from your man and give you the detonator." I lean forward on the table. "In exchange, I will get to Pippa and have her tell me how to disable the virus, and you hand over Jess."

Brute force won't work with Isaad, but negotiating makes him think he has the upper hand.

"I still need Pippa for the program." He counters.

I massage the offer. "This way, you get to keep your

supercomputers. You'll find someone else to write the program. There are plenty of hackers willing to do the work."

"Deal. But Sean. Don't cross me. Remember, I have nothing left to lose. Besides, my team will get the program." His eyes fill with dread, as if he can't wait for his end.

THIRTY-SEVEN

Sean

I PACE the room like a caged leopard. My mind keeps going back to everything Isaad lost over the years.

My family didn't have normal problems. Dysfunction ran rampant through each of us, one feeding off the other. One drop of alcohol could set off a firestorm of violence.

Neither of Isaad's children would have grown up in the house of an alcoholic. They would have had other crosses to bear. He used to be a kind and caring man. They tore away his shot at normalcy and changed him into a hard, bitter man bent on revenge.

The waiting game is killing me. I hope I bought enough time for the team to get in place, maybe even find Neil's team for a double whammy.

My hands flex, wanting to find Jess and get her out of here. I know they're planning an after-dark attack, and I made plans to meet with Isaad and his tech guy around dinnertime to take off the detonator. That should give me enough time to get Jess before the raid and meet up with Declan.

I load myself down with the weapons I brought in my

suitcase and dress in black from head to toe. The last accessory is my NVG, night vision goggles. I never leave home without them. My only focus is getting everyone out alive.

Heading for the door, I stop cold as if someone is watching me. As I look over my shoulder, a white envelope peeks out from Jess's suitcase. If there is one thing Jess would want me to keep from this room, it would be her letters to me. The genuine letters, not the words she thought I wanted to hear.

Her heart lives in those letters, and I want to own every ounce of her. I still need to earn her trust. Proving myself must be embedded in me. Thanks, Dad.

Grabbing the letters, I put them in one of the leg pockets of my cargo pants, slipping the letter I wrote to her in with them. Her black scarf hangs over the chair. I wrap it around my neck and let her scent calm me down.

For the first time, I don't want to die out here. When you're a soldier, you live, fight, and breathe knowing it might be your last time on earth. I want the firsts I have coming to me. Jess is going to get her first diamond from me, her first and only husband, and God willing, her first baby. This is a far cry from where I was only a few months ago, but I pray the stars are aligned for us.

Taking in a deep breath, I open the door to the hall. I should have paid more attention to Jess's breathing techniques during yoga. I could use some centering right about now.

The pink-purple color of dusk fills the windows looking out over the wooded area, which will fade to black any minute as it gives way to night. I can almost feel the energy of the team out there, waiting for their chance to attack this place.

Isaad stands in the dining room with his hands behind

his back. None of his guards is with him, which is unusual. The tech looks like he's about to shit himself.

"Thank you for joining us." His statement is formal as if I'm a visitor having tea with them.

I wave two fingers in the tech guy's direction. "Come over here."

My key unlocks the cuff, and it falls to the floor. This fake looks real. Peter is a genius.

Isaad's walkie-talkie crackles with a voice in panic. As I come up from kneeling on the floor, I hear the shots and ignore them. Isaad catches my eye and says something in Kati to whoever is on the other end.

"Looks like we have company. You wouldn't know anything about that, would you?" His eyes are hard yet vacant.

I lean against the table and cross my arms and legs. "How could I? I've been in lockdown. Remember?"

"You won't get what you came for." He runs out of the room.

The tech guy looks in my direction as his hands shake.

"Are you staying here or coming with me?"

"I'm going with you. He's dangerous and whacked." He pushes his glasses up on his nose.

I want to ask more questions, but there's no time. "Let's go. Stay close."

The heaviness of my Glock is like a glove for my hand. I've worn it for so long, it's become part of me.

Running for the panel in the wall, my hunch is he's keeping her in one of the rooms downstairs.

As I call out her name, it echoes off the rock walls. "Jess!"

I don't know what else to do. I know I'm drawing attention to us. It doesn't matter. There's no one down here.

As we move down the hall, I click open each door with the keycard, but she's not there. I'm about to head to the next door, Pippa's old room, as Isaad comes out with a gun to Jess's head.

Her eyes are wide and wild. This time I don't see my mother. I see my future, and no one will take that away from me.

"Let her go. You want me, not her." My calm voice doesn't reflect the sheer panic spreading inside me.

The tech guy stands behind me. "This is very bad."

"Thanks for the heads-up," I mumble.

"That's where you're wrong. I don't want you. I want you to suffer the way I've suffered all these years. Do you think it's a coincidence you're here together? I requested each of you to come here for a reason so you could be part of my plan. How does it feel to be manipulated and destroyed the way the U.S. manipulates and destroys my country?"

There's a slight shake in his hand, showing his lack of confidence, a struggle between the past and the present.

I aim my weapon at him and have the shot, but it's too close for comfort. I need to keep him talking.

"You should spend more time getting rid of the Taliban and restoring Afghanistan to what it used to be." My eye lines up with the sight down the barrel.

He laughs. "Our plan is so much bigger than the Taliban. It's global. We'll have total control over everyone and everything. It's such a shame Jess won't be here to see it. After I kill her, you need to reconsider your options."

He's holding on to the past, hoping I'll make the decision he made and succumb to power and greed.

An explosion from above shakes the house. Declan's calling card. Isaad loses focus and looks up. I shoot out the lights above us. We are left in the shadows of the lights, farther away. I maintain a visual on him and nod at Jess to move to her left, away from him. She elbows him in the ribs and rolls to the ground. I take the shot, and the bullet rips through his hand as he drops his gun.

I motion to her. "Grab his weapon and come to me."

Isaad grimaces and holds his hand. "Aren't you going to finish the job you started, my friend?"

"No. I'll leave that to my team. You won't make it out of here." My sense of loss is brief because I have hold of my future. I'll always choose her.

I grab Jess by the hand and run down the hall with the tech guy in tow. "I've got to get you out of here. The team doesn't know where we are."

We make it up the stairs and out to the garden. Dusk fades, but there's enough light for us to see. At the edge of the forest, I let her go as she stands behind a rock.

"Go to the cabin." Before I finish, I detect movement to my right. A guard aims at me, and I take him out with one shot to the chest. "Take him with you."

The tech guy moves away from us into a clearing in the woods as he makes a run for it. He doesn't get far, falling facedown with a bullet to the head.

Jess screams, and tears form in her eyes. "I can't do this without you. You need to come with me."

I hold her by the shoulders and pull us down behind the rock. I give her my SAT phone so she can use the flashlight on it.

"Go get Pippa. Let her know it's a go for her virus. I have to go back. I've got to help my team, and there are some things we need to get done."

She pulls my phone out of her shirt and hands it to me. "Here, I see I'm not the only one with a passcode from our past." Her lip curls to almost a smile.

The sound of a chopper overhead grabs my attention.

The little chopper hovers long enough for me to see who's in it. Rakesh is in the pilot's seat, and Isaad sits next to him with his hand wrapped up. We make eye contact through the glass. One man lives for his past, as the other lives for his future. We are a lifetime apart in how we see the world and how the world has shaped us.

Isaad reaches out with his other hand and points his gun at us, taking a shot. I push Jess to the ground and cover her as bullets ricochet off the rock. The chopper flies away toward the mine. If he's going there, a surprise awaits him.

Dirt covers the front of Jess. "I need you to do what I tell you to do. Go to the cabin and wait for further instructions."

"Are you meeting us back at the cabin?" She bites her lower lip to keep it from trembling.

I hold her face in my hands. In case I don't make it, I want her face to be the last thing I remember.

"I'm going to try. Knowing Mac, he'll have a chopper coming to get us farther out from here. You need to go with my team."

She grabs my shirt and grits her teeth. Tears well in her eyes, crest, and fall down her cheeks. "Don't you even think of leaving me again." Then her fingers gently touch my stitched lip. "Who did that?"

"I did. I know how to survive war." The lump in my throat is hard to swallow, and I will my tears not to fall.

I kiss her with an intensity that I've never felt before. My lip screams in pain, but I don't care. I plunge my tongue into her sweet mouth and suck on her lips. If I could physically give her a piece of my heart to take with her, I would. She already has my soul.

THIRTY-EIGHT

Jess

HE RUNS in the opposite direction from where I want him to go. I need him to come with me to safety. Instead, he heads into danger, ready to save someone.

That was always part of his DNA, and some things never change. I need him more than I've ever needed anyone. The "me against the world" attitude works up to a point, and then it gets tiring.

While Pippa was off doing her own thing, he was there for me, protecting me. He's not here to protect me, and I need to follow his directions. My obedience may save all our lives.

Darkness settles in on the forest, and it's hard for me to see the ground. I don't want to use the flashlight; it'll draw attention. The rocks and ruts in the path make me stumble to my destination, the cabin. My ankle catches on a tree branch across the path, and I fall hard on my hand, putting pressure on my wrist. I can still move my fingers, so I don't think it's broken, but it hurts to move it. I get up and dust myself off, moving toward the cabin.

As I get closer to the area, I turn on the flashlight on the phone on low. The light shines on the window and reflects as if something is covering it. I turn the door handle with my sweaty hands, and it opens.

"Pippa?" My flashlight shines on sleeping bags and lanterns on the floor. "Pippa?"

She's not here, but where could she be? Panic sets in, and I do my deep breathing exercises, trying to bring my heart rate down.

I close the door behind me. Darkness surrounds me, gripping me as if to say, gotcha. I fight it away, knowing the plan is still in play. The team will come back to meet us here and get their things.

My hands shake. I'm in the middle of the woods, looking for Pippa as a gunfight is going on back at the house. My only choice is to head up to the place where I hid in the cavern on the side of the mountain. This time, I use my flashlight to find my way. My left wrist throbs, and I move carefully to avoid falling again.

"Pippa? Are you out here?" I say it loud enough to be heard but not loud enough to be noticed by someone far away.

Fingers tap my shoulder. "Ahhhhhhhh!" I whip around and shine my light behind me.

"Jess, put that down and get it out of my face." Pippa's hands are up to shield her face from the light.

I turn off the flashlight. "Sorry." I can barely swallow and hug her tight.

"You have to let go at some point." I hear her muffled voice against my shoulder.

Letting go, I place my hands on her shoulders to steady myself. "Yeah, I know. I'm a little frazzled. Sean wanted me to tell you to release the virus."

"The team didn't want me to stay in the cabin in case

250

Isaad's thugs found me. I've been up in a cave in the mountains. Turn your flashlight on, but point it down. It'll be easier and faster to get there." Her head is together much more than mine.

She grabs my left hand. "Ouch," I hiss.

"What happened?" She lets go.

"I fell. I'll be fine. Let's go." We don't have time to worry about my injury.

We climb our way up the hill to a cave big enough for the two of us. I have a look around with my flashlight. Water runs down the side of the wall, and the air is raw and cool. It smells damp and moldy, but this will only be for a short time.

Pippa unlocks the phone, and it shows full power. She must have saved it for this moment. She holds it over her head and around, looking for the bars to show up.

"Shit! We have no service. Let's move out from under the rock and see if we get anything."

We move farther into the woods, looking for service so she can release the virus and destroy everything in the supercomputers.

"Nothing." Pippa sighs. "We need to get closer to the house." Her face glows in the light on the screen.

"That's not what I want to hear."

"In the cabin is one of Beck's guns. He left it behind. Let's get it and move toward the house." She talks as if she's done this a million times.

I'm in awe. "Who's Beck?"

"He's Mr. Beautiful." A smile crosses her face.

I roll my eyes even though she can't see it. "Do your hormones ever take a holiday?"

"No, why should they? From the looks of it, yours aren't taking a break either." She laughs.

She slips inside the cabin and gets the gun. I take it from her.

"Why should you get to carry it?"

"Because I've already shot someone."

The gun feels heavy in my hand, heavier than Sean's. It'll take two hands to point it and shoot.

"What the hell are you talking about?!" she exclaims.

I put the gun in my waistband. "I had to shoot Rakesh. He was about to… kill me."

"Oh." She puts her head down. "There were two sides to him. He saved his soft side for me."

I nod. "I'll be glad to leave this place. There are too many sides to everything. I can't tell what is what."

We use the flashlight on the path to the house until we get close enough to be seen and turn it off. At the edge of the wooded area, close to the house, we crouch behind the rocks and check for service. We hear pops of gunfire in front of us, in and around the house. None of them are close to us, but my gun is ready.

"Bingo. We've got service." Pippa taps a few times on the phone. "Voila. We're done. I have sent the virus." She taps a couple more times. "The app has been uninstalled, and now we have to take apart your phone and destroy it. I hope you have everything backed up."

"Yeah, I just didn't realize how much this trip was going to cost me." I sigh.

She shrugs as she disassembles the phone. "Your heart is your biggest expense."

I smile to myself. "He's worth every drop of blood."

Gunfire explodes, signaling us to get out of there. We run into the woods, staying on the path until we get to where the cabin is on the hill. Going past it, we hurry into the cave and wait for the team to come to get us.

We sit down with our backs to a dry part of the rock wall and huddle together for warmth and comfort. At some point, we must have fallen asleep. We wake up to a bright light shining in our eyes.

"Ladies." The man has a thick Scottish accent. "You need to come back to the cabin. We're getting ready to leave." He's covered in dirt and blood. I don't ask. I don't want to know.

"Where's Sean?" My body lacks energy.

He doesn't answer me as we follow him down the hill through the dark. He's wearing his night vision goggles and knows exactly where to go.

Lanterns light the cabin from the inside without detection from the outside. Two men are packing up their gear. But there is no Sean.

"Where is Sean?" I say with more force, demanding an answer.

The Scotsman reaches out his hand. "By the way, I'm Mac."

"I'm Beck, at your service."

"I'm Mr. Wonderful, Dean." The others roll their eyes.

"It's nice to meet you. You already know who I am. Now answer my question." My anger peaks.

Mac looks over at Dean. "He's going to try, but he may not make the rendezvous. We'll have someone pick him up later."

I open my mouth to protest as he pulls something out of the large pocket of his pants. "Here, he wanted me to give this to you."

He hands me the bundle of the letters I wrote to Sean, but never sent, wrapped up in a red ribbon, the way I left them. He knows they have special meaning to me. I put my fingers to my lips to stifle the tears and a groan.

"Thank you."

I don't want to think about what this might mean. He damn well better make it to the meeting place.

Beck stands with his hands on his hips. "Has anyone seen my .45?"

I reach behind my back and pull out his gun. "Sorry. We had to go back to the house to get service. We didn't want to go unprotected."

He smiles with straight white teeth that light up his face. "Good thinking." He puts his palm out for his gun.

"That thing is heavy." I hand it to him using both hands.

"It packs a punch. I'm glad you didn't have to use it." His British accent calms my nerves. There's something about him that's peaceful.

"We've got a hike ahead of us. Hopefully, you two wore shoes you can walk in. We have to climb around the ridge where the chopper can land. Timing is everything on this one. The chopper will land long enough for us to get on and fly out. I'll lead the way. Dean and Beck, you bring up the rear."

Pippa has been unusually quiet. "What about the women who were being kept prisoner? What happens to them?"

Dean looks at Mac. "We tried to get as many as we could. Sean and Declan, along with the special ops team, will do a sweep before they blow the place. We had them go to the other side of the mountains, and we'll get them picked up tomorrow. We did the best we could."

She nods her head, satisfied with his answer, and gives him a weak smile.

We start our climb as the men carry heavy backpacks, but they walk as if it's nothing. I keep looking over my shoulder at the house below. It gets smaller, and Sean is nowhere nearby. Pippa grips my hand.

"It's going to be fine. He's a trained SEAL. He knows what he's doing," she says confidently.

"I hope you're right." I squeeze her hand.

"Sean is one of the best, that's why I work for him. He can handle himself," Dean says from behind us.

We get to the ridge just as the helicopter lands. Pippa's out of breath, and they help her get to the chopper. I look behind me to see flames shoot out of the top of the house, followed by the sound of an explosion.

I lurch forward. "Noooo!"

Mac grabs my arm, and I struggle against him, beating him with my fists. "We've got to go. He'll meet up with us later. He'll be fine."

"How do you know he's not in there?" I yell.

He doesn't answer my question. "I made a promise to get you to safety, and that's what I'm going to do."

He whips me off the ground and carries me to the helicopter, only a few feet away. He plops me in a seat near the door and straps me in. The doors close, giving it finality.

I put my hand on the window. Anger heats my entire body. He's done it again. He left me behind, and I don't even know if he's alive. I give in to the fine line between anger and despair. Holding my head in my hands, I sob as my entire body shakes.

Pippa puts her arm around me for comfort. "Shhh, it'll be fine."

"I need everyone to stop telling me it's going to be fine. We don't know for sure," I mumble the words through a sob.

I turn to Mac. "Won't he let you know if he's okay?"

"Declan has a phone, but in this part of the country, I don't know how much service he has. Right now, we wait and hope for the best." Mac's response lacks emotion. Maybe that's what you do as a soldier to get through it.

The helicopter moves away from the mountain, traveling southeast toward Pakistan. The farther we get, the emptier I feel. I sag in the seat like part of my soul has been left behind.

THIRTY-NINE

Jess

OUR HELICOPTER LANDS IN PAKISTAN, and we hustle for the private jet awaiting us for the eight-hour flight to London. In flight, they attend to my wrist by wrapping it, and I mumble my thanks, numb to everything going on around me.

The next day is spent as a stopover so Beck can visit with family, and I buy some clothes for the trip home.

After sixteen hours of flying to get home, there's still no word from Sean or Declan. I've been told many times it will be difficult, if not impossible, for them to get word back to the team.

What they aren't saying is that it would be hard if one of them got hurt while they were trying to get out. I'm buried deep in my thoughts about the many scenarios that could go wrong.

Back in New Jersey, I throw my duffel bag on the floor in my apartment. I feel like I haven't been home in years. Pippa stays with me in case anyone is looking for her.

Mac and the team don't know if Isaad backed up his supercomputers somewhere else. Since we don't know what's on them, he may have blown her cover as Red Enigma, preventing her from working on the dark web.

Pippa stands beside me. "If you need to be alone, I can go to a hotel for a while until this blows over."

"No. I need you here. I know. It's selfish of me. Besides, you heard them. You're going to need to look for a new place to live, and you might even have to change your name, depending on who knows your real identity." I grab her hand and squeeze it.

My cat comes out from her hiding place. My neighbor across the hall has spoiled her while I've been away. She's a tawny Bengal named Mia because she's always missing in action, hiding somewhere in the apartment, and finding her moment to attack. Her curiosity gets the better of her, and she misses me. She meows and curls her body around my legs. I pick her up and hold her to me as we rub foreheads and noses. Pippa can hear her loud purr from across the room. She's a little feisty, but that's why I love her. She reminds me to always be a fighter.

Anxiety won't be my friend while I wait for Sean. Each day that passes without a word from him feels like an eternity. I slough through the day, unable to focus on my next big story. Pippa is convinced that writing a story about what happened in Afghanistan will lead to a Pulitzer Prize. I'm not motivated to write one word about it. Besides, it will need an ending.

My long-lost friend, Raquelle, contacted me a week later. "Sorry I didn't call sooner, but I wanted you and Pippa to get settled before I spring my family on you. Are you available for dinner tomorrow night? I would love to see both of you."

"Sure. That sounds good." My voice lacks enthusiasm.

Raquelle's softer side comes out. "Hon, he's going to

come back. It just may take a little while. I thought I lost Misha, too, and look where we are."

"The not knowing is what's killing me." My voice is barely above a whisper.

She tries to lighten the mood. "How about I have a car pick you up at seven?"

"That sounds great. It'll be good to see you again. It's been too long." I attempt to sound happy.

"You can say that again. Ciao!" She clicks off with her signature goodbye.

Some things never change, and that brings me comfort. She always makes me feel like family.

The following night, we get ready to meet with Raquelle and her family, whom I've never met before. I dress in a pair of dress pants and a light sweater.

Pippa walks into my bedroom and gives me a once-over. "Um, how about no. You're going to see Raquelle for the first time in years, and you're meeting her entire family. Besides, dressing up will make you feel better," says the woman wearing black Dr. Martens boots to accent her pink dress.

"Here."

She pulls out one of my favorite dresses, a tight-fitting lavender knit dress with a plunging neckline. Lavender used to be Sean's favorite color.

I hand it back to her as sadness pulls at my heart. "I think it's a little fancy for tonight."

"Who does it remind you of?" She holds the hanger on her finger.

"Sean." I stare at the floor.

"Then you should wear it. It will make you feel closer to him and take off the bandage on your wrist. You don't need it anymore."

Something niggles at the back of my mind. She's a little too pushy tonight.

"Fine, Miss Bossy Pants." I don't have the energy to argue.

A black town car picks us up at seven sharp and drives us into the city, where Raquelle lives in a beautiful brownstone. She opens the door before my finger rings the bell.

"Jess, it's so good to see you." She throws her arms around me and squeezes me tight.

"It's good to see you, too." I try to take a breath from her squeeze.

The memories of our vacation in Switzerland come flooding back to me. She was the wild one between us. I had to reel her in on more than one occasion, especially in the high-end nightclubs.

She gives Pippa a big hug, too, and shows us inside. I step into the foyer, and it's crowded with seven people, three of whom I recognize from the team: Mac, Dean, and Beck.

Dean has his arm around a beautiful blonde. She introduces herself as Leigha, Raquelle's sister. We go around the circle as I meet Mara, her other sister, and Mac's other half, Peter, and Raquelle's fiancé, Misha.

"Come on in. I've prepared an awesome Italian meal. I thought you might be hungry. If I remember correctly, you always have a raging appetite when you get depressed."

Raquelle was always good at laying it out there and calling me on my crap.

Mara, who looks like she's ready to give birth at any minute, pipes up. "Who prepared an awesome Italian meal?" She puts her hands on her hips.

Raquelle looks over her shoulder and pouts. "Well, I helped at least."

"Is that what you call it? You sat on the stool and drank wine." Mara's eyes bore into Raquelle's back. She's cranky.

Mac mumbles, "Let's get you comfortable on the couch with your feet up. You've had a long day."

"I'm so glad she's having a baby and not me," Raquelle quips.

She leads the way to the kitchen and stands behind the island with her hands on the black mica granite. That's when I catch sight of the diamond on her finger.

I grab her hand and hold it up to the light. In the time that I've known Raquelle, I've never seen her blush.

"Wow. What is it? A beacon in case you get lost."

We both laugh. "He went overboard. He tends to go overboard when it comes to me."

"That's a good thing. You deserve him. But seriously, how big is it?"

"It's a four-carat princess-cut diamond with sapphire baguettes on each side." She lowers her voice. "I didn't need something this big. I only need him." Her words catch in her throat, but the love in her eyes says it all.

Misha enters the room with authority. "I heard that. Maybe I want your clients to know who you belong to."

He's strikingly handsome, and they make a beautiful couple. My heart aches for Sean.

Raquelle rolls her eyes. "I don't think there's any doubt about who I belong to." She's glowing and can't keep her eyes off him.

I make my way into the living room and see Pippa standing in front of Peter.

"So, you're Red Enigma." He grins.

"Who might you be?" She leans over and puts her hands on the armrests of his wheelchair. "And you know that how?" She's not letting him off the hook.

"Wouldn't you like to know? I'm one of the partners,

and I love to roam the dark web. Your reputation precedes you. At least the name fits." He wiggles his brows.

I continue to the dining room, where everyone has been called to dinner. Loving couples surround me, including Pippa, who seems to have found her next conquest even as her eyes roam in Beck's direction. At least she has something in common with Peter.

Raquelle serves everything from salad and lasagna to cannoli. Laughter and ribbing are going on around the table. They are one big happy family. Being in this atmosphere is a welcome distraction from missing Sean. I eat enough not to offend her, but I'm not stuffed, and I can't wait to leave.

Raquelle stands up and announces that the men will clean up while the women move to the game room.

She takes me by the arm and whispers, "You and I have somewhere to go." Her move seems abrupt.

"If you could take me home, that would be great."

"Maybe." She smiles.

We drive in her burnt-orange sports car to the Upper East Side. Her driving scares the shit out of me. She gives new meaning to the phrase lethal with a deadly weapon.

We stop in front of a huge high-rise building with a large, black awning on Fifth Avenue across from Central Park, where penthouses go for millions. The doorman nods and lets us in. The lobby is spotless and accented with white marble.

I stop in my tracks. "Why are we here?"

"You'll see." She is giddy with excitement.

To the far left is a single elevator by itself. She presses the button, and we wait. The door opens, and she pushes me in from behind.

"Press nineteen. Then look for the number nineteen oh seven. Ciao!"

The doors close before I can ask her what the hell is going on. This building is an expensive high-rise with an address to die for. I don't know anyone who might live in this part of town.

I exit the elevator and sink into the plush carpet. The number I'm looking for seems to be around the corner. I stop halfway down the hall and think about turning around to make a run for it, but Raquelle wouldn't steer me in the wrong direction. She's always had my back.

When I find nineteen oh seven, it has two enormous doors, each with a knocker. I bang one of them three times and wait. When the door opens, I'm blown away.

FORTY

Sean

I OPEN THE DOOR, and her eyes go wide. I love the element of surprise. She drops her purse and rushes toward me, only to stop short when she sees my condition.

"What happened to your arm?"

"I had a minor mishap when the explosives went off. I got thrown to the ground and broke my wrist and some fingers. It's not a big deal. By the way, when you're coming toward me, never stop, no matter what."

She throws her arms around me and holds me tight. I hug her with both arms, forgetting the pain in my wrist.

"Your lip healed up nicely." She drags her finger across the place where I took out the stitches.

Her hands roam my face, my eyes, lips, and cheeks. She tilts her head and looks up at me.

I know that look. "What's wrong?"

"I thought I would never see you again. I worried you died in that explosion."

Her abandonment issues come screaming forward, and I need to extinguish them forever.

My lips meet hers to assure her I'm the real deal. Our

kiss deepens, full of passion as our tongues duel, each trying to convince the other that this will last.

Forever tastes sweet. We've taken a long time to get to this moment where she can be mine without question and where she knows I'll never leave her.

"You wore my favorite color," I growl.

"It was Pippa's—never mind. I know she was in on this. How long have you been back?" She rubs up against me like a cat in heat.

I tread carefully, but I can't lie either. "A couple of days."

She smacks my shoulder. "And you didn't call me?"

Backing away from her, I pretend I'm hurt. "I had things I needed to get done before I saw you again."

We stand in the foyer, taking each other in. I can't take my eyes off her as I grab her hand and lead her down the hall to the living room. The interior designer used distinct tones of gray and cream to make it soft yet masculine.

We follow the path of red rose petals, and candles of different sizes and shapes glow and flicker on every flat surface, including the live-edge wood mantel above the fireplace. Her letters are wrapped with a red ribbon on the coffee table in the center of the room.

She walks ahead of me and comments as we take our time getting to the living room.

"This is incredible. It's gorgeous. Is this what you were doing while you were back and didn't tell me, making me worry about you?"

"Boy, you know how to lay on the guilt."

She looks over her shoulder at me before we get to our destination. I turn her around and take her hands in mine.

"I wanted everything to be perfect for you."

My nerves get the better of me. What if she doesn't like what I've done or what I've picked out? What if she's had time to think about us and changed her mind, given what she knows about my background?

She gives me her total focus, and her eyes are soft and loving, something I haven't experienced since my mother was in my life.

"I don't want perfect. I want you just the way you are. You didn't have to rent this big, luxurious penthouse to impress me. I don't care where you live."

I'm unable to form words. There's a lump in my throat. She doesn't know. Pippa must not have done the thorough background check on me that I expected her to do. She frowns at my reaction.

"This is where I live." I stare into her eyes, willing her to understand.

A stunned look comes across her face. "I'm sorry. What? This is a high-end penthouse that overlooks Central Park. What haven't you told me?"

"When I was in college, I got into stocks and came across some great tips on big tech companies that have exploded over the years. I put together a portfolio, but then went on my first tour to Afghanistan. I watched it grow, but didn't pay much attention to it. When I came back, my portfolio was, well, very healthy, enough for me to buy this place and start my business."

Her face goes blank as I watch the wheels turn in her head.

"That explains why you're so snooty." She giggles. I love her giggle. It brings me back to when we were kids.

She stops laughing long enough to ask her next question, an investigative journalist through and through.

"Why do you still go on assignments? You could just run your business or not work at all."

"It's in my blood. If anyone needs to be rescued, I'm your guy. I like the challenge that comes with each assignment. If I get too far away from it, I feel disconnected from what's going on in the company and with my team. It's like asking why you're an investigative journalist."

I pull her close, pushing a ringlet behind her ear, and kiss her nose. "Any more questions?"

"Of course. I've spent my life asking questions."

"Yes, I know, but it will have to wait. I want you to see something."

My heart strums in my chest. I hold her shoulders and turn her toward the fireplace.

Her hand flies up to cover her mouth. "Oh, my God. That's my portrait. Raquelle did a beautiful job, as always."

I put my arms around her waist as my head rests on her shoulder. "This portrait reminds me of what I lost. Fate had a roundabout way of bringing us together. If I hadn't found you in Afghanistan, I would have hunted you down. That was my plan. The TV got moved to another room, so your portrait is the focal point of our home. I'll watch football somewhere else."

I push her hair away from her face and nuzzle her neck. She's smiling, giggling, and squirming around.

She stops moving. "Why are my letters in the center of the table?"

We sit on the couch in the middle of the rose petals. I pull her onto my lap, where she fits perfectly.

Kissing her neck sends a shudder through her, making me hard as a nail. "Did you look through the letters since you've been home?"

She shakes her head. "No. And if you keep this up, we're going to end up naked and having hot sex." Her eyes close, and she leans away, giving me more access to her neck.

"We'll definitely get naked later, and the sex is always

hot. Right now, I need you to untie the ribbon and take the top letter off the pile," I whisper in her ear.

Her fingers untie the ribbon, letting the ends pool on the table. She picks up the top one addressed to her.

"What's this?" she whispers.

"Open it."

She shakes her head as her hair falls like curtains to hide her face. She looks at me through glassy eyes.

I kiss her mouth with softness. "It's nothing bad. I promise."

Her fingers poke between the envelope's seal. She reads it out loud to me.

Dear Bug,

If you're reading this, it means one of two things has happened.

One, I've died and you're reading this with Pippa by your side. In which case, I'm sorry I've left you again. I never intended to let you go. But as I've witnessed one too many times, death gets its way when you least expect it. No one ever cheats death. Life postpones your trip.

Two, I hope you're sitting in my lap reading this letter to me. You have always been my universe. When I was suffocating, you gave me your air. When I was bruised and battered, you comforted me. When I felt unloved and unworthy, you lifted me and showed me I was someone worth fighting for. I didn't realize until years later that what you did for me came from your heart without ever knowing my circumstances. You truly saw inside my soul.

We were both masters at hiding, so we ended up hiding from each other, afraid to show ourselves. Protecting you proved to be a distraction for me, but in the end, it made me a kick-ass SEAL. The Navy gave me a place to shine. I owe you everything.

If I had to do it over again, I wouldn't change a thing. Without knowing it, you've made me the man I am today. Thank you.

I loved you then. I love you now. I'll love you always. You're part of my blood.

Forever,

Mr. Knight

Tears drop from her chin, leaving spots on the paper. Her eyes hold a tenderness I've never seen before.

"When did you write this?" Her lower lip trembles.

"I had some time on my hands when we were apart in the house. Since I didn't know how things would turn out, I kept hoping for the best." I hold her tighter to me.

She kisses me and strokes my face.

"Look what's behind the letter."

She unfolds a two-page description of a house in Connecticut. It's an enormous rambling ranch on five acres of land with a pool and a huge backyard. There's even a playscape for kids.

"What's this?" She wipes her tears to let her light shine through.

"It can be our house. I remember when we were younger, you said you wanted a house where everyone could be together and not separated by floors. This could be our forever home. I have a deposit on it, but I wanted you to have a say in it. This needs to be our decision. I'll sell the penthouse, and we'll move to the country with your white picket fence. I know it's not New Jersey, but it's your dream house."

"It's beautiful." Her fingers outline the playscape in the photo. "There's a lot of room in this house. I don't know what to say. This is more than I dreamed of."

"I was thinking we would have a couple of kids or ten." I shrug and give her one of my grins.

"Let's start with one and work our way up from there." She looks at me with gratitude. "Thank you."

I pick up the stack of her letters and put them to the side. Underneath them, in the center of the red ribbon, is a ring. I move her to the couch and settle on one knee, holding the ring in my hand. I've never felt this confident in what I was about to do.

"Will you do me the honor of being my wife, for eternity?" My heart hammers in my chest, not from nerves but from excitement.

"Yes. There was never a question."

She smiles through new tears as I slip the ring on her finger. The three-carat oval diamond has square rubies on each side.

"This ring has our story in it. The gold is from a nugget I found in the mine in Afghanistan. The rubies are for the wild red roses that remind me of you. I designed it for you when I knew we would get married."

"Well, I have a gift for you." She smiles and stands up.

She pulls her dress over her head and lets it fall to the floor. Cream lace bra and panties adorn her voluptuous body. The color accents her smooth brown skin, good enough to eat.

She steps out of her heels. "If you want it, you're going to have to come and get it."

I follow the laughter down the hall until she finds the master suite. Best gift ever.

Epilogue

Sean

WE SPEND the next couple of days confined to my penthouse, making up for lost time. I make love to her in every room, in every position possible. Right now, she faces the lush greenery of Central Park as I thrust into her from behind and tease her clit. The best view I've seen out this window.

I didn't know how much I missed her or needed her until I heard her say my name over and over again. My bond with her tightens with every moan and sigh, taking me to a higher place where just the two of us live. I like to call her Mrs. Bug Knight.

What makes me the happiest is her absolute freedom to be herself and walk around naked. She's not hiding anymore, and neither am I. This is the most honest I've been with myself or anyone else.

I've agreed to go to counseling for my PTSD, tired of the ghosts from the past chasing me and hunting me down.

They need to get knocked out so I can have the life I want with her.

I hold her hand as we drive to Connecticut to look at our new home. We outbid everyone else on it by a lot because this is the house she wanted.

I turn off the motor to my pickup truck and park across the street. The owners won't be out for another month, giving us plenty of time to plan what we want to do with it.

I hear a sniffle.

"What's wrong?" I still worry that I'm moving too fast.

"Nothing. Not a damn thing. That's the scary part. I'm used to the fight, the struggle, and I never in my wildest dreams pictured you, me, and this." Her hands clench in her lap, and she tilts her chin in the direction of the house.

Two kids and a dog run around the yard, laughing and rolling in the grass. They play hide and seek, but the dog always finds the one who's hiding. The scene resembles a TV show from the '70s.

"It's so far removed from how I grew up," I mumble as I continue to stare out the window.

She squeezes my hand. "I know what you mean. I didn't dare to dream because I wasn't used to dreams coming true."

My cell phone rings. I glance at the caller ID, not looking forward to this call. "Neil, what can I do for you?"

"I'm in the city and need you and your team to meet me at oh-eight-hundred tomorrow morning. We need to debrief." His voice is clipped.

"Got it. We'll see you then."

"Oh, Sean, bring Jess and Pippa." He clicks off without a goodbye.

Jess turns to me. "What's going on?"

I stare at the screen, unable to guess what he's up to

this time. "Neil wants to meet with us tomorrow morning, including you and Pippa. I got a bad feeling about this."

Her eyes go wide. "Do you think he has more information about Deep 8?"

I shrug. I'm not sure why he would share it with my team and me. This type of high-level operation is above our pay grade.

The next morning, I take Jess to the MBK office for the first time.

"This is a beautiful space. Very modern. And I might have failed to mention you look hot in a suit." She winks.

I lean down to her ear. "You needed to say that right before we go into a meeting? Maybe we should take a detour to my office so I can show you what's under this suit."

She smiles and laughs. "Slow it down, cowboy. Maybe later. Besides, I've had a full tour of what's under that suit."

"You mean reverse cowboy. I believe that's how you rode last night. I hope you're not sore." I feign concern.

She lifts her chin. "I can take whatever you dish out."

"We'll see about that." I smile so much around her that my cheeks hurt.

We enter the conference room, where everyone sits around the huge, oval table, leaving the head of the table for me. Mac sits to my left, followed around the table by Declan, Beck, Dean, Peter, and Pippa. I pull a chair over from the right for my better half.

The tension in the room is thick. "Do you know what this is about?" Mac asks.

"Not a clue." I unbutton my jacket before sitting down.

The receptionist interrupts over the phone. "Neil McFadden is here."

"Send him back, please." The group is eerily quiet.

We stand to greet him. Neil knows everyone but Pippa and Peter. He sits at the opposite end of the table from me.

He clears his throat. "Is this room secure?"

The room has no windows, solid steel walls, and a scrambler. To say it's secure is an understatement. "Completely."

"Good. What I'm about to say cannot leave this room. Your team is about to work for MI6 on a new assignment." No smile accompanies his statement as if it's good news.

Mac sits back. "Shit, McFadden. I just got out."

Neil smiles. "You're not exactly back in. The group called Deep 8 you came across in Afghanistan, is new to us. Isaad was on our radar, but for other reasons. He accumulated a lot of money over a brief time, which raised a flag, especially in that part of the world. He seemed to have his hands in everything, even the government, but not directly. There are very few links that lead back to him. Somewhere along the line, he evaded ABIS and has flown under the radar."

He gets frowns from most of the group. "ABIS is the Automated Biometric Identification System we used ten years ago to track almost everyone in Afghanistan, including fingerprints, retinal scans, and voice patterns. How he got by it, I'll never know." I was one of the team members gathering intel for the operation.

"I assume he's in custody?" I ask the question that's been gnawing at me.

Neil looks at me with tired eyes that have seen too much for a man his age. "I'm afraid we didn't get that far. We found his body next to the helicopter crash, along with Rakesh's. They made it look like a SAM had shot it down. Whoever Deep 8 is, they are sending a message. Otherwise, they would have made him disappear. I'm sorry, Sean."

I twirl a pen on the table. "The casualties of war."

I'm used to burying my sadness. I'll push off my grief like I've done so many times before, but he was my friend first, my enemy last. This one hits hard for many reasons.

"The casualties of being a little fish in a huge pond. We think Deep 8 is global and has woven its way into many governments. They seem to be extremely wealthy. I need this team to work with Scotland Yard to find out more about Deep 8. You'd be off-book, working in the dark. I'll be your only contact. They won't figure that we will use the top former military team to track them. The CIA has its radar up as well."

"It doesn't sound like we have a choice." Dean's voice has a bite to it. He's been backed into a corner before when he had to leave his beloved country of Australia.

"Not at this point. As they say, you know too much. Besides, we could use your anonymity to our advantage. They won't see you coming. Any movement by government agencies and we're dead in the water."

Neil turns to me. "The piece of metal you brought back has some interesting properties we've never seen before. We don't know what they want with it or what they use it for. We went back to the mines, and they were filled with it. I'd like you to inspect it and run some tests."

"Not a problem." He doesn't need to twist my arm to have me do what I love, investigating minerals.

"There is another piece of this that is a big problem. The data downloaded from the computers is heavily encrypted with a code we've never come across before. We're going to need a couple of hackers to figure this out." He turns to Pippa. "That's where you come in. You did excellent undercover work for us."

Jess's head snaps in Pippa's direction. Pippa smiles as if to say, "Gotcha."

Neil continues, unaware of their silent conversation. "I need you and Peter to work on this together. I can't afford to have anyone from the inside come across this."

Pippa's eyes look down. "Did you get the women out who were prisoners?"

"Yes, my team picked most of them up in the high mountains the next day. Some felt going on foot to Pakistan was a better choice."

Pippa nods and smiles. "Thank you. I'll be happy to work on this for you."

Mac speaks up. "My brother Campbell is a cryptanalyst and has a background in nuclear physics. He's looking for a change of pace. I'd like to bring him in. I know he can help. He's done some high-level encryption work."

"I'm well aware of Campbell. He's been doing some interesting work where the Chinese are concerned." Neil seems to have his fingers in everything.

"I can hire him as soon as he's available," I offer.

Neil nods. "Jess, I'm afraid your article about the incident in Afghanistan is on ice indefinitely. You can see why."

She throws her hands up. "And there goes my Pulitzer, but I understand."

"That brings me to Beck." Beck frowns at Neil. "You have an interesting family history, I don't think you know anything about."

Beck cocks his head to the side. "I know my parents adopted me in the UK when I was three years old."

"Do you know where you came from originally?" Neil taps his forefingers together.

"I assume I came from somewhere in the UK?" His words end with a question mark, not liking where Neil is going.

Neil stands up to leave and buttons his jacket. "It's time

for me to go. I'll be in touch. Your next assignment is about to walk through the door. Yes, we think Deep 8 has its hands in this as well."

Beck

The tingling at the base of my neck spikes like an alarm, a sensation I've learned never to ignore. Instinct has kept me alive more times than I can count, and right now, it's screaming at the top of its lungs.

The door swings open again, and a man strides in, draped in a red-and-black plaid shawl over a black shirt and skirt. His traditional attire starkly contrasts with the city's cold steel and glass, echoing something older, something primal.

He moves with the kind of confidence that commands attention without demanding it. Every head in the room turns his way, but his eyes find only me.

A strange, undeniable pull urges me to my feet. I've never seen him before, yet something about him commands my respect. His dark eyes are pools of wisdom, his white teeth gleaming against skin as rich as midnight. He is not much shorter than my six-foot-five-inch frame, but that doesn't lessen his presence. If anything, it makes it sharper and more concentrated.

I recognize his calm demeanor from within myself as he seems to float across the floor in my direction.

He stops in front of me and bows. "Your Highness, Dacari Touré Siwanda."

My heart slams against my ribs. The air in the room shifts, heavy with something I can't define. A ripple of murmurs passes through the onlookers.

"Excuse me. I think you have me confused with

someone else. I'm no one's highness." Growing up in the UK, his reference to me as royalty is sacrilegious.

The man straightens, his expression unyielding but laced with something deeper—reverence, maybe even sorrow. "No, I assure you, I am not confused. You look very much like your father."

The storm inside me builds to a crescendo. "My father is white." My words are clipped and controlled. "I don't look like him at all." But even as I say it, I know that's not the man he's referring to.

A muscle tightens in his jaw. "I'm Esquire Katoo Ole Kapiti here on an urgent matter. Your parents adopted you from my country. You are from Africa's earth, and it is time for you to return." His voice lowers, threading through the air like a whisper of fate. "Your biological mother and father have passed. You are the eldest son; therefore, you need to take your rightful place as the head of the Sai tribe in Zambia."

The proclamation of this man stuns me. He taps a familiarity, not in who he is, but in how he has presented himself. My soul takes notice and seems to recognize him.

"You have the wrong person," I say, though my throat feels like sandpaper. "I'm not aware of this, and I have no connection to it. There's no doubt your culture and customs are special. You would be better off choosing someone else." My hands clench at my sides, but my heart hammers against my ribs like a war drum.

Katoo steps closer and takes my hand, placing it between his own. His warmth seeps into me and calms me, grounding me when everything else feels like it's fracturing.

His face shifts, darkening like a gathering storm. "This is your calling, and we need your leadership. Things are not as they should be. You need to come with me immediately and take your rightful place."

The way he says it isn't a plea. It's a truth. An inescapable one.

He cocks his head to the side. "You've never been to your motherland, have you?" He smiles.

I shake my head, the world tilting around me.

"It's time to return home," he says, his voice a quiet thunder.

Zambia. A land of diamonds and emeralds. A land I know nothing about, but one that might hold every answer I never thought to ask.

And maybe—just maybe—my destiny.

———

SECRETS ABOUT BECK'S past are about to unravel, and someone wants him dead. Want to know more about MBK's adventures and Deep 8's conspiracy? Grab your copy of **KING in the Deep 8 series** now!

FREE Book

I love staying in touch with my readers.
Sign up for my newsletter for updates, giveaways, and
other exclusives, and receive **Silent Night** for **FREE** at

https://bit.ly/FreeBkKM

Caught between beauty's embrace and betrayal's kiss.

She must save her brother. He only sees her betrayal. Will
they find love or fall prey to a deadly rescue plan?

Chloe's dream of becoming a journalist gets crushed
when she can't secure a job. Forced to make ends meet, she
takes a job at a J. Luc Gallery. But when her brother gets
held for ransom, Chloe is thrust into a dangerous mission
to save him, jeopardizing her budding romance.

Desperate to save her brother, Chloe makes a heart-
wrenching decision, forcing her to betray Jean Luc. As
MBK Global Security races against time to make the
exchange, their plan teeters on the brink of failure, threat-

ening to leave Chloe in danger and Jean Luc's heart in pieces.

Please consider leaving a review

If you enjoyed **WILD,** I would love it if you let your friends know so they can experience the action-packed and suspense filled story of Sean and Jess.

Reviews are so precious to writers. Writing a review helps other readers find my books and is helpful when deciding what to read next.

If you have a minute, please leave a review. Thank you in advance for taking the time to help others find **WILD**.

Also by Kenzie Macallan

MBK Global Security

Truths

(Mac & Marbella's story)

Mara is hiding a terrible secret. He's on a dangerous mission. Can Mac protect the love of his life from a ruthless killer?

Edges

(Dean & Leigha's story)

Leigha is under threat. Dean is undercover. Will deadly family secrets ruin the romance of a lifetime?

Masks

(Michael & Raquelle's story)

Raquelle is investigating him. Misha is accused of fraud. Will a sinister conspiracy ruin their shot at unforgettable love?

Deep 8 series

King

(Beck & Pippa's story)

Pippa is a hacker turned agent. Beck will become king of a diamond empire. Can two unlikely lovers survive a sinister conspiracy?

Burn

(Declan & Olivia's story)

Olivia is a scientist fighting to keep her secret hidden. Declan is an ex-soldier with a tragic past and lost memories. Will the chemistry between them ignite lost love?

Risk

(Campbell & Quinn's story)

She created a game-changing nuclear weapon. He must keep her safe from a powerful enemy. As embers ignite between them, will their passion lead to an explosive meltdown?

Torn

(Roger and Harlow's story)

Harlow is undercover to find her father's killer. Roger must find his father before Deep 8 kills him for the software that will change the world.

About the Author

Kenzie Macallan is an author who skillfully weaves intricate action-adventure romances as art imitates life. Not really, but her vivid imagination often finds solace within the pages of her books. Having explored the diverse landscapes of Africa, Greece, Switzerland, Holland, France, England, and Scotland, her travels have ignited a relentless wellspring of storytelling.

This fuels her artistic endeavors, from painting captivating portraits to capturing moments through her camera, all while nurturing her green thumb in the garden. While culinary mastery may elude her, she loves to bake, much to the gratitude of her husband.

Kenzie's true passion lies in transporting readers to captivating realms, where flawed yet endearing heroes emerge, intelligent and resilient women take center stage, and unexpected endings leave them in awe. With each new adventure, Kenzie eagerly anticipates the opportunity to further enchant her readers and embark on a shared journey of discovery.

She loves to hear from her fans.

Join her newsletter for cover reveals, new books, deals, and giveaways.
Website: www.kenziemacallan.com

You can find her on:
Amazon: www.amazon.com/author/kenziemacallan

Goodreads: https://www.goodreads.com/author/show/ 15058012.Kenzie_Macallan
BookBub: www.bookbub.com/authors/kenzie-macallan
Instagram: www.instagram.com/kenziemacallan
Facebook: www.facebook.com/kenziemacallan
TikTok: www.tiktok.com/kenziemacallan
Pinterest: www.pinterest.com/kenziemacallan
X: www.twitter.com/kenzie_macallan
Email: kenziemacallan@gmail.com

Acknowledgments

As much as writing is a solitary experience, it takes many people to put it all together.

A huge thank you goes out to the readers who took a chance on me and read this book. If you left a review, I'm forever grateful because they are like diamonds, so hard to find and yet shine brightly. Your support is greatly appreciated. You make it all worthwhile.

I want to thank my husband who doesn't see me for many hours on end and still gives me his unwavering support. We seemed to have found a balance. You're wonderful!

I love this cover so much! Thank you, Tiffany Black.

Thanks to Elle and Karen who gave me invaluable feedback and changed the angle of the story, making it that much better.

www.ingramcontent.com/pod-product-compliance
Lightning Source LLC
Chambersburg PA
CBHW021216250626
47155CB00008B/2834